# The Other Side of Justice

*Hal B. Coleman*

SUNSTONE
PRESS

All characters, incidents, and dialogue in this book are the products of the authors imagination and are not to be construed as real. Depictions are fictional and any resemblance to actual events or persons, living or dead, is therefore entirely coincidental.

First Edition

Printed in the United States of America

---

Library of Congress Cataloging in Publication Data:

Coleman, Hal B., 1925-
        The other side of justice / Hal B. Coleman.—1st ed.
                p.              cm.
        ISBN: 0-86534-183-4 :   $14.95
        I. Title.
PS3553.047424P73      1992                            92-32567
813'.54—dc20                                          CIP
                                                     AC

---

Published by    SUNSTONE PRESS
                Post Office Box 2321
                Santa Fe, NM 87504-2321

Dedicated to my father
who was a lawyer and an author
in his own time.

# PART I

## CHAPTER I

It was more of a plain looking western type motel than any fancy chain type structure. Just white stucco that blazed eye-sore hot in the summer and gave new vents each year to the icy winds off the mountains. But to Russ Thurston, Manager of the Red Wing Motel, it looked like a real, honest-to-goodness haven in his own personal wilderness of frustration. He kicked at some gravel in a freshly opened crack in the asphalt parking lot and gazed absently at the small pool, still covered by dirty plastic with murky water slopping gently in the cold breeze. Maybe, for a change, his own dirty miserable life would change for the best, once more wake up and see blue sky and be glad, just glad to wake up. He swung through the portico and slowly walked past suite C. Absently he noted soft gentle sobbing and the low murmur of male comfort. He knew suite C would soon be empty.

The miserable bell clanged in the office as he walked in and the gum-chewing kid with the big high school letter began immediately to make new coffee, spill the old, and generally act like a teenage idiot.

"For Christ sake, son, ease up will you? I just walked in the door, that's all. If there isn't anything going on, just keep sitting on your athletic ass — who cares?"

As usual, the color TV was blasting away at some late afternoon tear jerker, and the small office hung heavy with the combined mixture of acne lotion and Russ' cheap Mississippi crook cigar. The electric heater was glowing red hot in the corner, by the desk, to make up for the long since deficient general heating plant in the old structure.

"Damn, it's still cold in this place. Get that heater out from under your feet and put it out in front where it will do some good. What's your name anyway?"

"Willis Walters sir, and I'm new here but I really will try hard, I can only work after school and —"

"Hold it, hold it. I only want to know your name, not your lousy life history."

The boy slumped miserably in the corner on the stool by the desk. He had failed, he knew it, the job was over before it began. Willis needed the job, needed it badly, just to try and help out and hopefully to put a little aside for college. It was funny how fast the set, simple security of life could change. Almost as the bursting of a big pink balloon, once full, round, gracefully moving on the whim of the wind, and suddenly with awful harshness and finality a great multicolored bursting, leaving only the wrinkled, shriveled skin of despair. The fight, and it was a fight, between mom and dad had been brief but horribly violent that winter night. Willis and his small brother and sister stayed at the dinner table and tried to eat, but the impact of it all was much too clear to ignore. As dad slammed through the dining room with his suitcase and coat, only three tear-streaked faces gave evidence that the balloon had burst. And now Willis, trying hard at sixteen to assume his role as head of the family and a sometimes provider, once more felt the sickening shriveled skin of despair and defeat.

He became suddenly aware that a buzzer on the switchboard was ringing incessantly. He leaped back to reality and clumsily clutched for the connection.

"Front desk."

"This is room 118. Any messages for me—? Well then, just be sure you don't let anyone know I'm registered here. By the way, get me some ice, a couple of glasses and a bottle of vodka."

"Yes sir, Mr. — uh — Mr. Room 118. Right away."

As Willis got up to leave, Russ moved over to take the switchboard. He put a big rough hand on the boy's shoulder.

"Don't give up, pal, we've all got problems, which accounts for my large bark with very little bite."

That famous Thurston smile was, as usual, infectious and Willis grinned half to himself as he flew out the door and banged it shut hard behind him.

The icy blast of cold air from the open door sent an involuntary shiver through Russ. "God damn this cold ice-box of a state." He roared at no one but the elements. He put his size 11 feet on the heater and folded his muscular arms around a broad chest for warmth. He mused that in spite of his sedentary, inactive life the past year he still was in darn good shape, better by far than the average middle ager. He knew this harked back to the days when he was the big man, the really big man, for the University of New Mexico and later for the Santa Fe Mustangs. Tight end on the pros was tough, just as tough as it slam banged through the television in living color. Even all of Russ' rock-hard frame of six feet four and two hundred twenty five pounds had reeled, bent and broken time and again during those three years. Tougher also, because after the grueling practices and the crushing games he would again bury himself in his law books. Night after night Blackstone, Justice Holmes and the Law of Torts gleefully tumbled into cursing action of 66 slant, 36 right, and down and outs. That final game when he had proudly shown the team his license to practice law, his whole being, both mental and physical, began to seep out of that mass of muscle and sinew. And that final game cost him two teeth, a three-inch scar over his right eyebrow, and a broken nose. But the spectators had stood and done final wild homage to this gladiator as he slowly came off the rain-soaked field. Russ smiled at the thought. He never would know whether that ringing in his ears had been from Ulysses Grant Lee's size 12 in his face or the spontaneous ovation of the crowd.

Once more the buzzer...."Where the hell is that kid for 118? I haven't got all day. I've got to be back at the office by 5:30."

Russ almost laughed out loud. The clock on the wall said 4:30. The mayor was some stud, and his little frustrated filly would be screwed, showered, and out in the New Mexico cold before she realized she had had it.

"He's on the way sir. Should be there now."

Willis wondered what vodka tasted like. It must be good because the motel winery carried twice as much as anything else. He noticed just in the two days at work that the businessmen at the motel didn't drink much of it but that mostly couples during the day did. He decided girls must like vodka more than men — it probably was sweet. Room 118 was at the back of the horseshoe shaped motel, where the rooms had garages with pull-down doors. The rooms weren't as nice and were smaller than the other rooms, but his instructions were to always rent these out first during the day. He knew someone had punched a small hole through the wall between 120 and 118, but he had always been afraid to peek through it. The maids always laughed about what went on in the rooms. Willis tried to find out, but they either talked in riddles or wouldn't talk when he came up.

He knocked importantly on the door and called out, "room service." He heard the lock turn and someone tried to open the door. As usual, it stuck so he kicked it to help.

It was the first time he had seen a naked woman! She had just slipped her black see-through panties off and turned toward the door as it flew open. She was beautifully bronzed with soft, silken, perfect skin. Her wide black eyes under a sheen of jet black hair only served to accentuate the perfect pink nipples. The startling beauty of her hips and thighs was broken only by a long scar low on the right side of her stomach, which pointed with arrow accuracy to the love laden joy of fulfillment between her thighs.

She shuddered visibly, and he suddenly realized that the chill air from the mountains had momentarily gripped this picture of purity, and he hastened to step inside.

He was stopped by "How much?" and he realized that they were not alone. She rushed into the bathroom, and he turned his attention to the bill. It was ten dollars, and he hoped a tip. Mr. 118 must have been twenty years older than the girl and a full, fat two hundred and fifty pounds, most of it in the expansive midsection. He looked absurd with horn-rim glasses, a cigar, and white boxer trunks that hung almost to his knobby knees with a pouch in the sprung seat. He pushed Willis outside and slammed the door while he retrieved his wallet. Willis stood with the memory of the beauty of the girl vividly held in his mind. The door stuck and once more he kicked it, hoping as it burst open that she would run to his arms forever.

"Next time don't take so damn long," growled 118, but he still gave Willis a dollar tip and slammed the door. As he hunched into the wind, he heard her laughing wildly and he glanced back just in time to see her briefly in front of the window. Then a long naked arm wrapped around her thighs and the drapes snapped shut.

"Why the hell did you want to stand there in your bare ass while that kid was here? Suppose he recognized me from the newspapers? Suppose he runs back to the office and tells that disbarred junky lawyer that the mayor's in here? Suppose ... "

"Oh, for Christ sake uncle, suppose, suppose, suppose. You sound like a broken record for cheap panty hose. Suppose I walked out of here bare-ass naked and had a press conference? It's no news going to bed with your secretary, but, by God, when his excellency the Major Bill Bascom throws a leg over his secretary and half-breed niece, that's front page."

Bill turned over inside. The very thought of that sort of press conference was enough to turn his red hot thighs to wilting echoes of yesteryear.

"Faith, hon, you're just upset today. Must be close to your time of the month. Here, suck on this vodka first and then we'll settle down for some serious lovin."

He knew what vodka would do to her. She would turn those black almond Indian eyes toward him and begin to chant the wild, eerie moan of love. In a frantic frenzy of love, despair and unleashed passion, she would drunkenly lurch toward him and rape him over and over, even when he could no longer hold his love hard within her. Her demands would force him to slap her back to reality, to violently throw her clawing, willful body away from him. Sobbing, sobbing with love, hate and uncontrolable addiction for the act of love, the spasmodic sensual sensation of his heat and love deep in her belly.

She lay on the dirty carpet where he had violently thrown her and as she opened her eyes slowly she saw a limp, long, sheet-white arm trail over the edge of the bed where it joined itself awkwardly to a carefully manicured hand, the great jewel encrusted ring of high office seated tightly on a blob of finger. The same ring, same finger, same hand and same arm she had seen ten years ago. It had fallen helplessly over the side of her mother's bed and harshly slammed her awake. She had crept into her mother's room late at night, frightened of the sudden fury unleashed by a summer storm. The lightning set its blue-green fingers dancing through the windows and marked carefully the big bed full of interlocked bodies. She had quietly lain down on her blanket next to the bed and in childish bliss dropped off into the warmth of security and nearness.

She knew it was Uncle Bill, and with childish love had held his hand. The room erupted in horrible action. Her mother, screaming in broken English, had dragged her wildly from the room. "Leave her here, leave her here. One of these days, I'll take care of both of you in this same old bed." He roared with laughter and she could hear him over and over, even after she had been locked in her dungeon of despair alone with her blanket, the horrible laughter and lightning. And so it was. He had them both, not in the same bed at the same time, but she knew she had been loved by him only after he had crept from mama's bed. She had gotten even with mama, but now was a true addict to love alone, and "fat-forty" Uncle Bill owned her body, mind and helpless sinful soul.

"I'm taking a shower. Quit quivering on that damn filthy floor. It's 5:15 and I've got to make a cocktail party for that idiot Indian Chief that wants the old armory for Indian housing. If he gets as drunk on vodka as you do, I'll end up chief of the whole tribe. Get up, damn it!"

As they went out the door in a blue blur of cigar smoke, the right honorable mayor thought he heard someone giggle. He looked sharply with trained eye for the intruder and then, with sun glasses in place, bolted into the car.

Phyliss took her eye away from the peep hole.

"I tell you sometin' for sure, Mildred, that li'l girl sure got to be part black to screw like dat. De mayor, he got to get hisself a bigger love machine if he spects to stay on that one."

As she began to change the sheets, she mused to herself that li'l girl could make herself a pile of money in one night just helpin out those poor men that got under worked and oversexed love machines.

"Yessir, that's just one big waste of talent on the ole mayor."


CHAPTER II

Russ knew there was a big conference set for 6:00 in the evening with the owners and vaguely he was worried. He had worked hard, handled the night shift to save money, and had still been there by 10:00 each morning for checkout time.

When Russ was hired by the new owners it was during the summer and business was day and night with no vacancies, either for the hourly rooms or the overnight travelers. Winter had killed the overnight business since there was ample room in the big chain motels just a block away. Naturally, the hourly business held its own, but even that, with all the college kids back at school, had suffered a little. Of course, there is absolutely nothing more drab and depressing than a wind swept, empty, local motel in the winter. Russ even had the help park their cars around at various rooms to make it look busy. This might have helped a little, but the cars they drove looked like they had come out with the Okies during the depression. He had cut the maids down to just four to take care of all of the one hundred rooms, but of course he knew the biggest part of that job was the hourly rooms.

He mused, to himself, how Willis would take to cleaning up rooms. He unconsciously smiled as he pictured the expression of shock on the boy's face when he changed the first bloody sheet, emptied the first wastebasket full of "cotton ponies" and "life like" limp used rubbers and read the rotten filthy "sex book" carelessly left behind. Lucky for you, Willis, that I'm not still riding my big heroin hooked balloon or by God that's just what I would do to you.

The owners had been habitually restless lately and he really didn't blame them, but again what the hell could he do about losing business week after week. He virtually prayed for spring and the return of the harassed and exhausted traveler, the rebelling college kid with his rebelling little lover who smoked haish and made love on the floor.

All he had left now that he could count on was one regular who had been with them since last fall and a crew of magazine salespersons coming in from time to time. The one regular, a lawyer in Santa Fe, never complained about service and kept to himself in Suite A. "A" suite was a little bigger room, a stand-up dressing room and a bathroom. Of course, you got two chairs, a couch and a table with this all for the bargain price of twenty dollars per day. Maybe that much more room was worth it. In any event, Russ knew John from when he was practicing law and had always liked him and certainly respected him as one of the really fine trial lawyers in New Mexico. He only knew now that he was going through a really tough divorce and that the frustration of prolonged separation without final action was slowly beginning to bring out the gray in that shock of blonde hair. John had problems, but they were his own and, typical of a good lawyer, they would stay his own until he was ready to make his next calculated move.

The office door literally burst open and in stomped a mountain of energy. Russ had just turned to the buzzer on the switchboard but could tell without looking that Ron White and his crew of semi-juvenile delinquents had just moved in on Santa Fe to unload every magazine from "Pornography for Parents" to "Tender True Lovers Journal."

"Front desk, Russ speaking."

"Hey, Russ, didn't we tell you we wanted you in the Conference Room at 6:00?" It was owner Lee Ladinsky.

Ron had immediately stuck a quarter in the pinball machine, and the racket of the siren and bells going off, as the ball hit a naked mermaid on her nipple, was too much.

"Damn it, Ron, can't you wait a minute. You'll have two whole weeks to fight that thing if your little delinquents don't burn down the motel before then."

The immediate sulking silence indicated that Ron had complied and would now look for a knock-down on the room charge to compensate him for his slander of character, verbal assault, and violation of his constitutional rights.

"Lee, I'm sorry. Ron White and his gang just roared in, so I will have to be a little late. If I don't get him off on the right foot, he may decide to pack everything that's loose into his trailers and head for God knows where."

"Russ, this is really damned important and it does concern you personally, so get him out of there as fast as you can. By the way, send that new kid over with some bourban and ice. We'll all need a few before we finish this one."

Russ felt his security blanket starting to slip into the slopping dirty water on the plastic pool cover. He instinctively massaged the heavy scar over his right eye, it throbbed and had turned a livid red.


CHAPTER III

"Now, Russ, you shouldn't talk to me like that in public. After all, I'm a businessman and you have seriously damaged my image before my loyal and trusted sales staff and the general public. It would seem only right and proper that in some small way you would make a monetary effort to ..."

"Ron, your salesmen and saleswomen, as you call them, are outside in the clear cold New Mexico ice box. Your public is me and that damned mermaid. And no, you don't get the rooms at any cheaper rate than you have before."

"Now, Russ, I can tell from that scar getting all fiery red that you are about to indulge yourself in a fit of uncontrollable temper which, as you know, is most unbecoming to men of business and high management such as you and me. I therefore graciously accept your humble apology and will take rooms at the same reduced rate that we had four months ago. Our requirements will be four rooms, one suite, a conference room, clean ..."

"Your requirements will be whatever I figure out after you give me a breakdown of male and female."

"Russ, you know damn well I run a clean show, nothing up the sleeve, no hands under the table, and besides there is no way you're going to keep some of these little monsters from snuggling up to a nice warm piece of female and vice versa."

"Vice you've got, versa I don't know about. Just give me the breakdown so I'll have some idea of who's where and where to send the cops."

"Mr. Thurston, once more you have affronted my dignity and shattered my calm pool of honest endeavor. Oh hell, here it is. I've got six blacks, three Mexicans and ..."

"Ron, you know I don't give a good damn about colors. All I want to know is male versus female."

"All right, all right. I've got fourteen male and six female, along with one pet."

"No pets allowed. You know that. Take it down the street to that old wind-wracked kennel."

"Russ, this pet is a little different. It's the baby of one of our more indiscreet young saleswomen. Unfortunately, the poor creature was born out of wedlock, the groom-to-be having just entered the gates of glory after dying a horrible hero's death in service."

"Oh, crap. He was probably the maintenance man in some motel that she trapped into fixing her plumbing. Why can't you come in here just once and register for rooms quietly and honestly without all of these extra-curricular problems? If I didn't feel that the public deserves, to a certain extent, the ludicrous con job you're about to foist on them, and if I didn't need the business, I swear I would put out the no vacancy sign when I hear you coming. What the hell does she do with this baby while she sells?"

"Oh the beauty of this blessing from heaven! Can't you see the soft moistened eyes of a housewife as this young woman stands before her door, burdened with literature and child. Her sales are twice those of any of the others. Since the baby had begun to grow some, she has taken to renting the small creature out by the day to other saleswomen. In each case, with one exception, the little creature has produced a bountiful monetary increase in sales."

"I assume the one exception was when you went out with the creature and they all thought you were a lecherous old fornicating grandfather — which you are."

"Russell, the sheer depths to which your once healthy and alert mind has sunk simply stuns me. As a matter of fact, that was not the case. The fact is one of simple miscalculation. The American public is still shocked to see a white woman with a black baby at their front door."

"You forgot to tell me the little creature was black."

"And, as I recall, my dear Russell, you just finished telling me you didn't give a 'good damn about colors.' Touché, which in sales language means 'screw you!'"

Russ mentally agreed he had just been "touché-d" by a real pro at the game of "touché-ing." Ron White actually had a beautifully logical mind when it came to making money for Ron. He had begun, quite simply as a runny nose runaway, hustling used magazines on a Chicago street corner. By sheer force of necessity, he had become a perfectionist at the delicate art of showmanship. He could cry on cue, smile with that blue eyed beauty that bespoke only the truth, and humble himself at a customer's feet, all for that thin piece of silver coin. He had then elevated himself into top management when he hired another runaway on a straight commission deal. He was always attuned to the ways of the public. What they wanted, he gave freely on cue; what was not wanted was just as easily kept from them. His ability to teach the fine art of door-to-door acting was as much a success as his special inate ability to act. And so at the old worldly wise age of twenty-nine, he was President, Board of Directors, Management and Owner of his own million-dollar actors group. His little company kept its home base in whatever motel they happened to bless with their presence and lived out of rental trailers. Each day he would send forth his little band of runaways, delinquents and homeless to act out their story for, "just one more subscription to Pornography for Parents and I can enroll in junior college," or for "just one more subscription to Tales for Toddlers and I can get my 'creature' a crib to sleep in." And so it would go for two full weeks from early morning until cold dusk when the runaways, delinquents and homeless would return to the security of Ron. And then as swiftly as these wayward Gypsies had appeared, so they would retreat to another corner of the country, leaving behind a city, town or village covered with magazines. The business was honest, the magazines would reach each destination. Only the actors were fictitious.

Russ was rudely jolted from his momentary flight from reality by the sharp staccato of a horn honking outside.

"Russ, you great, charming grizzly bear, could we possibly get on with this mundane problem of so-called registration?"

"Now listen, Ron, let's go over the ground rules just for old times sake. To start with, you require eight rooms and that includes four rooms with a roll-away. No roll-aways in the girls' rooms because they say it is too crowded, although I frankly think it interferes with entertaining their boyfriends. I don't know where 'creature' will go, but if you'll send in this flower of purity I'll figure out where she and the baby can stay. Next, since all these kids are still kids, no drinking in the rooms or giving my bartender a bad time next door. If the cops come in for one of the kids on a complaint, turn him over to them without a fight. Do your fighting at the station house. Next, if we would happen by the grace of the almighty to get one nice warm day, I don't want these kids raising hell all over the motel, just in case we might have an unsuspecting guest. And finally, we do have one regular customer in Suite A. He's a lawyer, minds his own business and has enough problems without your sales company adding to them. Because of the shortage of help, two of your girls will be in the room next to him. Pick a couple of nice ones that won't try to hustle him for money or otherwise. And Ron, just because I do like you and because I do know you try hard to run a tight ship, for God's sake take it easy on the sauce. You are really the devil's handiwork when you fall in the sauce bottle. The last time you were here, you broke your fourth wife's nose. And I understand she just got rid of you last month."

"Mr. Thurston, if you are completely through reciting the constitution and by-laws of this den of destruction, I trust you will turn over the keys to these cherished rooms. My feet are freezing in this plush executive front office."

Russ blocked out five adjoining rooms on one leg of the horseshoe and then blocked out three rooms on the opposite leg for the girls. He mentally decided to put the flower of purity and creature in a separate room next to Suite A in the forlorn hope that at least there wouldn't be any wild monstrous parties with "creature" in there. He turned and handed the well-worn keys to Ron and then turned to his register.

"By the way, Russ, in case my wife should arrive, we will need a suite."

Ron smiled that "honest to God" smile.

Russ frowned momentarily, "Ron, I'll give you a suite, but don't give me that wife type crap. I know you just got a divorce." He reached for Suite C, he knew it was empty and cleaned up ready for action.

Ron smiled and started out the door.

"Honest, Russ, she's a sweet little combination of Dr. Jekyl and Mr. Hyde, just like me. Wife number five. Sorry she can't be here to enjoy your charming hospitality."

The door slammed shut as Russ yelled, "You're an absolute idiot. Don't forget, no checks — just cash when you leave."

Chapter IV

As Russ walked into the Conference Room, he was really more worried about leaving Willis in the front office than the meeting itself. But then he got that panoramic shot of all three of them and it reminded him of the front line of defense for the Denver Broncos. Grim was the only way to even come close to describing it. Once again, he felt that tell-tale throbbing over the right eye where Ulysses Grant Lee had left his autograph. He hated himself for his self-conscious involuntary gesture of massaging it. Anyone who really knew him well would know that this was his Achilles heel, his outward indicator of that pent-up nervous tension. It was just such moments as these that Russ hated the most. The game was about to begin, but the players were strung up tight waiting for the kick-off.

Russ moved toward the proffered chair with studied casual-ness. He carefully fingered some ice cubes into a tall glass and splashed a healthy jolt of bourbon over them. As he sloshed the bourbon gently around the glass, it took the form of a great brackish brown whirlpool. The great eye in the center seemed to menacingly beckon and force him back to the unpleasant memory of days gone past when he had lived in the eye of a whirlpool. Sucking, pulling, tormenting him, never quite releasing its clammy superior grip on his mind and body. At first, it had begun casually, almost without notice.

After that last bone wracking, vicious game, he had begun to have sickening throbbing headaches. The intensity grew worse almost by the minute, and finally he submitted to a battery of tests to try and find the real solution to his unending misery. The trainer had been liberal with potent shots of morphine to give him temporary relief and he had found himself more and more dependent on these to give him those moments of deep relaxation. Electroencephalograms, blood letting by what seemed to be the gallon, spinal taps, unending interviews and tests and more tests finally led to one of those "within a reasonable medical certainty" diagnoses.

The doctor's office bore the hush of a courtroom just before the verdict is read, on that day of diagnosis. Russ could see around the perimeter of this diagnostic dungeon all of the medieval tools of witchcraft, sorcery and psychology. Great heavy books with gold lettering, all in Latin, sharp instruments of torture lay neatly placed on a clean white towel, the shadow box that would clearly show fractures both old and new, as well as many other internal secrets of the body, and of course seated squarely in the middle of this great diagnostic center was the man himself. Russ always wondered how a doctor could pull the shade of detachment across his face when he was about to tell you that your body and mind were almost at the eye of the whirlpool where one great greedy gulp would suck you under to eternal circular wandering. And so it was that awful moment before the kick-off, up tight, strung out with screaming guts retching for the game to begin.

Dr. Mendelson seated himself squarely before Russ and meticulously cleaned, polished and re-cleaned his black rimmed glasses.

"Russ, your days of football are over." There it was, flat on the desk.

"Doc, it may come as a surprise to you, but that last game was my last game. I am now very carefully starving while I practice law. And I do mean practice."

Russ smiled at the thought of his gross income for the past six months. "What my income has been wouldn't even keep you in cigars. Would you believe $822.76 and a free tune up on my car?"

They both laughed, but it was apparent that it was as unnatural as the laugh of a condemned man on his way to the gallows.

"This is even more serious than just not playing football, Russ."

Dr. Mendelson frowned absently at an invisible speck on his glasses. "What I am actually saying is that any violent physical activity is absolutely out. As a matter of fact, any severe traumatic blow over your right eye might well cause blindness, complete amnesia, or even death, as you lawyers say, "jointly, severally, or in the alternative."

Another invisible speck was carefully examined. Russ was stunned. His right hand instinctively reached for the heavy scar on his forehead.

"Doc, you've really got me on the defense, so maybe now's the time to unload your whole game plan. I am reasonably intelligent and have been known as one of the "guts boys," so let's get it over with so I can figure out the offense."

It was big talk, but Russ knew his voice had trembled ever so slightly and his mouth was as dry as moon dust.

Dr. Mendelson got up and carefully adjusted the venetian blinds as he turned his back to Russ, momentarily diverted by a wind whipped mini-skirt. The crackling tension raced ahead explosively. He turned abruptly. "Russ, you have a bone pressure on the right frontal lobe of your brain. It is completely inoperable. The internal pressure of the brain has to some degree, slowly, almost infinitesimally, pushed the cranial fracture back into a quasi-healed position. As you know, your extremities of pain have become less frequent. But I do not, within a reasonable medical certainty, believe that you will ever totally be without some severe attacks of pain. The area of the fracture will always be highly susceptible to trauma and in medical fact is, and will be, a continuing weakness in the cranial structure."

Dr. Mendelson smiled, almost sadly, "Fortunately for you, the practice of law is a highly refined form of combat. The combative use of words most certainly won't trouble your present physical deficiency."

Russ took the offered cigar and meticulously lit it to the symmetrical round glowing tip. The palms of his hands were clammy slick and his tongue touched delicate beads of sweat on his upper lip, the pain and throbbing was there but it could be overcome. He stood up slowly and looked down at the small, frail man of medicine. "Well, Doc, as they say in the legal field, 'you can't win 'em all.'"

"That's exactly right, Russ, and perhaps the worst is yet to come."

Again the invisible speck. Russ felt his entire being tense. He was strung out as tight as an electric guitar plugged in a 220 current. He violently wanted to rip the perfectly manicured medical head from this demon of medieval torture.

"For Christ sake, what could be worse!" His brutal fists ripped into the solid mahogany desk.

"I'll tell you what's worse. What's worse is what you are just proving right now."

He was no longer a doctor; he was Harry Mendelson against Russ Thurston. He wanted to hurt Russ in those words any man can understand, those words that begin in the worst sewer and rise to respectability through repeated daily use. He was mad and gave himself freely to the white-hot maddening rush of viciousness through his body and brain.

"Now get this straight and don't ever forget it. You're a fine specimen of a man whose body has served him well and whose brain can serve him well the rest of his life but..." He deliberately paused and then with the subdued sureness of a calculated killing, "... but you are strung up, strung out, hooked and an almost junkie."

"Junkie! You're no doctor. You're a God damn sorcerer, a miserable Merlin the Magician."

Russ' whole body screamed wildly, unsensibly for revenge, brutal, devastating and uncontrollable.

"You're a miserable, insufferable medical hack, hooked on your world of witchcraft and medieval medicine. You tell me I'm hooked, a junky. Look at me! I'm twice the man you are or ever will be. Do you think I got this body by taking junk? Do you think I got through night Law School being hooked?"

Dr. Mendelson had fixed his pale blue eyes steadfastly on Russ and held him there unmercifully.

"Nobody or nothing puts Russ Thurston down. I shagged golf balls and rat sacked at the country club when I was twelve. Pumped gas at a truck station at night, crawled in cow manure to plant bulbs at the greenhouse, swung a sledge and was a "Gandi dancer" just to get through high school. But I made it, God damn right I made it. I've broken almost every bone in my body and some of them twice playing college and pro ball, but by God I made it. I was beaten and exhausted physically during the day and beaten and mentally exhausted in Law School at night. But I'm a Lawyer and I'll be the damn best one in New Mexico!"

Russ heard Dr. Mendelson's voice from far off somewhere, "Russ, you will be absolutely nothing but a junkie if you don't break the needle."

Russ could hear his own cursing, flailing, incoherent words, but they came from somewhere else, not this body. He hurt, and he knew in the depths of his used-to-be guts, he knew, his craving, willful body had wrapped itself serpentine around his mind and will and was demanding the relief from pain and worry that only the shining needle could give.

The roaring rush of the whirlpool was on him. He felt himself reel and stagger unsteadily into the endless circle of the ever decreasing pattern of oblivion. The eye of the whirlpool gleamed menacingly up at him beckoning with promise of peace and eternity.

"Russ, if you stir that drink much more, you won't be able to taste the bourbon." Lee was smiling easily at Russ but the business at hand had begun.

"I'm sorry Lee, I guess my mind drifted off to that crazy Ron White and his troupe of Gypsy delinquents," he awkwardly lied, "If the big problem is no customers, I'm afraid I can't be of much help."

"If that was the only problem we had, we could probably battle that out until tourist time." It was hard-bitten Jack this time, the ramrod of the tight-knit organization. "Admittedly, we could use some more income, but we know you are doing all you can and we can't fault you for the way you have managed this windswept whore's dream." He paused to relight his soggy green cigar. "No, there's a lot more to it than just customers. We have figured out that there is just one way to make this deal go and go big. As you know, Interstate 25 will be completed this fall and that will transport the happy little travelers within a half mile of our front door."

Russ absently wondered what all of this had to do with management. This was really out of his hands and undoubtedly would all be put into proper perspective by the owners. His eyes moved restlessly to Doug Kruetz, who sat quietly in the far corner, a never-ending drink in his hand. It really was a very neat little package of owner-entrepreneur enterprise. Jack Cahill was the tough pock-marked driving force. His job was to put the deals together and then switchblade out the fat from the lean basic operation. Lee Ladinksy was not only a shrewd manager of money, but had the basic connections to get the loans they needed to feed the tenicles of the octopus with new acquisitions. Doug Kruetz was just pure blue stocking and if he didn't drown in the sauce, he would probably suffocate under a mountain of money. But he was a "must" factor since it gave the CLK Corporation necessary high quality prestige and, of course, ready cash.

It was Jack again. "We also are just as sure that the old familiar local motel is a thing of the past. In short, we have got to hook up with a chain and shoot our best deal right now."

Jack chewed his cigar and Lee continued to clean his finely manicured fingernails. It was curious to watch Lee since he had lost half of his forefinger and middle finger on his left hand years ago cutting meat in a Jewish delicatessen. He would carefully begin by cleaning the little finger, ring finger, and then oddly enough, the same motion across the missing middle finger and forefinger, finally making contact on the thumb. Lee was terribly sensitive about his misfortune and frequently would either cover his left hand with his right or carry it inside his coat, Napoleonic style.

"I've made arrangements for the money we will need," said Lee, "for completely tearing this monstrosity down and rebuilding it with an additional two hundred rooms."

"Of course, we will do it in stages so we keep some income coming in all the time, so you are assured of a job during construction." Jack had said this with nonchalance, but the tell-tale voice of impending disaster seemed to whisper quietly in Russ' ears. "During construction" seemed to indicate a purely temporary condition, but before Russ could say anything Doug had moved ahead.

"Truth is, Russ baby, we can make a deal with the biggest chain motel in the southwest if we can get the rest of the property we own re-zoned to commercial and rebuild the whole God damn thing." Doug stretched out full length on the couch and eased off one loafer at a time.

"I've done some checking and it looks like the planning and zoning commission will go with us on the re-zoning and rebuilding, but the approval of the board of alderman looks like a real cliff hanger." Jack looked disapprovingly at Doug as he mixed the last of the bourbon with some ice.

Russ felt the rush of excitement now as he quickly envisioned being manager of a beautiful first-class shiny new motel with a chain name to back it up. After all of his recent rotten luck, it looked like he had really fallen into a feather bed full of money and prestige rather than a snake pit.

"Naturally, we will want all of the help you can give us. You still carry a good name from the old days as all-pro tight end."

Russ noticed Lee had carefully not mentioned his abortive effort as a lawyer. "And it looks like the real pressure play will have to be on the Board of Alderman and the Mayor. We know full well that the

Mayor controls three votes out of the six and if he says squat, they'll piss."

Russ smiled since this was a well known fact throughout the city. His high and mighty excellency, the Mayor, had kept his fences well mended and carried the favor of those dedicated voters in town. If there was a tie vote, the Mayor, after an appropriate ten minute speech of how he really hated to have to break the tie, would promptly slam his great seal of office in the direction he had already known the vote had to go. To an outsider it was a truly dedicated man at work, to those who really knew him it was the great fixer affixing the fix.

Lee went on, "The real problem we have is getting enough pressure on his highness to make him go our way. He continually bitches in public about this eye sore but oddly enough he has never taken any steps to close us up. I never could figure out why he doesn't make life miserable for us?"

Russ knew, full well, why there hadn't been any trouble. It also was crystal clear that he still had some use to the organization and that had to be to control the Mayor. He felt his anger beginning to rise but put a death grip on it until he heard it straight.

"I sure as hell can't do anything with old "fat and forty," it was Jack now - "the last time I even tried to get a parking ticket fixed he gave me a long lecture on the honored and sacred duties of a public official. I have never been so embarrassed in my life - right in front of all the clerks in his best, God damned, Baptist baritone," Jack was on his feet now preaching from his own pulpit, "The very next day, so help me, the next day - he had the God damned gall to ask me if I could send over our maintenance man to do a little tree cutting at his house. I laughed in his face, and told him maintaining this place was a job for twenty men. I told him, incidentally, I had paid the damned parking ticket."

Russ knew that the next day his Honor had made it a point to see him in front of the motel and failed to mention to Russ that he had already asked Jack about free help. Naturally, Russ had sent the man over figuring it was good public relations to do so. Russ had never mentioned it since it didn't seem important and certainly wouldn't swing the Mayor to their side on a zoning problem.

"Russ, you must have some way to get him, to really set him up for the vote we need. You've been around this town forever and there must be someone, someplace that can get to Big Bill. If it takes money, that's no problem, but I understand that he already has more than he needs. Not that a greedy son-of-a-bitch like him wouldn't want more."

"Jack, I really don't know how to get to him," Russ lied, "I have pretty much stayed out of politics since I gave up the law business."

"Russ, let's just lay it right on the line," Lee said, "you are at the end of a hanging rope, one you made yourself when you couldn't get off the needle and blew your law practice as well as your ticket to practice law. We gave you a job in a run down shack joint because we knew you finally broke the needle and you came damn cheap." Lee let it sink in just as hard as it had come out. "Now you've got one last shot to stay with this organization, get to the Mayor. You get him for us and you have a guaranteed job with us running the new motel."

Russ could only stare absently at the floor. What was one more fix in his life. The whole world was made up of "the fix." Pressure was the name of the game. Put the heat on the right person at precisely the right time and then sit back and watch it build into unrelenting pressure. So CLK had put it on Russ, at precisely the right time, and now they would sit back and see if the pressure would carefully force its way through devious crevices into the final affirmative vote.

Russ had been in the pressure plays before and knew the game was always like a very quiet tense game of checkers. One move, simple as it may be, always led to a counter move and from there the game of who owns who got complicated. Well, this was one time that Russ didn't want the ball, it was time to punt and get out.

There was a frantic knock at the door and in burst Willis. "Honest to God, Mr. Thurston, you've got to come right now. All those sales people are switching rooms and Mr. White just plays the pinball machine. I told them —"

Russ was on his feet concerned only with this real present pressure and on his way out the door.

"Russ, I assume we can count on you to find the way," said Jack.

"I've got to think about it. I told you I don't know any way to get to him, but I've got to think about it."

The first crevice had opened and was ready to receive its initial injection.


CHAPTER V

Russ was not a man to be treated lightly when he was aroused. His white teeth were set in a grimace as he roared across the parking lot to the wing of the motel where the sales group had been sent. Willis was jabbering nervously that he had to get home to eat dinner and help out at home.

Russ swung around and told him to get the hell home and eat dinner, that he could handle this alone. But now Willis felt his first duty was to the motel and wanted to help Russ, although his eyes were wide with fear of the unknown that was about to happen.

Russ banged on the door indicated by Willis. Then he roared that if they didn't open up the police would be here in two minutes. The door opened slowly and revealed total, mass, utter confusion. Clothes everywhere, wild posters on the walls, radio blasting and the reeking smell of marijuana. Two young Mexican boys, neither over 15, were standing in the hallway in nothing but a smile and undershorts.

"O.K., I want the woman and I want her right now, with no smart talk or "no comprehende" crap.

"But, Senior innkeeper, we have only been preparing for a hard day's work tomorrow," said the tallest of the two.

"Listen, Pedro or Gonzales or whatever the hell your name is, you've got exactly two seconds to pull that broad out from under the bed or wherever she is. If you don't, both you and your buddies' chocolate asses are going to be in the middle of that swimming pool." The fiery red slash above Russ's eye gave him the appearance of the devil's own messenger.

Both men leaped for the closet door and pulled the naked protesting girl out from behind the clothes hangers. She was as black as the New Mexico night and obviously high on marijuana. She started to laugh wildly and lurched against the astonished Willis. He flattened himself against the wall where she promptly pressed herself against him and deftly began to unzip his pants.

Russ reached around and slapped her hard on her firm round buttocks.

"I ain't going to hurt him, Boss, just play with him some and then I'll give him back to you. He's cute white boy, let me just have him for tonight," but she backed away and began to throw on a shirt and pants when she saw Russ coming at her.

"All of you leave the God damn help alone and leave each other alone or you'll be out of here by night fall. Now I mean it. I don't care how big a stud you are or how hot your crotch is, you do your screwing games somewhere else. Willis, get the hell out of here and go eat dinner, I'll see you tomorrow."

Russ turned to the door and grabbed the girl by the arm and headed her toward the outdoors. She smiled up at him and moved closer to him, "I like you too, Boss, I just bet you make a girl happy. You going to take me to my room, make sure no bad men under the bed waiting to screw me? I just love to have you spend the night."

As Russ shoved her out the door, the Mexicans laughed and called out instructions on just exactly how to make her happy in bed. They obviously had laid her before.

As Russ was leading her in the direction of her room he saw Ron White lurching toward him. Ron was full and damn near fell in the pool as he stopped Russ.

"Got a hot one there, Russ baby, better watch her, she gets pregnant from just kissing, at least that's what she told me."

The girl laughed hysterically and ran toward her room while Russ turned on Ron.

"Now, Russ, no harm done. Just some kids getting rid of that extra sap that raises their peters. Better this way than laying some sexy, unsuspecting housewife tomorrow. Once again, Ron White comes to the aid and assistance of this great flower of a town, always mindful of his civic duty, he keeps the screwing for his black beauties."

Obviously pleased not only with his statesmanship but also with his poetry, he threw his arms wide in an expansive gesture to the whole world. Russ grabbed him by the coat as he lost his balance and prepared for a backward swan dive in the pool and lifted him off his tiny, almost feminine feet and onto the parking lot.

"Now, listen, twinkle toes," Russ began, knowing that Ron's Achilles heel was the daintiness of his feet, "for all I care your little troupe of fornicators can attack the whole town and come back in nine months to claim their Creatures but not one pregnant broad is coming out of here when you leave. And that means just one thing, no screwing in, on or about this motel."

"Russell, as the great god of fertility is my witness, none of my elite sales organization will split a thigh without first obtaining permission from you. Now, if you will, kind sir, I shall depart for the Presidential Suite and take my repose," he began to move away in mock dignity and righteous indignation. Russ had to smile to himself as he mused over the ability of this man to turn any situation to his advantage.

"Oh, Russ. I want general quarters sounded for these little bastards at six o'clock sharp in the morning. After all, the time to sell the best is just after the old man has left for the office and momma comes to the door with her nipples showing through the nightgown. One look at these leering faces of my lecherous little group will mean a sale or a screw, either will do the same, put money in my pocket."

Russ shook his head in silent exasperation. He knew Ron meant every word of this and, of course, it was a truism that had been proven time and time again. Any unsuspecting woman who answered her door still feeling the warmth of her bed and her gown clinging precariously on her willing breasts was faced with a threefold decision, a slam, a sale or a screw.

It was true that frequently the doors were slammed before the first words came spilling from these pearly mouthed midgets of mirth. But this was usually from either direct fear or from some unforeseen emergency that was in progress within the home.

Actually, the feeling of fear didn't arise until they began to charm the unsuspecting victim with their gentle yet persistent pitch. And just as gently they would move in closer to the open door and shudder slightly in their light weight suit coats, hunching into the biting crosscut of the wind. A willing smile, clear eyes locked onto the victim and an honest plea for help always began to produce the maternal instinct in the breast of the darling of domesticity. It was only then, when she found herself feeling the surge of womanhood, that she would see with horror that he was in the door with those eyes locked firmly in place on her uplifted nipples beneath the sheerness of her gown. Now she must buy, now she was caught in the very dilemma she had seen so many times on television. Any subscription for a year was cheap compared to the price she was sure she was about to pay. More than once a single woman had hastily bought "Psychology and Parenthood" or "Your Child and You" in the seemingly desperate effort to be rid of this renegade rapist. Yet curiously enough there was, in fact, the so called Code of Ethics imposed on these runaways by Ron White and their fellow deceivers. A distinct part of this code was that no male forced himself on an unwilling prospect nor would Ron permit any of his females to be forcefully taken by some horny husband alone for the night. For as much as the women were trapped by the early morning con men, so too were the men unsuspecting victims in the evening. And so it was that again in the evening Ron would shuttle his heavy, high breasted teenagers into the subdivisions and apartment complexes to slip through the doors to display their baubles, bangles, books and bodies. Caught flat footed by a young braless teenager standing at his door, there was no way a man could turn them back out into the bleakness of night. Once inside, these little darlings virtually had a sale one way or the other. If a wife was present, they would perch demurely on the edge of a deep cushioned chair and carefully tug at their short skirts. But as the wife would look away or tend to a wifely duty, the thighs were delicately opened to the keen eye of the husband who perceived the glory of womanhood welcoming his fixed stare. And just as adroitly this bush foliage would disappear with a deft crossing of cool limbs when the wife reappeared. But the job was complete now as surely as the man had mentally laid her, he would buy the subscription for one more glimpse of the smooth young thighs leading to the virginity of this dear, hard working victim of society. And again should this poor dear child chance upon a man alone in her evening wanderings, it was effortless for her to succumb to his overwhelming generosity of satisfying this sex starved, misunderstood child. Once the act was accomplished her deft fingers found their way into trousers and dresser drawers while he checked to make sure his wife was still at the bowling alley. And then sweetly and demurely she would promise to call him tomorrow to give him more delights, but tomorrow never comes.

The rape of the rapist was not unknown to Ron White, he had been there and knew the wild desires that could be set upon a door to door mag boy. And as surely as the front door was opened just enough to reveal a naked leg and breast, so just as surely she would rush from the door to "slip into something" while the door opened to its full expanse. Once inside he could smell her body even to the close aroma beneath her arm pits and between her damp lips of love. He could feel the swelling between his thighs and the regular throbbing that tells him it won't be long until sex has begun and the sale is done. The "something slipped into" is only enough to provoke him to an animal desire and the something slipped into her is all wild throbbing animal and just as she would have it. Once more the deft fingers move across the dresser while she prepares herself to leave for shopping and lunch with her husband. And once more the promise to return tomorrow to provide new voyages on the sea of sex — but tomorrow never comes.

CHAPTER VI

Most of the world thanks God for Saturday. At least, a part of that same world gives thanks to God on Sunday. But Russ did neither. Saturday and Sunday were absolutely no less than pure hell. This was, of course, compounded by Ron White's troupe and the shack up jobs that came in heavy on Saturday night. These were always the worst because they seldom got to the motel until they were so drunk they could barely drive, much less do any better at driving home their sexual prowess. The result was a disaster area left in the wake of a man-made hurricane.

The first problem child had hit about 9:00 Saturday night. Russ saw the car coming at a very slow pace but unfortunately, it was a relentless forward movement that only stopped when the car hit the corner of the office. Willis fell off the swivel chair behind the switchboard where he had fallen asleep reading Chaucher, and came up screaming "Jesus Christ, it's an earth quake." The car was relentlessly pushing at the old building and new cracks appeared readily in the corner exposing one headlight from outside. Russ vaulted outside to shut off the engine while Willis frantically began to reconnect the mass of jumbled wires on the switchboard. It was river ice cold outside and in spite of his anger, Russ shivered involuntarily as he opened the door to the car. He saw immediately that it was "T.J." Mitchell, the number one son of none other than Thadeus Joncliff Mitchell II, the very son-of-a-bitch who had been Chairman of the Bar Committee that lifted his license to be a lawyer. Ironically this Friday afternoon he was to appear, with his witnesses, to try to be reinstated as a lawyer before the same Committee.

"T.J., what the hell do you think you are doing? Driving your old man's tractor? You're not out on your wide open estate now, you're just trying to get into a motel to get a piece of ass and you're doing a damn poor job of both."

The girl giggled and promptly threw up all over the dashboard.

"What the hell you wanna go and do that for? Can't you hold your booze like a man? Sit up so you don't get your hair in it. You think I wanna screw you when you smell like puke?" T.J. began to start the car again.

"Wait a minute, friend. I'll get the boy to drive you to the room. You've already damn near demolished my home in the west. Speaking of home, why the hell don't you just let me get you a taxi and send you two victims of society back to mamma and pappa?"

T.J.'s glazed eyes almost focused. "The main reason is because mamma and pappa are out victimizing society and could care less about receiving their son as a guest right now. Gimmie a key, a bill and a beer."

"You want to pay for the damage now or have me send a bill to your dad?"

"Come on, Russ, you know I'm good for it. I'll be back as usual and pay for it but I can't write a check to this crappy motel. Now can I?"

T.J. began to look a little green and pale so Russ hurried on with it, "T.J. sign a check and I'll hold it until you come in and pay up. If you don't, I'll fill it in and run it through."

T.J. already had a check book out and scribbled something on the bottom that would pass for fly specks on the indoor wall of an outdoor outhouse. Russ took it and the keys and went back in the office.

"Willis, I want you to take T.J. and his pussy down to Room 28. You drive and make sure they get in the room and make sure the heat is turned up so they don't freeze to death. Oh, and collect twenty bucks in cash from him for the room." He handed Willis both sets of keys and turned to the cash drawer.

Willis knew T.J. well, he thought. But this was a side he had neither heard about nor frankly even thought about. T.J. probably would have been a nice guy if his old man had just let him be himself. But he had pushed T.J. hard in high school and insisted on straight A's as well as captain of everything. When he got to be a senior he just quit everything — except drinking and wrecking cars. Well, now Willis could see he had added one more — shacking up.

"Would you please move over, sir, so I can drive you to your room."

T.J. already was pawing the girl's left nipple and she had a frozen smile on her face. T.J. moved over and flopped his head in her soggy lap. She just sat there smiling stupidly with her delicate pink nipple exposed to the night air. Willis ignored the mess in the car and backed up carefully and headed the car into the parking area. When they reached the room it was freezing, just as Russ had told Willis. He got T.J. and the girl in the room where T.J. gave him $20. He turned up the heat and turned around in time to see T.J. unzipping the girl's dress while she grinned stupidly. Suddenly she bolted by Willis for the bathroom and almost made it before she threw up again.

"Will that be all, sir?" Willis was all professional and felt complete indifference toward the present mess or the orgy that was about to begin.

T.J. stared blankly at him and then tried to light a cigarette. Willis offered a light, "Yep, guess that's all ole buddy, that is unless you want to help me screw her when she quits puking?" He fell on the bed laughing and promptly passed out as cold as the outdoors. Willis took the cigarette from his hand and stubbed it out in the cheap glass ashtray with some other motel name on it. As he left, he looked back to see the girl standing in the bathroom door grinning stupidly with her dress down to her waist, both naked breasts swaying gently as she moved toward the bed and her sleeping stud.

The office door crashed shut as usual and Willis cringed knowing how Russ hated the noise but Russ was busy trying to get a maid to clean up room 12 so it would be ready for the man at the desk.

Willis asked politely if the man would need any help with his luggage. He smiled back but his neck showed color above the collar as he declined saying he was sure he could handle it. He asked for ice and a bottle of Scotch if it was available. Willis went in the other room and produced both while Russ was still on the phone and thanked him for the tip. Willis went to the front window and gazed absently out at the car by the front door with the motor purring quietly. It was a real beauty and looked just like one he had seen next door to his house occasionally. He glanced up at the woman waiting in the passenger seat and just caught a glimpse of her before she turned away. "My God, that Fred's mom" he thought. He looked hard now but she continued looking out the side window. He turned sharply and looked at the man in front of Russ. Now he was sure. The car, the man and "My God, Fred's mom."

The horn sounded briefly out in front and the waiting customer stepped outside. Willis was afraid and embarrassed to look but he could see their reflection in the picture window when he looked at the pinball machine. The man looked hard at Willis while "Fred's mom" gestured and then he quickly got in the car and backed out. Willis was hot all over. They were gone but he stood there in silent embarrassment for Fred. How could this happen to him and why did he have to be there when they came in? He knew he could never look at her again without seeing the motel and all the writhing naked bodies that are its paying population.

He felt someone close to him and suddenly, yet gently, a great hand was on his shoulder, "What's the matter, pal, you see someone you know? Or even worse than that see someone you know and respect?" Russ was looking warmly into his shattered mind. "Now, Willis, let me just tell you something. First of all, this is a vast overwhelming world we live in. It is full of the goodness of life and yet it overflows with apparent, evil inconsistencies. Father loves child, child hates father. Man loves woman and woman loves man but later each loves someone else. Love between man and woman is not a static, stationery solid state of being. It is a violent, exacting movable object that bounces crazily in a pattern of highs and lows that lead to irresponsible acts by one person that, in turn, lead to further retaliatory over reactions by the other. Frequently the actions are done in haste with the thought only of vengeance and that can lead only to the front door of our motel. Again it can be a deep hurt to someone by a person they love deeply that will virtually drive them to the solace and warmth of another. This motel is only a temporary stop for the poor souls who just want to be warm and wanted for one night. Whatever their reason is for being here, it is not our position nor our right to stand in judgement of them. The cross they have borne or may be bearing now is no more than a silent black shadow to us but we know not the weight of this shadow without having walked in their shoes. I found out this truism, while I was a lawyer. There are two distinct sides to every story and the reason for each side has normally come about from a very complex chain of circumstances many of which were out of the control of the individual. I firmly believe that there is some good in all people and given the proper attention and encouragement it will overcome all else. So whoever it was that you saw, believe in that person as you have in the past and hope that your belief and friendship in the future will bring out the goodness."

Willis reached for the now forsaken Scotch bottle to return it to the back shelf and vaguely wondered at Russ's ability to believe in "some good in all people" when he knew full well Russ had been put down again and again. And yet with all the rotten rumors about Russ, Willis knew there was an abundance of good in him and that had to be the proof of what Russ had said.

CHAPTER VII

Mayor Bascom faced each Monday with a mixed feeling of dread and delight. He absolutely dreaded the mealy mouthed crap that he knew would be waiting for him at City Hall from the weekend high rollers. The only delight in the day was the fact that he knew as usual he would get a great screwing from Faith. That is, unless it is the wrong time of the month. Hell — he never really worried too much about that since she had the softest mouth in the business. While he carefully shaved the dimple in his chin he was sure that sexually, she was the greatest. His reverie was abruptly interrupted when Elsa walked in and promptly plopped her oversized ass on the stool. She smiled up at him blearily while he heard her urine splash wildly in the bowl. "Here I sit in silent bliss, listening to the trickling piss." He must have been ten years old when he first heard that old cliche.

"Got a kiss for mommy this morning?" Now, just how unromantic can you get? Sitting on the stool, dripping urine and breathing last night's booze and cigarettes all over again.

"Of course, my darling," he bent over and pecked her on the lips, being careful to smear some shaving cream on her cheek.

"God damn you, Bill," she shrieked, "you know I hate that slimy shaving cream on me in the morning." As she jumped up, her tits flopped about wildly. One thing Bill could say for her, she had a set of tits second to no one and no matter how hard he pulled, sucked or just plain jerked on them, they always stood straight out with hard, full nipples. He even admitted to himself that when she started going braless he was more jealous than nervous. He reached over and grabbed a firm nipple and let it slide between his forefinger and thumb.

"Ouch, you son of a bitch. Why can't you just for once in our marriage act like a man instead of an oversexed ape?"

Yes, there was the whole trouble. All of that beautiful breastwork was lost to the frigidity of the north pole. At best, when Elsa wanted to get screwed it was, "I'll lie here and you work on me." Never once had he made her reach her climax. When he would unload in her with the fury of a hurricane, she would stroke his hair and say, "That was a nice boy, now let's go to sleep." Oh well, if you had a wild Indian to make up for it you could stay married and hold your respected position in the community.

When he went back in the bedroom, Elsa was carefully powdering her crotch and then dabbing perfume on her inner thighs and just under her tits. He had often wondered about this and almost hoped she had a lover somewhere out there. At least, they would be even if she ever caught him with Faith. But as cold as Elsa was, he was sure the best she could do would be to have an immaculate orgasm.

He dutifully kissed her good-bye and vaguely asked about her day while he slipped on his overcoat. She was still telling him her plans for the day when he went out the door, brief case in hand.

Faith met the new day with an odd sense of foreboding. She knew full well that Uncle Bill would be tight between her legs by noon time and depending on how he felt, she might get enough screwing to last for a day.

The whole thing had begun as a simple game to Faith. It was as old as adultery and was simply called "get even." She had gotten even, alright, and now her mother was a welfare case, fat and drunk with only a blur for a memory. The sheer irony was that the money Faith gave her on the side each month came from Uncle Bill. If the devil himself had two legs, a diamond ring and a small prick, he would surely be called "Uncle Bill."

She really didn't just look at her body in the mirror, she admired herself and enjoyed what she saw each morning. A smooth, natural tan skin, graceful long fingers, with square firm shoulders holding her breasts high and full. The sheen of jet black hair hung sexually across her shoulders accentuated by a full sensuous mouth, the softest mouth in New Mexico. But all of this led to her crowning glory, that full black bush between her thighs that throbbed with intensity at the very thought of screwing. Any man who had ever been in her knew she was truly the best he had ever had.

She smiled as she carefully powdered her thighs and perfumed her body preparing for "just another day at the office" with the good ole Mayor Bascom rooting and grunting over her body like a backwoods boar. Well, it sure beat the hell out of typing cause you sure as hell can't screw a typewriter. She laughed at the thought and began to throw on the usual mini skirt and white blouse. On the way out she grabbed a cup of coffee and headed for the door, still smiling at the thought.

Elsa sat in the sun room slowly sipping her coffee and absently staring out at the purple haze across the mountains. It was so odd how fate had played such a dramatic role in her life and really, in the lives of others who were involved around her. She had married Bill in the very best tradition, big wedding, big booze and a drunken bride-groom who viciously stabbed her virginity and wrenched it from within her. She could still remember that awful night and the next day when he mounted her with bulging eyes and drunken saliva hanging from the corner of his mouth. She wanted to leave him and return to the silent security of her Puritan home but she knew she would be the laughing stock of all of her friends, so she endured. All the books she had read, all the stories she had heard in the girls john bore no resemblance to the agony and sheer horror she had of another night in bed. She found herself thinking of her shopping list for the next day or who she should write to while the rhythmic in and out continued between her thighs. She would feel him shudder and moan and then that hot something flooded inside of her and she knew it was over. One good thing about it was that in a few minutes it was over and he would roll over on his back, spread eagle and begin to snore. She was safe now and she would carefully bath herself and put on her flannel pajamas so she could sleep secure.

It wasn't long before she knew there were two women in her husband's life and the other most certainly was not his mother. This normally would have driven Elsa to her family but oddly enough she found it most enjoyable. The massive attack on her body now began to slow and finally stop altogether. She found that she could even disrobe in front of him and still there was no reaction. She finally began to enjoy her sexual freedom and would tease him just to see if his dangling stump of manhood would come to attention and throb against his belly. Often at night she would wait until he was flopped out naked on the bed reading the paper to slowly take off her clothes. Only the paper moved. Then beautifully naked, she would stand in front of the mirror and massage her full breasts. This failing, she would lie on the floor next to his side of the bed and do her exercises. First she would lie on the floor and pull up one knee at a time to her full bosom exposing vividly her ample pussy and this failing, she would then pull up both knees to her bosom in the classic position of submission. The stump of manhood lay like a sleeping night crawler between his legs. She showed him her body in every ecstatic pose she could think of as she writhed and jerked through the wildest of exercises. And the final move was always the same. With the warmth of her body exuding from her, she would casually walk over to the night table next to his head on the pillow, pick up a cigarette and slowly light it and as a gesture of finality blow a heavy ring of smoke at his limp love maker. No words were ever spoken about either his non-performance or her sexually oriented exercises. She knew there was another woman and he knew for all her female animal gyrations she was as cold as a New Mexico winter. And so night after night they played their careful charade to the final twist of the lamp switch and a grunted goodnight.

The coffee was hot and the wind off the mountains blew loud and cold and Elsa involuntarily shivered in her short negligee, as she thought back to that day that fate crossed her path. They always said the wife was the last to know but she knew this was a saying from the dark ages. She knew it was a regular occurrence with her husband. The lingering smell of perfume, a blur of lipstick on the shirt or even his shorts at times, and of course those regular hours on Monday, Wednesday and Friday when he couldn't be reached at the office and had a meeting out of town. Of course, the final proof was that limp, uninterested stump of manhood that found sleep more desirable than even a bad screw, and she did admit to that.

Even though Elsa knew there was someone, she didn't know who it was until fate stepped in to show the way. She had been out to see her mother on a beautiful spring afternoon just south of town in one of the fashionable suburbs. They had enjoyed the day sewing and chatting, with Elsa willfully lying about everything being just wonderful at home and how they hoped soon to get a family started. She almost smiled at that thought since she was sure she couldn't get pregnant without some male assistance. When she was ready to leave, the battery in the car was dead so she simply took her mother's new convertible home. As she pulled onto the highway she thought for a moment she saw Bill's car pull out of an off-beat motel so she slowed slightly. The big red Cadillac was coming up behind her and moving erratically. She could see him clearly in her rear view mirror and next to him, intent on something in his lap, was the "across the tracks" niece whom she had begged Bill to give a job so she could help her widowed mother. The girl's head disappeared onto her husband's lap just as he pulled around her and as he got beside her, she could see the girl working furiously with his pants while he stroked her long black hair. He was intent on driving and on the girl as he passed her rapidly without a glance. That night she took particular relish in rubbing her body next to his in frantic desire, she knew she was safe and would be from now on.

So the fate of a dead battery in her car had given her the knowledge of who it was, which really didn't matter except from a pure ego point of view. She should have known that being the brutal animal he was, he would take particular delight in virtually contributing to the delinquency of an innocent minor. Her feelings for herself and her marriage were overridden by a sincere sorrow for the poor innocent who had succumbed to her husband's power of office. She was sure the job was given only in return for a willingness to become a sex slave to his honor, the Mayor.

The next day after the fateful happening, she stayed in bed until after Bill had gone to the office. For some odd reason, she now felt disgusted to even act out the part of the sensuous woman in front of him. He lit a cigar and puffed goodbye and left her to a re-living of yesterday. But this day was a day he would come to regret.

She listlessly got up and started to prepare coffee and then decided to mix a stiff Bloody Mary. What the hell, why not get drunk, who cares? Elsa was not what you would consider a heavy handed drinker and a few good ones would normally either put her to bed in a stupor or she would suddenly throw up, neither of which was too satisfactory, at least from the male point of view. She had once passed out with Bill before they were married and had come to in the back seat of his car with his hand bringing forth the warm juices from between her thighs. She couldn't move at first for the joy of it all, but then reality overcame the alcoholic content in her blood stream and she sent Bill writhing in agony as she clawed at his erection. She laughed crazily when she thought about it. "I should have torn the whole damn thing off for all the good it's done me," she said to her antique clock. "Screw 'em. They are all bastards and his pompous excellency, the Mayor, is the prize of the male sex hounds." She mixed another double and flopped whorishly on the couch willfully exposing her body beneath the shorty nightgown to the front door. "I think I'll just open the front door and see how long it takes to get raped." She raised an eyebrow, "Raped? Who's gonna rape who? Or is it "Whom?" There must be a rapor and a rapee for there to be an honest to God rape." Her stomach felt funny, she hadn't eaten, "Now, if I do the rapin, I'm the rapor and the man rapee will have to have me arrested." She swished her legs apart, "Your Honor, the Mayor, we beg leave to inform you, sir, that your wife has just been arrested for raping a big stud." She roared with absolute glee at the very thought of his frustration as his sweet, darling love making secretary looked on. Oh, it would be a fun scene but it would make Momma cry so instead, I'll just wait here and hope for a lover. By now she was completely preoccupied with sex and all the writhing, seething scenes in the X-rated movies and double X-rated paper backs. It seemed the whole world continually revolved around man loves woman, man loves man, woman loves woman, they all love each other in the same bed, a mad wild scene of sex, and she was willfully wallowing in the middle of it.

The door bell ringing had jerked her to a strained awareness. "The hell with it, let it ring," she thought but its persistence was unbearable. "Just a minute, I'll be right there." she swayed momentarily as she gathered her slippered feet under her. As she passed the hall mirror, she involuntarily gave her hair a fluff and tugged her shorty down an inch. "Ah, a fine good morning to you, Miss," Ron White was in his finest form.

"It's not Miss, it's Mrs., now what is it you want," Elsa had only exposed her head and one full breast behind the sheer gown as she peered around the door.

"Had I been correct at the outset and it had been Miss, I would have said it is you I want, but being a taken woman I can but remain loyal to my code of honor to never walk in another man's slippers, particularly when his wife's feet are in them. And so to the business at hand." Elsa couldn't tell whether she blushed or if it was the Vodka rushing to her head.

"I have with me this poor orphan boy who wishes to learn the trade of sales in my vast organization. Naturally, experience is the best teacher, don't you agree, my dear?" He smiled that bright blue eyed smile implying something vague and impish.

It was then for the first time that Elsa saw the small boy to Ron's left. He was neatly but cheaply dressed and had the look of a Saint Bernard puppy on his face. He looked at Ron like a child would his father and hung on his every word. Elsa felt more at ease now and took a drink from her Bloody Mary.

"I have taken it upon myself as the head executive to help this poor forgotten son of no one to enter into the fabulous world of free enterprise," Ron for all his talking had not missed the heavy full nippled breast, the Bloody Mary and the gently swaying door. "As a simple mechanism to the greater world of salesmanship, this waif has come to your door to simply sell you a subscription to your choice of your favorite magazine. Frankly, at the moment, luv, I can't tell whether he stands there in dumb-founded awe of my salesmanship or your astounding morning beauty." Elsa laughed and suddenly, rashly asked them both to come in out of the cold, New Mexico morning. It wasn't until they had almost bolted at the opportunity that she realized she still had on her shorty from last night, she quickly sat in an easy chair and tugged at the shorty while Ron's sparkling eyes never left her thighs.

"My husband will be down in a minute as soon as he is finished shaving," she lied poorly.

"Oh, really, well then, my dear, I must admire you for getting your lover out of here before your husband got up, that is truly a test of salesmanship at its best," Ron laughed loudly as Elsa looked at him in bewilderment, "You see, my dear, this young Horatio Alger and myself were at the corner of the block when we saw, shall we say "your lover" waltz out of the house with no less than his briefcase and a cigar."

She knew she was caught, trapped in a stupid lie because now he had to know she was afraid, and yet now that she was caught she was no longer afraid, now just curious about the next chapter in Ron White's magazine.

"Oh, really, well I'm sure that was my husband, he must have had an early appointment and left while I was fixing coffee."

Ron paid no attention, it was an old story, an old excuse, but the people were always different, "Ralph, show this beautiful woman what you have to offer her and remember to give her the sales pitch I taught you, son." He winked at Elsa who suddenly smiled back and finished her Bloody Mary.

Ralph stood close to her while he began the sales pitch and she obediently nodded and smiled at the boy. All this time, Ron had fixed his eyes alternately on her full blown bosoms with fresh morning nipples staring back at him, and that patch of promising joy between her thighs as she carelessly opened them to accommodate the magazines on her lap.

Ralph chattered on while Elsa made appropriate remarks and Ron eased into the kitchen and mixed two double Bloody Marys. He noted with an experienced eye that the coffee pot stood idly in the corner of the counter.

He handed a drink to Elsa who deftly took it and took a long drink from it before she realized what was happening. Ron could see stuffy wealth and frustrated sex crammed into the house side by side and he fully intended to take care of both of the problems.

"Very good, Ralph, I shall grade you accordingly even if—," Elsa interjected as if on cue, "Please call me Elsa, both of you," as she touched Ron's hand in an overwhelming feeling of friendship. He held her eyes glowingly with his as she rushed to get away, "I'll get my checkbook," she almost screamed hysterically. As she rushed up the stairs, Ron stared boldly. She reached the bedroom with her head swimming and her legs trembling. She knew she couldn't write a check so she jerked open the dresser drawer and took out two $20 dollar bills from a stack that was under the socks. She rushed for the closet and slipped on her heavy quilted robe and felt the trembling subside. She started by the great brass bed with the canopy and momentarily swayed and fell loosely on it. Her mind knew she had to get them out of her house. The room zoomed past her as she caught the brass headboard and pulled herself up. Slowly she came downstairs and took her place in the easy chair.

Ron sat easily on the arm of her chair and whispered "I'm delighted you put on your robe for the child's sake. All of that beauty beneath such a sheer gown might give the child an emotional problem, it certainly did me." He smiled at her as they toasted each other.

She bought two six month subscriptions hurriedly and told Ralph where the bathroom was upstairs. As he galloped up the stairs Ron carried on a never ending banter about nothing and she felt her head beginning to turn rapidly on its axis. Ron waited patiently until he saw Ralph coming down the stairs and got the signal that the cash had been cleaned out and how much. It was a good return for a short hours work and he was ready to move on.

Ron got up from the arm of Elsa's chair and gently patted her hand, "You are a complete dear to help this poor lad, my darling Elsa," he could see now she was about to pass out, but her glazed eyes were locked on his and her hand held his tightly. He was sure she was about to fall off the world and the only way to stay on was to lock herself in his arms while he jammed his locking bar deep inside of her to hold her secure.

He sent Ralph back to the Motel with the money and told him to stay in his room until he got back. Ralph almost drooled at the thought of what he would do to the big titted broad in her condition, but the boss got first choice and he had obviously chosen Elsa.

Ron turned back to his darling of the day, "Now my precious jewel, the time has come for us to learn all of the beauty hidden within us."

As he reached for her hand to help her to the bedroom, her head fell back listlessly on the chair. She was mumbling quietly while she smiled up at him. He bent closer to her, "to bed, to bed—carry me". Ron reached under her and felt the warm comfort of her thigh in his hand while the other reached under and around her to hold her breast firmly. He lifted her gently so he wouldn't get her excited. She smiled and whispered at first as he began to climb the stairs. Her robe fell open and her entire body was his. His mouth went to her parted lips as he felt a stirring in his groin.

Elsa's whispers were louder and louder and finally booming through the whole house, as she begged him to make love to her. She was on the bed moaning and writhing. Ron was so excited he almost felt sick to his stomach and he visibly shook all over. He threw his coat and tie on the floor and fumbled with his belt and zipper. With his pants still around his ankles he jerked his throbbing erection from his shorts and lunged at the open pulsating slash of joy between her legs.

Elsa felt only the first wild lunge by Ron as he penetrated into her belly and numbly realized that he had filled her with a surging load of love on the first stroke. She drifted off to the race of the rapor and the rapee.

And so it had been with Elsa and Ron on each visit to town. Her true warmth and willingness as a woman almost smothered Ron and she was afraid he would soon stray to other bedrooms in town and that would be the end. She had been a good pupil and Ron had taught her the fine art of being a dedicated lover. She had known but two men in her sexual life, one a boorish louse and the other just a louse. But at least the "louse" was a lover and her cup runneth over for him.

She got up from the couch, emptied her coffee cup and went to her bedroom. She reached in the dresser drawer for her panty hose as she recalled Ron's shocked disbelief the next day when she confronted him with the fact that $460 in $20 dollar bills had been stolen from the dresser drawer just coincidentally while he and Ralph had been there. She was just as shocked to see Ron and Ralph at the front door of her home within the hour. Elsa was glad she was fully clothed in blue jeans and a flannel shirt when they arrived, at least there would be no repeat of the day before.

Ron grabbed the boy by his tie and jerked him inside the door. "This Madam is a former, I repeat, former salesman of mine." He gave another violent jerk on the tie that sent the horrified boy to his knees before her. Ralph began to hold his breath so his face would turn red and purple. "Now you rotten beggar wrap yourself around this good woman's feet and beg for her forgiveness."

"My God, Ron, you're choking him to death. Let go, he's turning purple. Please, Please!"

Ron gave one more tug that sent the boy to her feet where he lurched against her body and locked his arms around her knees, "Oh, please maam don't call the police, I'll work for you, I'll be your slave, anything, just don't call the police. I sent the money home to my mama and eight brothers and sisters. I love you, I love you!" Elsa shuddered it wasn't true, this was a wild neurotic dream. Her life was set, secure and solid until yesterday when she found herself wildly making love to a man she had known but an hour and now today this chapter from Oliver Twist with a wild eyed urchin wrapped around her trembling knees.

Ron slowly and deliberately removed his wide belt, "This then must be your choice, my dear Elsa, the bastion or the belt." He somberly handed her the belt and he bent to pull the boys shirt up.

"Ron, have you lost your mind? I can't and won't do this to this child. His only wrong is wanting to care for his family. He knows he was wrong and I am sure he won't repeat this act of burglary."

"Oh, no Maam, never, I promise, I promise. Oh, I love you, I love you!" Ralph was trembling for all he was worth since Ron had promised him $20 for a good performance. He put real feeling into "I love you" since Ron had said she was a great lay and Ralph truly would like to love her, with a big stiff prick!

"Get up boy and thank your Gods, whoever they are, for the gracious generosity of this fine lady. Now take yourself from our sight and never set foot in this town of righteousness again. Get out, out!"

Ralph raced for the door and lurched outside where he had carefully hidden his magazines. He whistled aimlessly as he headed for the next victim, knowing he had earned his $20.00 from Ron.

Elsa began to lecture Ron but it was too late, his lips were on hers with both hands, under her buttocks, pulling her thighs against his hard solid erection. They went hand in hand to the big bed upstairs to rework, revive and refine yesterday's efforts.

Elsa carefully pulled on her panty hose and smiled as she remembered the next day when she picked Ron up at the Motel and there sat Ralph in his room. By now it made no difference. She knew

Ron was a beautifully perfect con man and while in bed he confessed that he and Ralph had set up the one act melodrama. She laughed so hard he lost his erection.

She explained to Ron that really she could care less since this was money that had been paid to the Mayor in cash for a few deft moves on his part. When the Mayor came bellowing that the money was gone she simply said she had used it to buy magazines. "For Christs sake Elsa you would be up to your ass in magazines for $500."

"I know, darling, but you see I bought the magazine man too," she replied, and smiled up sweetly from the pot. He didn't believe her but decided to let it drop since she knew where the money had come from.

Ron stared in disbelief and then rocked the motel room with laughter, "You know, between us, we could blackmail that old son-of-a-bitch into running this town just for us."

Now, as she pulled on her skirt, she mused that it hadn't just been a happening that Ron had not been run out of town long ago. Elsa made sure of this, she had Ron back again and again and both she and this god-damned town were his on arrival and Ron had arrived.


CHAPTER VIII

Russ knew that Ron had been seeing Elsa and at first he thought it was just one of Ron's ways to con the Mayor, through Elsa, to let him sell in town. He probably should have known better, at the outset, but good ole trusting Russ really didn't want to believe that sweet frigid Elsa was playing "sucky-fucky" with Ron. Damn near the whole town knew Elsa was a cold fish since the Mayor would loudly and drunkenly proclaim in public that he was, "the only damn man that lived with an Eskimo and didn't eat blubber." Not very funny, but since the only time Elsa was out in public with him was at his swearing-in ceremony, Russ guessed maybe he was right and Elsa didn't give a damn.

Ron still had a so-called wife that appeared and disappeared with some regularity but Russ assumed that this was probably just a marriage in name only. This time when Ron came in town almost the first call that came through the switchboard for him was from Elsa. Ron had always had standing orders that if any woman called him he was out on business. "If I want any god-damned broads, I'll call them. Ron White makes the choice, no one else."

So when Russ told this woman Ron was out on business, he was stopped cold when the voice said, "Russ, this is Elsa, the Mayor's wife, and I want to talk to Ron. Now get that shocked look off your face and get his ass on this phone."

Russ knew that Ron was busy doing nothing so he put the call through and told Ron who it was. At first he protested but finally said he would take it and to forget he ever heard her name.

Since then Elsa had called frequently and Ron obediently left after each call and returned looking two inches shorter and ten pounds lighter. Russ knew Ron well enough that he could tell something was churning inside of him but Ron wasn't the type to talk about his personal problems and Russ knew better than to ask.

And so when Ron came in on Thursday, one week to the day after he had arrived and told Russ he and his gang of guerillas were pulling out early Friday, Russ was visibly upset.

"What the hell, Ron, you were supposed to be in here for two weeks and here you are telling me you're pulling out a week early." Russ knew this would hurt the business and also that he had turned away others who wanted to come in during the time Ron was supposed to be here.

"Russ, I've know you a long time and you know I wouldn't do this to you if I didn't have to, but there just isn't any other way," Ron wasn't his cock-sure self and betrayed the look of a loser in his eyes. Russ didn't like the look because there was also a look of desperation and that meant real trouble for Ron and most certainly for someone else.

"Ron, you couldn't pick a worse time to pull out. In case you didn't know it, I appear before the Bar Committee on Friday for a hearing on reinstating my license to practice law. You know I need to be here when your troops leave." Russ was visibly upset. "Not only that, I've got problems with the management and if you pull out early they will raise all sorts of hell with no one but me." Russ flopped his big frame heavily on the torn leather chair.

"Russ, I know all this and that's the reason I'm in here today so you can work up the billing and make arrangements for tomorrow. Believe me, old friend, if there was any other way, I would help you out but," he saw the question in Russ' eyes, "All right, since you once were a damn good lawyer I guess I can confide in you but I want you to treat whatever I tell you as confidential and never divulge it to anyone, agreed?"

Russ felt a flow of pride as he once again was addressed as a lawyer and readily agreed to the confidentiality of the conversation.

Ron began to pace the floor and Russ snapped off the television and turned on the "No Vacancy" sign.

"As you well know, I have been seeing Elsa — well, hell I've been doing more than that, I've been screwing her ass to the mattress almost daily. Well, you probably noticed how her ass got smaller and her big tits bigger, and her whole self sexier. Well just chalk that one up to ole Ron. I have to admit it has been a good deal because she's not only a great jump but has money oozing out her pores and the old Mayor jumping through a hoop since he knows she knows he's laying some broad." Ron stopped and slowly lit a cigar. The blue smoke rolled around the room and disappeared out the crack in the wall, compliments of T. J. Mitchell.

"Well, you know how I am, Russ, I just can't stand sticking one girl too long, I need some variety. I never mess with any of these kids in my entourage, but little ole Elsa has got me so tied up that even some of these little heavy chested whores are looking good. So anyway, I finally lay it out cold, to Elsa, today while we were shacked up at her house. Honest to God, Russ, she went out of her head. She used words and combinations of words that Creature's mother taught me." Ron stubbed the cigar and spat in the waste basket. "I asked her what the big deal was, that she knew all along we were just lovers and she could sure as hell find another man with all the tricks I had taught her. She held onto me for dear life and even promised to go to a doctor and have it made tighter for me. I just laughed and crawled out of bed and began to put my clothes on. I told her again a new lover wouldn't care how tight it was the way she handled it. That he would be as good as I am and she wouldn't know the difference once he gave her a good screwing."

Russ shifted in his chair and from his past experience as a lawyer he knew the worst was about to come.

Ron stood slumped looking out at the bleak pool with the dirty slopping water, "That's when she let me really have it. She said he probably will be as good a lover, darling, but he won't be the father of my child like you are."

The world stopped for just a split second, and then began to turn again.

"So there it is Russ, she says she's pregnant by me and she's going to have the child. You know she's never had a child and you sure can't have one by a husband that doesn't screw you. Oh, I said all the neat things — like, how do you know it's my kid, go fall down the steps, tell him it's his, but she just sat there smiling saying she was going to get a divorce so she could marry me and have the baby."

Russ had that same old feeling you have for a client when they pour out their troubles. They aren't your troubles but that something special and different in a lawyer makes you feel as if they were your own problems.

"Now, Russ, I'm talking to you as a client but I don't want any god-damned free advice. I know you would do the so-called honorable thing and that is marry her. But there just ain't no way, my friend. I'm doing my honorable thing and that's getting the hell out of town for good. So figure up the bill and the cost of repairing any damage and I'll pay you in cash as usual. Oh, and by the way, good luck tomorrow. If you need a character witness I'll tell them you're a hell of a fine listener." With that the door slammed and he was gone.

Russ slowly unwound from the chair and routinely began to total up the bill. People and their problems. Sex and its slamming impact on people — not just some, but all, people.

## CHAPTER IX

"Now, darling, there's no sense in carrying on about it, I'm pregnant and it's not yours. It doesn't make a damn whose it is, the pure fact is that you and I both know it isn't yours. So let's just go ahead and dissolve this unholy marriage of convenience so you can marry your squaw and I can do what's right by my child." Elsa was strong. She was full with child and the knowledge that hopefully Ron was waiting for her to carry her off on the wings of love and fulfillment to an eternal life of sex and sun signs.

"What do you mean marry my squaw? What the hell are you talking about? I have been true and loyal to you these years upon years as only a man of great faith and courage could with a woman of your frigidity and unabashed rejection.

"Crap — pure crap. Don't you know your little Indian niece wears Chanel #5 and I wear Musk. Don't you know she leaves little souvenirs all over you, such as long black hair on your shirts, short black pubic hair on your shorts and above all you both always seem to be out of the office at exactly the same time. Crap and more crap, Bill Bascom," she furiously lit a cigarette and inhaled deeply. Her fury was not so much directed toward "his excellency" as it was the fact that she needed Ron now! She wanted to be with him this moment and have him stand with her in defense of their child and their pure and simple love.

"But, Elsa, that doesn't prove a thing, this is all circumstantial evidence. You know it is possible —"

"Bill, it is possible that you are Jesus Christ and I am the Virgin Mary about to have an immaculate conception, but the truth is I saw your secretary and niece, Faith, sucking the life out of you while you tried to hold the car on the road. Call her, call her now, and she will be the first to admit it and enjoy every minute of it." Elsa knew Faith would dearly love to see "Big Bill's" face when she rolled her black eyes in that adoring way and said "Why, Uncle Bill, you know we are great lovers—si?"

"Well at least I didn't get her knocked up like your son of a bitch did." Bill felt he had gotten to her on this one.

"Bill, I wish you could have knocked me up, I really do. And as far as your niece is concerned I hope you marry her and make her an honest woman."

"Marry her, are you crazy. The Mayor marries his niece, and she's a god-damned, half breed, Sioux on top of that! Elsa, for Christs sake, let's be reasonable." He began to pace and bite his left thumb. Pressure and more pressure building. "You get an abortion in New York, take a vacation in Mexico for a month, come on back and we can try and make a new start."

"So now it's 'let's try again' time, and while I'm snuffing out the life of the only child I have ever borne, you will sit home and mourn for me. Bull shit!" The whole scene was a cheap drama, a prelude to the damned of divorce. "No, Bill, I have my total fulfillment. I want out of this mess, and I am going to marry the father of my child. Just one more thing before you explode. I have already taken all the money out of the savings account, cashed in our certificates of deposit, cleared all the cash out of the safety deposit box and transferred the checking account over into my name alone."

Bill was flattened. Was it possible that sweet frigid, dull, dumb Elsa could really have done this to him.

Elsa's voice knifed him once more, "You see darling while you have been shacking up for afternoon matinees, I have been watching the television, 'Divorce American Style', and that's just what this is, honey." She flipped her cigarette in the dead fireplace, "Of course, I will let you off the hook and not ask for alimony, but I want this house deeded over to me or I'll do a rain dance with your darling niece in front of City Hall." Elsa was exuding all of the charm of a coiled diamond back rattler as she gently swayed toward him. "And in case you're thinking of pointing your stubby finger at my pregnancy I will sweetly say it's yours, and still zap you for the divorce and child support and alimony and castrate you in the process."

Bill, for all of his failings, was not stupid. The great American legal device of divorce was a pure bitch on wheels when the time came to separate a man from his accumulated savings of a lifetime. Emasculation was the name of the game and lawyers in their sanctimonious roles would sit on thrones as high priests as they gleefully separated man and wife, money and man and finally man from manhood.

"You lousy rotten bitch. You useless unpaid whore." He reached out like a giant cat and grabbed a handful of blouse and bra. She flew across the room against the wall. He threw her shreds of clothing at her as she sat there stunned and horrified. He was coming at her again and she screamed in terror as she folded her arms across her great tender bare breasts. He grabbed her hair and dragged her to the center of the room and to her feet. "Oh, God Bill, please, please be sensible." He began to slap her bosoms back and forth until she shrieked in both pain and terror.

"So you're going to clean me out. Well, you may do just that, baby, but at least I should get something for my money." He was dragging her toward the big bedroom. "If you're such a hot piece of ass then you must have been holding out on me. I want a fair return for what you have taken." He ripped off her skirt, pantyhose and threw her shoes across the room. First he tied her hands and then her feet with her pantyhose. He rolled her over on the floor and her bruised breasts throbbed wildly. She heard him leave the room and desperately she struggled to free herself. She rolled under the bed for protection and began to weep and moan, "Oh, Ron, my God, where are you. Help me, help us. Oh, my God." She was sure Bill wouldn't kill her but he was sadistic and this alone was enough to frighten her. He had gotten drunk once and had forced her to make love to an imitation penis. She had hated herself for months afterwards because she had reached her climax over and over.

He was by God going to find out just how good a lay she was. He found some rope and an old rubber hose in the garage. He cut off a piece of hose about a foot long. In his rage he stumbled on the steps and cursed violently. Elsa moaned and shuddered as she saw his feet at the side of the bed.

"Come now, my little pregnant pussy, we are going to play Doctor." He reached under the bed to grab her and she clamped down hard on his hand. Blood ran warm in her mouth, and she hung on like a bull-dog.

His hand was ripped in a ragged wound and blood flew across the bed as he jerked her out by her feet and threw her on the bed. "God damn you, I'll kill you for that. I'll kill you, do you hear me, I'll kill you," he screamed. He wiped the blood off on her round belly and began to tie her hands to the bedposts. He untied one leg and jerked it up and tied it to the top of the bottom post of the four-poster. Then the other leg the same.

"Oh, God, Bill, please, please. I'll give back all the money and you can have the house just don't hurt me any more, don't hurt the baby." Uncontrolled tears dampened her hair and soaked the sheets.

"Sure you will. Just like they all do." He leered at her, casually taking in her naked body while he wiped a bloody paw on her inner thigh. "Let me see, baby. I figure that you just took me for the grand total of about one hundred thousand big ones and I don't intend to let you get away with it just so you can marry your stud and have this love lust child." He was flushed with eyes bulging as he bent over her, "Now give your Billy boy a big kiss so we can have one for the road before I beat you black and blue with this piece of hose."

She turned her head away from his hot cigar breath. He violently jerked her head around and kissed her dampened lips. She bit his lower lip and screamed, "You son of a bitch, you never could make love to me so don't think you can start now." She saw the fist with the hose coming from above her as he spat blood from his mangled lower lip and grabbed her by the throat.

When she came to, she could feel warm salty fluid trickling from the side of her mouth. It was blood. Her eyes focused on the canopy above the four-poster. She was sure she was going to die. Why was it this was never in the television series. Divorce American Style always came out in favor of the woman. But what was it that the paper said about crimes of violence, that the majority of the crimes of violence, beatings, mayhem, murder were between husband and wife or estranged husband and wife. My baby, my baby, my God, Ron, can't you hear me, feel me, know I need you.

She realized that he had left the room. She looked desperately for a way out. She was flat on her back, arms above her head tied to the bedposts. In a haze of pain she realized that she was still bound both hand and foot unable to move without terrible wrenching pain in her stomach. Suddenly, as she rolled slightly to one side she felt a warm gushing flow. Elsa was aware something was inserted well up into her. She moved again and knew it was long and cylindrical and warm. She tried to look at the precious place between her thighs but could only see her full breasts, now bruised and discolored. She rolled and looked at herself in the mirror on the door as she lapsed into unconsciousness. "Dear God, have mercy!"

The postman heard what he thought was a scream for help, and then gentle moaning, but after all it was none of his business. He really wouldn't blame the Mayor for straightening his wife up with a heavy hand the way she had been laying around with that man and God knows how many others. Anyway it sure as hell wasn't any of his business. He rang the door bell and moved on to his appointed rounds.

CHAPTER X

The hearing had really been tough. Russ was exhausted and felt the need for dim light, soft music and a cold drink. He eased into the Motel bar and found a stool near the end of the bar. He muttered to himself as he noted the leather cushion was so old it had cracked open exposing the cotton guts. It was still early since the hearing had been completed by 11:00. Funny how many words can be said in two hours, how many years relived, how many memories rekindled.

"Hi Russ, what can I do for you?" Manny had been a bartender at this same location since it opened nine thousand years ago — or whenever it was. He had that bright red nose and a puffy face that comes from partaking of his own wares too often but he never got loaded, at least not so the general public could tell. Russ always knew because he would start to lisp ever so slightly when he over-indulged and the more he drank the worse his lisp.

"Hi Manny. I should just have a beer but since today will be a special day, whichever way it goes, I guess I'll have a Vodka on the rocks with a twist."

Manny, deftly, put the drink together, "You look all pulled out, Russ, this joint getting to you?" The drink came up on a clean cocktail napkin.

"No, it's not really that. Course this joint would get to anybody sooner or later, but I think it's already gotten to me, wrung me out, wiped its ass with me and thrown me out with the soggy used towels." Russ swished his drink with a long forefinger and gently lifted it to drink, "Well, Manny, here's a toast to today. May Russ Thurston be a better man no matter what decision comes down."

Manny smiled blankly and went to the other end of the bar to check his inventory on hand list. Russ swung around on his stool with his back to the bar, long legs dangling, feet almost touching the floor and stared a tired blank stare at the empty bandstand. Some day is right. The bar association disciplinary review committee had started off right at 9:00 on the dot. Russ was truly thankful he had hired a lawyer to represent him in the hearing. He was sure he would have blown his cool without a cautioning glance or a timely interruption now and then. Jim Ross was one of the straightest and most highly thought of lawyers in not only the State but the entire southwest territory. He had at one time been on the Bar Association grievance committee and it was said he was the only member who used some reason and common sense in the application of the Cannon of Ethics in disbarment proceedings. Jim took great pride in the legal profession and was one of its purest defenders, not failing his duty when called upon but at the same time cautioning that too rigid an application of its Cannons, as well as unwarranted and unjust punishment for those lawyers who strayed could, in fact, bring about a breakdown of justice through it's misapplication. In Russ' case Jim felt strongly that justice had indeed been meted out and properly served. It was now time to reinstate Russ on the rolls as a lawyer. No further good nor purposeful example could be served by refusing his reinstatement. Ten years in the prison of disbarment is enough, let justice be done!

The hearing was held in a private suite of the Downtowner Hotel in order to attract the least possible attention. Whatever took place at the hearing was extremely sensitive and of a confidential nature. The chairman of the committee, Bart French, was a jovial looking man from out-state. Only one member of the committee was from Santa Fe and that was D.J.'s father. How tempting to lay it on his pompous dad that D.J. had damn near drunkenly, single-handedly demolished the front office of the motel last weekend. But Russ knew he would play this hearing straight and the hell with the old pressure politics.

"Gentlemen, this hearing will come to order." Bart French turned to his left. "Mr. Reporter, are you prepared to take notes of the testimony given here? Very well we will proceed. Mr. Thurston, you are represented by counsel, I should say very capable counsel, Mr. James Ross, is that correct? Very well. Now, Mr. Ross, you, of course, are aware of the reason for Mr. Thurston's disbarment some ten years ago, are you not? Very well. May we then assume you will waive the reading of those charges and the disposition therof? Very well. You may make an opening statement if you care to, or waive same and proceed with your first witness. Frankly, since we are all lawyers on this committee I think I speak for the committee when I say that opening statements do seem a waste of valuable time."

"Bart, I quite agree with you and will so waive my opener and get on to our witnesses." Jim turned to Russ and in a loud clear voice said " Counselor will you step outside and call Bruce Robert as our first witness."

Russ was as startled as the committee at being addressed "counselor" but with a reassuring wink and nod of the head by Jim he arose and stepped outside to summon Bruce.

"Now Mr. Robert you know Russ Thurston here don't you?

"Yes, I do Mr. Ross."

"And just how long have you known Russ?"

"Oh, I guess about fifteen years. I knew him when he was a pro-football player and going through night law school," Bruce remembered that all too well.

Jim stood and slipped his hands in his hip pockets, "And have you had occasion to see him in action. By that I mean have you ever seen him try a case in court?"

"Yes, sir, I have."

"And your opinion, sir, as to his ability at that time as a trial lawyer?" Jims blue eyes pinned the committee to their chairs as he waited.

"Why, I definitely felt he was an excellent young lawyer with a great deal of talent in the courtroom."

"Are you a personal friend of his?"

"No, sir, no more than any other lawyer in town. We never went out socially."

"By the way, Bruce, perhaps some of the members of this committee are not familiar with your background. Would you please enlighten them?"

Bruce obviously took pride in his forthcoming answer as he sat up just a little straighter in his chair, "Well I was admitted to the practice fifteen years ago. Since then I have been on my own and now am the senior partner in the firm of Robert, Randall and Rouse. I was President of the Metropolitan Bar Association and named the Outstanding Lawyer in Santa Fe last year, this being based upon an attorney's ability, performance and integrity before the bar. I am a past International President of Optimist International, a service organization, and I am presently chairman of the State Judicial Committee for revision of our judicial process."

Jim had been careful to let the impact of Bruce's credentials sink in before he posed his final question, "Now Bruce, I will ask you if you have an opinion as to whether or not Russ Thurston should be re-admitted to the practice of law and if so just tell us what that opinion is and your reasons for it."

It was a foregone conclusion that Bruce would ask for the re-admission of Russ or he wouldn't have been called as a witness, but the reasoning behind the opinion would be interesting.

Bruce looked directly at the chairman, "Yes, sir, I do. I feel that Russ Thurston should be re-admitted and reinstated to our Bar Association. It has been a long ten years and any additional time on top of this could not possibly serve any useful purpose as a deterrent to Russ Thurston or serve as an example to the Bar in general. He has served his sentence, done his penance and should once more stand proudly before the Bar of Justice as an attorney."

Jim turned to the chairman, "Mr. French I have no further questions of this witness?"

Bart French leaned forward with a slight disarming smile and addressed the witness, "Now, Mr. Robert, if I may ask you a few questions. First may I make it clear that this committee takes no position on either side of the fence. We only know at this point that Russell Thurston was disbarred some ten years ago and that this disbarment was based upon competent evidence and ultimately ruled upon and determined by our State Supreme Court. We have acquainted ourselves with the transcript of those proceedings and we are, therefore, fully aware of the charges brought against Mr. Thurston, presented to the grievance committee, and which led to his ultimate disbarment. I shall, therefore, ask you if you are generally aware of those charges that were brought against Mr. Thurston?"

Bruce hated to go back to those bad times in front of Russ and he involuntarily glanced at the big man who was gently rubbing that scar over his right eye. God what a football player he had been and Bruce only hoped his guts would hold up during this ritual of the damned, "Yes, of course I know what they were and we might just as well get them out on the table right now. Russ Thurston got hooked on every narcotic you could pump in him. His habit demanded more money than he could supply from his law practice. He lost all of his savings from pro-football, lost his home, lost his wife and lost his license to practice law."

"Do you know the reason for that loss of his license?" Bart French was the exquisite high priest now forcing the rotten details out in front for Russ to relive and Bruce hated him for it. He glanced at Russ again and was stunned to see Russ smile and nod at him.

"Of course I do. He was handling a damage suit for a man who lost his leg in an accident. It seems that Russ had a one-third contract but when the case was settled for $60,000, and the check endorsed by his client, the money never got back to his client. In common parlance he ripped off his own client for $40,000 and blew it on junk for his habit. And, yes, I do know his client ended up on welfare and died five years later in a rest home for mentally ill." Now it was all out and we could move on. Damn some of these sanctimonious bastards from out state. You would think purity was a virtue reserved for country lawyers only. Russ was still smiling but it was a vague, frozen look and the bright red scar stood out like the devils own handiwork.

What wasn't said was the fact that during those five years Russ had seen to it that his client wanted for nothing. He was drained on a regular monthly basis by payments to the rest home and keeping booze in front of this one legged maniac. Be that as it may it was just what he had coming for such a way out move. He was just damn lucky he hadn't been thrown in the slammer besides losing his license to practice law.

"Now, Mr. Robert, you stated that ten years was enough. Let me ask you if this hearing had been called for by the defendant, pardon me, Mr. Thurston, one year after he had been disbarred — would that have been enough?

"Mr. Chairman, I can only say that had this hearing been called for one year after the disbarment of Russell Thurston I would have testified in the same honest and forthright manner as I have today but what my opinion would have been then would be purely speculative. I will say this though. It is my opinion that once a lawyer is disbarred and such disbarment is published to the general public and the general membership of the Integrated Bar Association, that the length of the disbarment can never exceed the mental degradation the lawyer must carry the rest of his life. He will relive past history each time he shakes hands with another lawyer, or hears the whispers as he walks into the courtroom.   Society is basically cruel and unforgiving. The very scandals blasting at us from the front pages of our newspapers tell us that the great mass of people on this earth relish the downfall of the hero, not his difficult climb to the pinnacle of success. And so it is with Russ Thurston. Will they remember him for his greatness or for the one time he stepped out of bounds? I think, unfortunately, we all know the answer.  Thank you for your attention, Mr. Chairman, members of the Committee."

Russ shook his head and smiled to himself as he put the empty glass on the bar for a refill. Yes, sir, just like that ole Bruce had laid it on them and then gotten up and walked out. You really don't have to say kiss my ass when you pull something like that, your point is made. He knew Jim was upset that Bruce had walked out and Russ was too since it might prejudice the committee against his case, but, God damn, you sure had to enjoy the drama and the old guts play.

Russ laughed at and with no one — just laughed, "screw 'em, screw 'em all." Manny just shook his head and filled the glass with Vodka and a deft twist of lemon. Russ turned around, elbows on the bar and two big hands all but covering the glass. He stared into the glass and slowly swished the lemon twist around the rim.  The eye of the whirlpool seemed to gleefully beckon to him, holding out all the joys to be found in the depths of delirium. "Not this time baby. I've got one more shot at the big brass ring and I fully intend to hang on to it for dear life." He gulped down the Vodka and slammed the glass down on the time worn bar. "Manny, that's the best damn martini I've had in years. Someday you'll have to give me that secret mixture." He swung around and before Manny could answer was out the door.


CHAPTER XI

Willis looked up with unseeing sleep-laden eyes that suddenly popped open when Russ came in.

"It's no wonder you're half asleep in here — the goddamn place is hot as hell." Willis pulled the plug on the electric heater and opened the door briefly.

"What time did Ron and his band of bastards get out of here? He usually is on the road before breakfast." Russ was slowly sorting out the junk mail from the bills and complaints.

"He left later than usual. I wondered about that but then Creature's mother laughed and said Ron had fallen headfirst in a Vodka bottle and couldn't drag it out of bed this morning. I buzzed his room for early wakeup but he didn't answer. I just figured he was already up and in the shower so I didn't buzz him back."

Russ agreed it must have been Vodka since this was the first time Ron had failed to roust out at sunrise, come hell, high water or Bourbon and water. The switchboard lit up and Russ easily picked up the phone. "This is Russ, can I help you?"

"Russ, this is Thadeus Mitchell, II, T.J.'s father. I was wondering if you could possibly enlighten me on a couple of points." Before Russ could stammer out an answer he went on "Right after we concluded our hearing this morning my son, T.J. III, made an unexpected call at my office. The last time he was at my office he wet his diapers on a Supreme Court brief. His regard for the law and his father has been thus ever since. So you would agree that his visit now was quite unexpected and unusual, wouldn't you? Yes. Well —" Russ thought you bastard let me answer the question, if you really want an answer; "Well, be that as it may, it seems that I mentioned your hearing in his presence and he just dropped by to see how it went and to let me know what one hell of a great guy you were."

There was a long deliberate pause. This time Russ knew it was his turn to answer the unasked question but he fingered that pulsating scar and kept his silence.

"Well now, Mr. Thurston, I am sure I don't need to remind you that tampering with a committee duly appointed by our Bar Association and working in behalf of the best interests of our judicial system, is a criminal offense and would, of course, prohibit any consideration of your reinstatement as an attorney at law."

Russ couldn't stand this pompous bastard and he wanted to scream at him that his no good pot smoking kid should keep his Goddamned nose out of other people's problems and business. Deep down inside of him he pulled the lever marked "Lawyer" and replied in his most senatorial voice, "Why, Thad, I really am surprised. I have met your son a time or two under the most pleasant circumstances. I am pleased that I conveyed the proper image of an attorney to him. I might add that regardless of your son's physical expression for the law it would appear his sense of duty and honor follow those so often expressed by his father. I would only hope that any son of mine would follow such an honorable cause as T.J. has. Please thank him for his unsolicited assistance and I do hope his injection into this matter won't bring the wrath of the committee or his family down on him."

The silence was ear splitting only that throb told Russ he was still alive and every inch Russ Thurston not the mealy mouthed fink he had just portrayed. Anything for that reinstatement. If he ever got that license back to practice law he would chew it up and swallow it so no one, but no one could take it away from him again.

"Well, Russ, I am sure T.J. would appreciate your thoughts and, of course, I do. Your explanation is quite satisfactory to me. Incidentally I have some feeling that the committee as a whole is looking with favor on your application for reinstatement. I shall go directly from here to the hearing room for our final decision."

Again, the long thinking loaded silence, again, Russ bit his tongue and squeezed the phone so hard his knuckles turned white.

"Incidentally, Russ, just in case it should happen, I would appreciate your refusing my son admittance to that so-called Motel you manage, and that includes the bar. Thanks and good luck."

Russ held the phone tightly and heard the distinct click and then the hum of the disconnect. He very carefully placed the phone in its cradle and stared at it. That son-of-a-bitch knew about T.J., pot and pussy all the time, and now he knew Russ would keep that knowledge locked up, he knew Russ Thurston was a man of honor even when his license was on the line. Well bless little T.J.'s pot pickin ass! He laid it on the old man and watched him perform like a puppet on the string. Let's hear it for T.J. one more time. He looked up at the old noisy clock on the wall it was 11:30 a.m. and the committee was "looking with favor" on Russ Thurston.

## CHAPTER XII

The Mayor had on his "grieving for the citizens" look when Russ flipped on the faded corner TV. The usual unexciting 6:00 news was about to begin its usual unraveling of the tangled web of nothing that went on endlessly in New Mexico. Russ turned the volume up so he could hear it while he busied himself at the adding machine to figure out the payroll for the week. It never ceased to amaze him that week after week he could continually come up with different totals on the wages for the same employees working the same hours. As a lawyer he was a rotten accountant.

"This is an exclusive interview with the Mayor of our city who is still dazed and shocked by the grizzly events of the day" Russ glanced up and lunged forward to clear up the picture.

The front door of the Mayor's home hung unceremoniously open with a tangled mass of cables running in and up the stairs to an open bathroom where an unquestionable bloody hand print was on the white marble sink. The camera hit a tight close-up of the print and then fanned away to the corridor appointed in light blue carpeting leading to a bedroom with a beautiful lace topped brass four poster bed. It was a scene from *Gone with the Wind*, the grace and beauty of the old south, and suddenly the horror of Sherman's bloody march to the sea. The faint "Oh my God" gasped by the veteran cameraman was enough to warn the glassy-eyed public that this was no bedtime story. The bed was a soggy mass of bright red blood with great globs of discharge intermixed. One bed post at the head of the bed had been snapped off like a broken toothpick. The death throe had been unparalleled in frantic strength.

"And this horror greeted our first citizen when he returned home to retrieve a forgotten savings account passbook this morning. Irony is hardly the word for his happening upon the scene apparently only moments after the attacker had left. An errant passbook for an anniversary present has led police to a suspect now being held in maximum security. Bill Wells has the story."

"The Mayor called the police immediately when he found his wife of fifteen years dead in the upstairs bedroom. The grotesque figure of his wife twisted and tortured has left the community in a state of shocked disbelief. The Mayor could only sob out "My god, on our anniversary." Mrs. Bascom died of massive hemorrhaging induced by the insertion of a short section of garden hose into the vagina with tremendous force. The final report from the Coroner has not yet been received. Here, at County Security, the police have a suspect who is being held for questioning. Apparently this suspect was seen near the home at about the time the Mayor arrived home. Security here is extremely tight to prevent any leaks from within as well as to safeguard the prisoner. Emotion in our town is at the lynching level. This is Bill Wells at County Security."

"Thank you, Bill, and back here at the scene, the Mayor has asked that cool heads prevail and anyone who can be of assistance to the county police to please come forward immediately." He turned to the Mayor.

"Mr. Mayor, only a brief word or two from you on this solemn occasion."

Russ couldn't help but admire the old bastard. There he was with his most stricken yet brave chin up pose. Russ had seen this same pose when he stood next to the demolished school bus after the onslaught by the Union Pacific express train, and again after the great fire had leveled the old city hall. This was the only genuine part of the pompous white-collared crook. Even so Russ felt a tightness inside for his grief now oozing out of the scratchy T.V.

"The horror, oh God, the horror of it all. My poor, May God have mercy. I'm sorry, I just can't talk, I just can't —"

"We all understand your horror and offer the unbounding sympathy of your city. Thank you, back to you Reggie."

"In the mideast, Sadam Hussein once again has taken a stand —" Russ switched off the set and stared out the window at the dirty winter landscape. He wondered who the suspect was and also wondered just how the police had come up with an arrest so quickly. Must have been fingered by an eyeball witness or he blew the whistle on himself. This had to be a crime of extreme passion — a way-out thing from the little he had heard and seen. Well, it wasn't his problem. He was just glad they had caught the son-of-a-bitch that went berserk and killed her.

Willis roared into the office and slammed the door loudly. Russ winced and inwardly regretted the fact that Willis was beginning to act like some of the hot shot shack ups that made the overnight scene.

"God damn, Russ, did you hear the news. The Mayor's wife was raped, mutilated and murdered by a mag salesman who worked for Ron." Willis flicked on the television which Russ promptly flicked off.

"Willis you are an absolute wealth of information. Now which program did you watch from which you glean this story of hell and damnation. The living color I saw only said she was dead and they had a suspect in tow. Now enlighten me."

"Hell, I haven't even seen the TV. You know where all the straight copy is. Back in the laundry room. I took a bottle into Black Helen and all the girls were talking about it. Helen says that the word was out that Elsa was makin it with some other guy who would come around during the day always with an armful of magazines. Now you know that has to be one of Ron's little heros doing his extracurricular activity for a little pin money. Well Helen says that Billy Jo Washington had more than just pin money last time she saw him and disappeared before Ron pulled out not to be seen again. So there you have it, must be Billy Jo down at County Security."

"Willis, why would Billy Jo rape her if they were lovers, and why kill her or torture her if she was giving him money anyway? I'm sorry but my long lost latent talent as a lawyer tells me the girls in the laundry fell in the gin bottle and came up cross-eyed and doubled headed."

Russ got up to leave just wanting to forget the whole mess. It still wasn't his problem even though as a lawyer he could see the earmarks of a hot case with the whole town in an ugly mood ready to convict just as easily as Willis had done.

Willis grabbed the phone, on its first ring then motioned to Russ as he studied the TV guide.

"Russ, that you? Listen I can only talk a minute but I have got to get help. You are the only one I know that I can rely on — will you help me?" Ron sounded desperate.

"Ron, you know I will if I can. I thought you were long gone on the way to Texas. Where the hell you calling from?"

"Russ, did you ever try a murder case? Don't bother to answer, I know you haven't but you've got one now."

"Ron, what the hell goes on. I'm not even reinstated as a lawyer."

"You will be and when you are I'm your first client. They have me fingered for the murder of Elsa Bascom. Don't just say "bull shit" tell me what to do."

"Ron, don't make any statements. Don't talk to anybody, not the cops, not your cell-mate, not me until I tell you to. I'll see about a bond for you if they will even set one. Right now the town is so upset the best place for you is right there in County Security."

"Ok, Russ, I've got the picture. You know how I like to talk but this time I keep it shut. You call me 'cause this is the first and last call they will let me make. See ya."

# PART II

## CHAPTER I

It was one of those unusual dry hot winter days in Santa Fe. Unusual for this time of year but it was not unusual that the air conditioning was not working in the turn of the century old courthouse. The voters saw absolutely no need for a fancy new courthouse when this one was still solid and had plenty of room for the jurors. As far as air conditioning was concerned it worked most of the time and besides it just didn't get that hot when the courts were is session. Well at least that was the consensus of opinion by the voters who continually turned down bond proposals for a new courthouse. This definitely was not the opinion of District Judge Rachael Rawlings as she stood totally naked in front of her full length mirror on the door of her court room chambers. She carefully admired her thirty five year old body and proudly stroked her flat stomach just above her beautiful flaxen mound. She gently swept her blonde shoulder length hair back and dabbed at the perspiration as it trickled between her pink nippled breasts. She was proud of the fact that she had kept her body in the shape of a twenty year old. At least the smart ass new lawyers, admitted to the integrated bar, couldn't call her old lard ass or some of their other choice sayings. She slipped into her favorite bikini panties with pink bows on them, picked up some sheer panty hose and then stuffed them back in her desk drawer, it was too damned hot to worry about her personal decorum under her heavy black robe. No bra either, since it was a cinch her thirty six c's couldn't be detected swaying gently under the unflattering robe. As she made her way to the small bathroom with the antique fixtures she picked up the criminal docket to see the days line up. Mondays were always fast and furious in the criminal division. The day would be full of preliminary hearings and a multitude of motions, most of them of the bull shit variety.

On Tuesday things settled down as the jury trials began that took up the rest of the week. Rachael really preferred to stay in the civil trial divisions but since she was the junior member of the twelve division district courts for Santa Fe county, she had to take the least desirable position. Not only was it the least desirable but it also meant that she had to deal with the prosecuting attorney, James "Buzz" Rawlings, her ex-husband. This invariably caused her some discomfort since the news media was constantly looking for ways to claim that she was prejudiced in favor of the State and against the defendants.

She and Buzz had known each other in law school and had studied together. He was typical of the western breed that make you want to smoke a Marlboro. Tall with blonde hair, penetrating blue eyes that told the jury to damn the defendant to purgatory and a disarming brilliant smile that totally swept you away. He was the essence of a trial lawyer. Not to be outdone, Rachaels beauty made her the delight of every professor in law school. Invariably she would take a seat in the front row and promptly display her magnificent feminine charms. Some of the senior members of the faculty were said to have found a new sexual urge they hadn't known for years when Rachael attended their classes. Fortunately Rachael was as talented intellectually as she was sexually which led to her graduating at the top of her law school class. The resentment among the male students was understandable under the circumstances but this did not deter Buzz from taking this class charmer as his wife on that same graduation day.

Rachael was offered the prestigious job of law clerk for the United States District Court which she promptly accepted at a most respectable salary. Buzz, on the other hand, hired on as an assistant prosecuting attorney for the district courts of Santa Fe county. Although his duties at first were primarily mundane, of the tote and fetch variety, he rapidly moved into the courtroom as a trial prosecutor. It was at this point that the marriage began to come apart. Rachael was deeply into legal research and brief writing for the U.S. District Court and enjoyed a top drawer reputation among the blue chip law firms. Buzz was recognized as a flambouyant non scholarly street fighter type prosecutor with an excellent conviction record.

Buzz decided to run for the office of prosecuting attorney with the blessing of his boss, who was retiring, and he was deemed to be a sure thing at the next election. He was unopposed in the primary and the news media had endorsed him all the way.

In the June before the fall election, Judge Connelly of the District Court of Santa Fe County was stricken with a heart attack and died shortly afterward. Through Rachaels connection with the U.S. District Court and because of her reputation as a brilliant law clerk, the big law firms of New Mexico suggested to the Govorner that she be appointed to fill Judge Connellys' division. Since she would be the first woman judge on the District Court of New Mexico it would certainly enhance the Govorners position with the female voters at the next election.

The offer was made and Rachael, flattered beyond belief, accepted immediately for fear someone might change the Govorner's mind. She immediately called Buzz to tell him the good news. He was more than cool in his response and simply said, "We'll talk about it when you get home" and hung up. Rachael couldn't believe his attitude and took off work early to be at home to greet him with his favorite dry martini. The six o'clock news came on and, of course, there was the announcement of her appointment. When Buzz finally came in the door an hour later, it was apparent he had already had his share of after court cocktails. Rachael smiled and gave him the usual peck on the cheek. He whirled around and faced her and his flashing blue eyes sliced across her face like the cutting edge of a whip.

"Rachael, for Christs sake, what were you thinking of to accept the judgeship? Don't you know what position that puts me in as the prosecuting attorney when I win this election? How in the hell do you think I can bring criminal cases in front of you to be heard? There would be an automatic change of judge and probably a change of venue to another county."

Rachael knew immediatly that he was right but she also knew she wanted this new honor as a Judge. "Buzz, I really don't see what difference it will make." she lied, "Just think this through and you will see that most lawyers would love to have you in front of your wife, in court, just to have an automatic appeal for prejudicial error should they lose the case."

"Rachael, this isn't one of those legal briefs you write for some snarling Federal Judge where you play cat and mouse with one theory against another. This is the real world and this is my career you are fucking with." He was flushed with anger and martinis.

"Your career, big deal, and how about my career," she whispered, "just who is fucking with whom? It seems to me while I sat in a musty library writing legal briefs, you were on the loose as Mr. Hotshot prosecutor, charming the public, who looked back over his shoulder on occassion at "Rachael who?" Her lips quivered and her voice began to choke up as she reached for the now warm martini she had mixed for him.

"It won't work. You know it won't work so you might as well just call the papers and retract your acceptance of the job." He slumped into a soft leather sofa and rested his chin on his thumbs and looked up at her with soft pleading eyes, but it was too late. It had probably been too late even months before when they both began to follow different shining lights as they warily moved ahead in their chosen fields of expertise.

And so it came to pass that a very quite dissolution of their marriage took place in a county far removed from Santa Fe County, where they both came forward under oath to admit the irretrivable breakdown of the marriage. The irreconcilable differences certainly were there but at least the parting of the ways was accomplished with dignity and decorum befitting a Judge and a Prosecutor.

She sighed heavily in her reverie and came back to the realization that she once again was faced with another week of rape, incest and murder. The Judgeship had really turned into a nine to five job punctuated only by "overruled" and "sustained" as the gladiators on the courtroom floor below her bench jousted to charm the jury of their peers and hopefully keep the Judge awake. She slipped into the black robe and discreetly left two buttons open at the top to let those two full beauties breath during the long day ahead. Then she slipped on her low heeled very unbecoming but comfortable loafers and with one last glance in the mirror was ready to open her chambers door to the howling masses in her clerks office.

A gentle knock at the door told her that her clerk, Hannah Nolan, was there with her first cup of coffee and the latest run down of the days work that lay ahead.

"Come in, Hannah", the door opened to a rush of hot air, cigar smoke and the usual arguments over the week-end basketball games.

"Morning, your Honor. Would you believe I even got here early enough today to grab a couple of danish rolls down in Division Four before those cheap ass lawyers got all of them. Cost me half a buck though. That god damned bailiff down there is building up the coffee fund again."

Rachael opened the top drawer of her massive oak desk and moved her panty hose over to get at her petty cash and flipped Hannah two quarters, "Never let it be said the Judge, in Division Six, is a cheap son of a bitch." She leaned back in her high backed leather chair and took a slow willful sip of her coffee and felt the sweat run down the back of her neck. "Hannah, the most important business today is to get the god damned air conditioning working. If that can't be accomplished then you have an all day job of locating a fan to put behind my bench to blow some hot air up my ruffled robe to keep my ass from swimming in sweat on that hot leather chair. Do you realize it is ten degrees warmer up where I sit looking down on all the peasants on your level?"

Hannah had a mouthful of danish and sticky fingers but she nodded dutifully and began to pull out the morning docket. "Well, at least you can get your day off to a fast start. We've got that Murder One case to set for a preliminary hearing. You know the one where the Mayor's wife got the hell beat out of her. This is really a bad one and as you know the whole damn town is up in arms about it."

"I guess the Marlboro man, himself, will be handling this one. This will be his next step on up and away to bigger and better political achievements. All I can say is I am sure glad he won't have little ole

Rachael tagging along", she absently threw her paper napkin over her shoulder at the waste basket behind her.

"So just who is the hot shot for the Defendant and who the hell is the Defendant anyway?"

Hannahs eyes sparkled with delight as she handed the docket sheet over to the Judge to see for herself.

"You've got to be kidding me. Russ Thurston is back in court? I don't believe it. When the hell did he get his license back? How did I miss out on that little goodie of gossip?"

Hannah deftly reached across Rachaels' desk and answered the phone. "Yes, the judge is in, no, she is busy, yes, she will open court as usual promptly at nine o'clock and no, she does not permit television cameras in court." She dropped the phone in its cradle and smiled at Rachael, "The usual bullshit from the great Santa Fe news media which is about to swarm all over this normally quiet little ole Division Six. Anyway, Thurston got his license back late Friday afternoon so as usual it made about one inch on the back side of the sports section. Remember he used to be some big time football jock."

Rachael knew all about Russ Thurston and his days of glory as the Mr. tight end in the NFL. She had even had her hands clamped onto that naked tight end as he made her flounder and thrash with total sexual upheaval. Those were the days when she was one of the cheer leaders for the Santa Fe Mustangs. It didn't take long for one Russ Thurston to see a very finely tuned piece of equipment frolicking on the side lines. The rest had been history, with the usual bed and breakfast routine, the eternal professing of love forever and then the agonizing relinquishing of your lover to another. Rachael stared absently at the clock on the wall while she carefully relished the memory of this great powerful, yet tender, lover. Odd how you can remember where the lover made you a part of him. A small party, just three couples, at the managers mansion looking over a beautiful lake with snow dusting the tops of the mountains in the background. Russ was almost out of it on drugs so she took him off to the bedroom to calm him down. The door closed and he was on her like a maniac. She kept her cool and slowly stroked his swollen groin with expert fingers while her tongue wrapped around him. He shuddered and begged her to take him in her mouth. Gently she stroked him toward bed, then carefully worked his shirt and pants off and suddenly jerked down his shorts to expose his throbbing erection. He was reaching for her desperately and she quickly slipped out of her clothes unleashing her magnificent full up turned breasts. He grabbed her panties and pulled them away from her soaked, steaming box of love and slid inside of her. She gasped and pushed him back on the bed. As his legs clamped around her he came in great moaning gushes. He fell slack on the bed, his head off of the pillow but his throbbing erection stood tall and straight. She took it and held it while she mounted him. She lowered herself on him and exploded with love over and over again as he sucked her sweet nipples now as hard as his erection. Then with one final massive lunge they both came together and again shuddered in spasms as they slowly became uncoiled.

She held herself involuntarily in her great leather chair and knew that her nipples were hard under the black silk robe. "Yes, I remember Thurston alright, quite a guy but what the hell is he doing trying a murder one case on his first time out of the chute since he got back in the arena? He doesn't know his ass from third base about the trial of a murder case."

Hannah shrugged and got up ready to start the days parade. "Well all I can tell you is that this defendant, some kind of con artist mag salesman, is supposed to be a friend of Thurston so I guess ole Russ latched onto the case to make some quick bucks. It's sure got to beat running that flea bag motel."

"Let's get out there and see what the great world of crime and catastrophe has brought us this week." Rachael swiveled around in her chair and got to her feet with all the grace of a lovely lynx on the prowl. "Give me a few minutes to put on my Monday morning judicial face and then hit the buzzer right at nine o'clock and Hannah please beg that maintenance man to get the God damned air conditioning fixed, my robe is already stuck to the crack of my ass." She moved toward the wash room and her make up.

"If I had a sweet ass like you have I wouldn't mind showing these courtroom cowboys a little clinging robe routine." Hannah pointedly shook her flabby cheeks as she ducked the pencil Rachael let fly. She squeezed out the door into her office past the usual complaining lawyers. It was easy to single out Russ in the small office. He towered over most of the lawyers and still had those massive shoulders, large but graceful hands and the cutest tush in the Southwest. He was particularly silent today and it was no wonder this being his first day back in the courtroom. Not to mention that he had a murder case staring him in the face. Hannah caught his eye and gave him a quick wink. He returned it with that gleaming sensual smile and a quick wink that brought the blush to her face. Face hell, to her entire body. God he was still some hunk of heaven.

"Well is the old girl going to be on time today or is she in her usual Monday morning mystery mood and has decided to punish the integrated bar by being an hour late for the docket call?" It was Buzz Rawlings with his usual entourage of female law school graduates hanging on his every word as they caressed his files and briefcase.

Hannah continued to pull the files for the morning docket from the old beat up four drawer legal filing cabinets. She threw an armful of files on her desk, glanced at the clock and then back at Buzz.

"She will be on the bench at precisely nine o'clock and you had better be ready to fish or cut bait when we start through this mass of files or we will be here until midnight. And since her honor is well aware of your propensity to chase pussy all night she just might enjoy holding court tonight. After all it is with great infrequency that we are honored with the presence of the great prosecutor himself."

With that she slapped her hand down on the buzzer and picked up the docket sheet while the bailiff, Harry Bates, picked up the heavy files.

Hannah moved past Buzz who had a "hurt to the quick" look on his face but she still felt the quick pat on her ass as she looked into the face of innocence.

"Don't mess with what you can't handle Buzz boy. I have been known to rope and throw some of the bigger studs in this sun baked heaven on the hill. Just one little pat isn't enough to keep me from suggesting a night session to clean up the docket." She fell in line with the stream of lawyers exiting from her office through the rear doors of the courtroom. It was the usual Monday morning full house with all the chairs taken in front of the spectators rail and even the jury box filled with lawyers. She laid the docket on top of the files just as Harry banged down his gravel.

"All rise please." The door behind the judges elevated bench swung silently open as her honor gracefully stepped from her chambers around her high backed burgundy leather chair and then stood motionless with her long fingers folded easily before her. Harry banged the gavel down once more to quiet down the legal gossip of the week end. "Order, order in this court." Harry was big, black and a retired Marine Sergeant with much Vietnam time behind him and thus when order was called for, order there was, and a hush fell across the courtroom like a cold blanket of heavy wet snow.

"Oyez, Oyez, Oyez. This honorable district court, Division number Six of the great state of New Mexico, the honorable judge, Rachael Rawlings, presiding, is now in session. All those with business before this court may now draw near and be heard. No talking or smoking while this court is in session." There was a pause while Rachael lowered her head in silent prayer as did some of the attorneys present, and then with a quick nod to the bailiff she seated herself behind the bench of justice.

Harrys' gavel crashed down like the crack of lightening in the now silent courtroom as he intoned, "You may be seated." All of the lawyers now had on their serious faces as they began to look through their files and anxiously look out over the court room for the appearance of their clients who were out on bond.

"Now, gentlemen, we have an enormous docket to handle today. So I would suggest you keep your impassioned speeches for the benefit of your clients, brief and to the point." With that the judge turned to Hannah who was at her desk to the right of the judge and some four feet lower and asked her to call the first case. And so the system began to slowly grind out the problem people of the great state of New Mexico. The whispered conversations between attorneys as they awaited their call before the judge, gave a constant air of urgency to the whole proceeding. Some judges resented this whispered background music, found it disturbing and contradictory to the bailiffs explicit order of "no talking while the court is in session." Rachael on the other hand had often heard her ex husband, Buzz Rawlings, state that many cases were settled with these whispered conversations between prosecutors and defense attorneys at the last minute before the case was called. For some unknown reason it was always felt that the "best deal" could only come about when the pressure was on both sides to "fish or cut bait." Of course it must be said that this whole process caught the unsuspecting alleged criminal totally unprepared for the awe of the high ceiling court room with it's fine mahogany walls and many somber bearded past judges glaring down at them from their framed pictures on these sacred walls. The plea bargaining process was therefore hard at work in the arena of justice as the court continued to call those cases that could not be disposed of by settlement.

Russ was lost in his own thoughts as he watched the now unfamiliar drama unfold before him. Why in the hell he was even in here representing Ron was beyond his own belief. But Ron still insisted, even after Russ had explained that a criminal lawyer was as much a specialist as a brain surgeon. All Russ could hope for now was that somewhere along the way to the trial Ron would agree with him and at least get a top drawer criminal lawyer to assist in the trial. He had a chance to talk to Ron on Sunday and really all that came out of the conversation was that Ron knew nothing about the murder, was innocent but did have a torrid affair with Elsa and was sure it was his child she was carrying. Other than that Ron spent a good deal of time asking Russ questions, most of which were still unanswerable. One thing was for sure though, because of the undeniably horrible nature of the murder it was going to be a charge of first degree murder or as they say in the legal arena, Murder One.

He felt a heavy hand on his shoulder and turned around to see a solemn faced Buzz Rawlings looking at him. "I hear you have the son of a bitch that butchered up the Mayor's wife. All I can say is that you sure picked one hell of a way to get back into the law practice. Oh by the way, I do assume you got your license back after the hearing Friday?" The smile was a smirk and Russ knew there wasn't now, nor had there ever been, any love lost between them.

"Well, Buzz, I don't have the sacred card with me with my name on it but if you want you can check with the District Clerk to see if I am properly enrolled to practice in New Mexico. In the mean time maybe you and I can do a little talking about this case just to make sure you have the right person charged with this murder."

"Listen, Russ, I am going to personally handle this case and I am personally going to see to it that the guilty verdict is also the death penalty. So you can save your breath trying to work out a deal for your hero — he is on the way to the Gas Chamber." Buzz turned and walked away with his bouncy bunch of assistants following in lock step. Russ really didn't know enough about the case to tell Buzz to shove it and make it sound like he meant it. So the best he could do at this point was to believe his own client and file the usual pre-trial discovery motions to find out what the State had against Ron as solid evidence.

The guards had brought Ron into the courtroom where he was seated with the other prisoners. They were all wearing bright orange jump suits with large black P's on front and back. The manacles which were on the other prisoners ankles were removed but not those that Ron had on, nor were his hand cuffs released. He looked strangely sad as he sat next to the heavy jowled guard and his eyes seemed to move frantically around the court room looking for a familiar face. Russ walked over toward him just as the clerk called out, "State of New Mexico versus Ronald White, all step forward please."

Russ held Ron's arm in order to help him shuffle across the courtroom to the judges bench where he faced the Judge. Russ was tall enough that he looked straight into those bright blue eyes of Rachaels' as he approached the bench, flanked by the prosecuting attorney and his staff.

Rachael smiled pleasantly and greeted Russ with a little more warmth than the usual judicial demeanor. "It is so good to see you again Russ. I heard the good news just this morning before opening court. We have all missed you and we welcome your return to the practice."

"You are most gracious your honor and may I say that I can't think of any other courtroom I would rather be in to start the second half of my career."

Rachael could feel the flush to her face and the droplets of perspiration between her breasts rolling across her flat stomach to be devoured by her downy full mound. God could she still have these feelings about her once upon a time lover?

"I am sorry though that it has to be an appearance of such a somber nature that brings me before your honor. May the record show that I am entering my appearance as attorney for the defendant Ronald White."

"The record shall so reflect your entry on behalf of the defendant." As Rachael was making the minute entry on her records she could feel the presence of Buzz as he leaned well forward and whispered,"Are you sure he has his license back, maybe you should check with the District Clerk's office?"

Without looking up Rachael told the bailiff to declare a fifteen minute recess and told Russ and Buzz to come back to her chambers. She stood and glared at Buzz, then turned and left the courtroom.

Down came Harry's gavel with a crash,"All rise, this court is now in recess." and the gavel crashed down once again. Both attorneys gathered up their briefcases and hurried back to the courts chambers where they knocked and were promptly admitted.

Rachael was already seated behind her desk with a handkerchief wiping her forehead. "Have a seat gentlemen. Now I want to get a few things straight before we go one step further in this case. Russ if you have any objection to my hearing a murder one case where my ex, and I emphasize ex, husband is the prosecutor then let's get it out now."

"No objection, your Honor."

"Next, the fact that Russ was disbarred and out of the practice for a period of time will have no bearing on how I view the evidence or rule on the questions of law in this case. Understood Mr. Rawlings?"

"Of course Rachael, you know—"

"I know one thing for sure. I am not Rachael to you and you will henceforward in this case address me as Judge or your Honor!"

"Yes, your Honor."

"Now let us get down to business. Russ I know for a fact you have never tried a criminal case, much less a murder case. Now are you sure you are in this case for the duration because I intend to move this case along. There is alot of public pressure here and I see no reason for any undue delays. The fact that you are a novice in the criminal justice system will not in anyway change the usual procedures followed by this court. As for you, Buzz, your comment to me out in the courtroom was totally uncalled for and certainly is not becoming of your office as Prosecuting Attorney. I suggest that if you have any doubt whatsoever about Russ Thurston's privilege to practice law in this state, that you send one of your trained camp followers to check it out!"

She turned to Russ and said, "Since your client is accused of the murder of Elsa Bascomb I must assume you will plead not guilty to the charge." She stood and shook some air up under her robe.

"To be real honest about it your Honor, I really haven't been able to see my client long enough to make a solid judgement as to his guilt or innocence. So in answer to your question, yes he will plead not guilty to the charge and we request that bail be set at this hearing."

"Let me assure you Russ, you will have access to your client at anytime of day or night in order for you to properly prepare your case for trial in a timely fashion. I am disinclined to set bail at this time due to the nature of the crime, the public outrage, and the fact that at the moment this is a murder one case." She turned to Buzz who had just lit a cigarette, "Now Buzz why don't you turn over the evidence you have in this case as well as the names of any witnesses you anticipate using at trial, to Russ without alot of pre-trial motion nonsense?"

"Well lets put it this way Rach—your honor, I intend to cooperate to the fullest with the court and defense counsel in order to enable this trial to come to its conclusion at the earliest opportunity. But —"

"But, bull shit—just stop right there without any buts. I am sure Russ will cooperate in the same manner—right Russ. Good. Why don't you both shake hands and come out swinging but no punches below the belt or I will step in to use my contempt of court powers to straighten things out. Now let's get out there and hear your motion for bail Russ, which I am going to deny." She was on her feet and headed for her private door to the bench when she suddenly turned to both lawyers who were still at her desk, "and Russ if you have any problem with this overgrown tit sucker you come direct to me — I sure as hell know how to straighten him out." With that she was out the door to the bench waiting for Mr. Ronald White and the attorneys.

CHAPTER II

True to her word the judge had opened the gates of the jail to Russ so he had no problem seeing Ron. The difficulty now was getting Ron to really tell him all he knew about what did take place on that Friday morning. Oddly enough for someone like Ron, who talked constantly in his sales scam, he now seemed to have a silent horror of what he had seen that morning. Russ was sure that Ron had been at Elsa's that Friday but was really not sure whether Ron had killed Elsa and if he had was it done with intent or in a sudden fit of anger. Certainly the cause of death pointed to a sudden uncontrolable rage and if so, just as certainly the case should be one of second degree murder committed without malice or even a plea bargain of manslaughter would seem a likely balance of the scales of justice. On the other hand the fact that poor Elsa had been tied hand and foot to the bed would imply a coolness that would show the intent necessary to charge the perpetrator with first degree murder. The preliminary hearing was now set for trial on March thirty first, just thirty days away and Russ already was beginning to feel the panic that sets in the final day before trial. Those dreaded Sunday nights before the Monday morning trials began. Sunday was a day of rest for the majority of the great American public but not so for pro football players and Monday morning trial lawyers. His Sundays had first been filled with total violence on the field. Then they were filled with working and re-working the final touches to the case that might just make the difference between a winner and a looser, re-reading all of the depositions and again preparing that all important opening statement to the jury. And finally the fitful sleepless nights with brief dreams of judges with no faces and trials with no verdicts. Russ was once again moving with awful certainty toward that Sunday before the Monday morning trial of a murder case. The usual nagging question was whether or not Ron White was in fact the perpetrator of the crime or was he really the victim of the criminal justice system. As of this moment, as he waited for the steel door to open into the visitors area where Ron was waiting, Russ was not a bit sure that Ron had not committed the crime. Nevertheless he had taken the case at Rons insistence and as long as Ron professed his innocence then it was his duty as a lawyer to give it his best shot and go for acquittal. The jury would make that final decision of guilt or innocence.

All jails smell the same. First there is the smell of lysol that is constantly being used to disinfect the floors. The usual trustee is in the hallway slowly wielding a mop with the usual non-filtered cigarette loosely held between his lips. The haze of cigarette smoke hangs across the whole area. There is never total silence on the prisoner floor. Steel doors clanging, a TV blasting a useless soap opera and constant talk between cells.

The steel bars suddenly began to move and the door swung open automatically. Russ stepped into the visitors area just as Ron was brought in through a solid steel door on the opposite side of the room. The guard lit a cigarette for Ron and then left the room with a clang of the door.

"Jesus, Ron, you really look like hell. Aren't you eating anything?"

"Let me tell you about the only thing anyone is forced to eat around here is some big black cigar hung on the crotch of the head honcho. Hell, he has it so good in here he doesn't want to leave." Ron snuffed out his cigarette on the floor and looked up with watery eyes. "God. Russ, you have to get me out of here. Please see the judge again. Do something! I can't take this constant racket and some guy always trying to stick it in me or make me suck him to sleep. I swear if they get me I couldn't live with it. I'm just scared all the time. I can't sleep because I never know when the trustee will open the door and let some bastard in to rape me."

Russ could tell Ron was in terrible shape and vowed to make another try at getting the judge to set bail. He knew unless he had some solid evidence to put some doubt in the case about Rons guilt, the judge would continue to refuse to set bail.

"Ron, I will do my best to get you out on bail but for now we have to talk about this case and see just where the hell we are going. First of all did you talk to the cops when they picked you up?"

"No, I talked to you on the phone and that was it."

"Well, at least that's one break in our favor. How about anyone in the cell with you. Did you talk to them about the case?"

"They did put some spook in with me who kept asking me a million questions but I just made small talk. I figured he was a cop or a snitch so I just laid the usual bullshit on him."

Russ offered Ron a cigarette and then gave him the pack. He lit up and inhaled deeply. "Now, Ron, let's get to where you were on Friday. Now take your time and think back. Don't guess at things just give me the straight facts. Also, give me the names of any possible witnesses who can back up your version of where you were at the time of the murder."

"Lord knows I have thought of this enough. You remember I told you I was leaving early on Friday morning. Well that was because Thursday afternoon I had decided to call it quits with Elsa. I know you know I was into her hot and heavy. As you know she was pregnant and I am sure it was mine since she and the Mayor weren't making it. Anyway she told me that he couldn't make a baby because of some problem he had from childhood. So there I was just like a high school kid who has knocked up his girlfriend. I really didn't panic too much because I was sure she could get it aborted but then all of a sudden instead of just a good lay while I was in town, now she was talking about divorce, marriage and what name to put on the kid. I couldn't believe it but rather than get into a big fight I simply crawled out of bed put on my pants and told her I would see her the next time I was in town. Well she did her usual hugging and trying to get me to stay but I said no, that I really had to get ready to leave early on Friday. Well now she wanted to come with me so we could tell my wife about us and the baby. Russ my God damn knees got weak so I just flat out told her this was all bullshit and she had better get rid of the kid. Well you can imagine what happened then. I finally just walked out the door with her screaming and crying."

Russ looked up from his legal pad and nodded, "Now when you left what time was it and did you see anyone who was a witness?"

"No. It was about four in the afternoon and I was in a hurry to get out of there because the Mayor could be coming in the door at anytime. I always parked my car in her garage which had an automatic door closer so I would just get in, open the door and back out the driveway to the street. So I am sure no one saw me leave that afternoon and if they did they wouldn't know who I was."

"You didn't beat her up before you left?" Russ looked Ron straight in the eye as he slowly exhaled a large smoke ring.

"Hell no, why should I do that? I knew we were finished. Naturally I felt sorry for her and I told her the usual crap about how much I loved her, which was probably true in a different sort of way." Ron got up and shuffled around the room his leg irons noisily clanking against the concrete floor. "Now I know the next question will be what happened on Friday. Right?"

Russ really had a bad feeling about what was to come so he put down his pen and just stared at Ron waiting for his alibi.

"OK. On Friday I was all set to get out of town early. Well I got sentimentally drunk Thursday night. The drunker I got the more I needed to get laid. I kept thinking about Elsa, who believe it or not, really was a fantastic animal in the sack. So I got blasted, told all my little rag-a-muffins goodnight and that they could sleep in tomorrow because ole Ron sure as hell was going to split the sheets until noon. Well I woke up the next day, Friday, about nine o'clock in the morning. I not only had a throbbing hang over I also had a throbbing hang over hard-on for a good final lay by Elsa.

Russ looked at him with studied incredulity. He just couldn't have gone back.

"Yes—that's right, I went back for one final fuck fling. The garage door was open as usual with her car in there and the Mayor's gone, just like she knew I would be there in the morning. I even laughed out loud as I put down the garage door and called her name. Of course there was no answer so I let myself in and walked through the kitchen. I could still smell the cigar smoke so I knew the Mayor had not been out of there too much ahead of me. This also meant he was late leaving since it was now ten o'clock. I called again but no answer and I began to get a kind of creepy feeling. I looked in the bathroom from the hallway and saw the water running in the sink. I went in and turned it off and then opened the door to the bedroom. My God, Russ, I have never seen or smelled a dead person. I retched and then turned around and threw up in the sink. I sank to my knees and sobbed. Then without thinking

I went to the bed and screamed at Elsa to look at me, to say something. The bed was a mass of blood and excrement and this horrible rubber hose was stuck up in her. I grabbed it to pull it out, then I suddenly realized that I would be a prime suspect." Ron shuddered and held his head in his shackled hands, "I had blood on my shoes, on my pants and on my hands from grabbing the hose. I panicked then and started to slowly back out of the room. The phone suddenly rang. I jumped and bolted down the stairs as the phone kept ringing. I opened the garage with the automatic door opener and got out of there as fast as I could. When I got to the motel I changed cloths and laid down for awhile to think. Then I called Angel and told her to go ahead and leave with the others. I told her to check in to the usual motel in El Paso and that I would meet them later."

Russ got up and stretched, then turned on Ron. "Just why do you think the cops picked you up? Do you have any idea why?"

Ron suddenly began to pale, it was beginning to sink in that this really was a murder one case. "God, Russ, I can only guess that Elsa had my name and the motel address with her at home."

"Ron, that isn't enough to arrest you and charge you with capital murder. Did anyone see your car arrive or leave on that day? Did you leave anything at the house to identify you? Think about this man, your God damned life could depend on it!"

"Christ, Russ, I have tried to think it through step by step, but all I can see is Elsa in a bloody mess, in her own bed, where just the day before we had made love. You don't know what a shock that is Russ." Ron was about to lose control so Russ decided to ease off and call it a day. No sense in pushing too hard. Just take it one day at a time. "One final question, Ron, and this is the usual one, do you have any idea who could have done this to Elsa, anyone at all, no matter how far out it might be?"

Ron stared at the floor and slowly shook his head, "I never knew any of her friends or people who were there when I was gone. Of course she and the Mayor didn't get along or she wouldn't have been sleeping with me, but apparently everyone knew this."

Russ could feel the let down in the room, "Ron, is it possible that Elsa was sleeping with someone else when you weren't in town? You know you are out of this town alot."

"I don't know Russ. I guess it is possible. I am certainly not that naive or egotistical to think I was the only lover in her life, — but if there was someone else she sure fooled me."

"Well whoever it was they went into a rage about something, either sex, jealousy or money. Maybe someone else, the other lover, found out she was going to have your baby and blew his top? Anyway let's both keep thinking about the details in this case. Right now I don't know too much about what the prosecution has in it's bag of tricks. I will keep you informed as we go along."

Ron got up slowly as the guard was signaled that the conference was over. Russ reached out to shake Ron's hand and saw the bandage on his hand, "What happened to your hand, Ron?"

"Thursday night, when I got loaded, I tripped and fell going back to my room from the bar and cut my hand on some glass in the driveway. No big deal except it won't heal."

The door clanged shut and he was gone. Back into the personal hell of noise and internal violence preserved only for those who invoked the system of criminal justice upon themselves. They would all be waiting for him, waiting for the chance to take "Ron Baby" in that sacred jailhouse marriage.


CHAPTER III

In all cases, criminal or civil, the discovery of evidence can make or break your case. The painstaking and often boring process of investigation is high on the agenda of things to do before trial. Time slips away and so does the evidence that once was readily available. The preliminary hearing for Ron Whites case was set down as the only matter to be heard by the court on March 31st. Russ knew there would be no continuances and he was sure the state would be ready to unload on Russ at that hearing. So in the meantime he had to do his best to formulate some strategy to shake the foundation laid by the State for Murder One. He used his pass key to go into Ron's room at the motel. Since Ron had called him to represent him he had told the cleaning girls not to touch Ron's room. It was a drab dark room with only windows on the north side. The rug stunk of old whiskey and bug spray. The arm chair was grimy from over use and the heating unit only worked half of the time, then only at half speed. Russ could only shake his head at such a miserable way to live. Day after day from one town to the next with each successive motel a carbon copy of the one before. It was a wonder Ron had kept his sanity all these years.

In the corner were some dirty towels and a pair of worn out sneakers. He guessed these were Rons but other than these the room was in it's usual unkempt condition. Certainly no clothing or other evidence to assist either side of the case. He went out the door and headed for the laundry room. When he opened the door the girls quickly covered up the card game and began to fold towels. "Did any of you remove anything from Ron Whites room after he left on Friday?" They all looked at each other and shook their heads. Russ looked down at the pretty young girl with the gold tooth and said "You won't be in any trouble if you did but I just need to know in order to help Ron out." She raised her hand as if in school, "Yes — is it Lucille? Please go ahead and tell me." Russ smiled easily at the young Mexican.

"Well, I saw Mr. White and he took what looked like old clothes out to the dumpster in back and pitched them in it — but I never went back there to see what they was cause the cops came up pretty soon. They asked me which room was Mr. Whites and I showed them. They went up and tried the door, then looked in the window. One came back and asked me where we dump the trash so I pointed to the dumpster. I saw him go back and dig around and then he came back with what looked like the stuff that Mr. White had just thrown away."

Russ felt his temple throb, there went the filthy pants with possible blood on them and probably his shoes. He thanked the girls for their help and headed back for the front office. He had to sit down and put the pieces together as best he could, but he really had very little to go on. He despised this motel and the front office because he had no privacy, but one case sure as hell didn't make a law practice. Whatever Ron could scrape together for a fee wouldn't pay for an apartment and a law office.

Willis opened the door for him and told him one of the owners, Cahill, was looking for him and wanted him to call as soon as he could. Russ nodded and told Willis to handle the front desk while he did some work in the back room. If he had an emergency he could interrupt him but otherwise to leave him alone. Russ poured a thick black cup of coffee and disappeared into the back room. He pulled out a legal pad and turned on the old green shaded desk lamp standing on the gray steel desk.

It really was discouraging to think of the possible clues that Ron could have left at the scene of the murder. Finger prints, threads from fabric in his pants, pubic hairs from the day before when he had made love to Elsa, and possibly blood from the cut on his hand. Not only that, there was no telling who in the neighborhood could identify him. He sure as hell had no alibi. As a matter of fact Russ could pretty well see where the State was coming from on this one even before the preliminary hearing.

Willis banged furiously on the door and yelled that it was Mr. Cahill on the phone. Russ sighed then took a deep breath and got ready for the usual ass chewing.

"God damn it, Russ, we can't keep waiting for you to take care of this re-zoning problem. I guess you weren't aware that the planning and zoning commission approved the total package at their last meeting."

As a matter of fact Russ did know that the project had received approval but only on a tight split vote of the commission. The word was out that the project didn't stand a prayer on a vote by the board of aldermen. Russ held back an impulse to tell Jack just where to stuff the phone and the project.

"Jack, there really hasn't been an opportunity for me to approach the Mayor. I am sure that with his wifes murder the last thing on his mind is re-zoning this little jewel."

"Russ, I don't spend alot of time around your ill begotten motel but I can tell you one thing — at least a million dollars is at stake. Now there is a slight rumble that Russ Thurston can get to the Mayor and God damn it, I want him gotten to now! I don't give a damn about his wife being murdered by some sadistic sex maniac. I don't give a damn about your gentlemanly sensitivity. All I give a damn about is me and money! Have I gotten through to you that this is where you get the ball to run with it — like it or not?"

Russ could feel the heat in the phone, see those bulging eyes and the green cigar with the green spittle sliding out of the corner of Jacks mouth.

"Jack, I know how important this is to you and believe me I will do my best to see the Mayor before the final vote of the board. You know that there has to be a public hearing on this before the formal vote is taken. So it is my guess that the final vote won't come up until around the end of March or first part of April at the earliest. I will find out the exact date and get back to you. I want to figure out the best place to see the Mayor so we can have a little serious private discussion."

"Russ, its no secret that you are all involved in that murder case representing that sleazy magazine route man that killed the Mayors' wife."

Russ finally had enough of Jack Cahill and his pompous attitude, "Now get this straight, Jack, Ron White may be accused but he sure as hell isn't convicted."

"Bull shit. In this town being accused of murdering the Mayors' wife is as good as being convicted. That loud mouth whore monger is on his way to shake hands with the devil." Jack snorted a short laugh and choked on a piece of loose cigar. He was enjoying sticking it to Russ. "And by the way, Russ, just remember you have a full-time job running that motel and we don't pay your salary and provide you a suite of rooms just so you can spend time with your new client."

There was a pause then Russ said, "If you want me out then just say the word and I am history. If not, then you let me run this show my way. By that I mean leave me alone and let me get the job done. I will see the Mayor when the time is right and you can bet your ass he will talk to me whether I represent Ron White or not." Russ started to slam the phone down but gently placed it on the desk and covered it with his hand so all he could hear was the continued muffled moaning by Jack as he raved on about the glory of CLK.

Russ knew exactly when and where he would go after the Mayor. All he had to do was wait for an afternoon after Faith had finished working him over and he would be all set up for a little friendly conversation about the re-zoning matter to come before the board of aldermen. Naturally the meeting would have to take place at the motel while Faith was still repairing any damage done during the matinee. No need to mention anything about adverse publicity should the newspapers get wind of these matinee sessions. Just a quiet one on one conversation about the advantages of re-zoning.

Russ hung up the phone, now only identified by some computer chip telling him his phone was off the hook. Where to begin. There had to be a beginning just as surely as there would be an end to this night mare of melodramatic murder. He wanted to believe Ron. That he was in fact a very innocent victim of circumstances that now led to the even larger and more compelling victim of the highly flaunted judicial system. The system up to this point had only been fair to the enforcers. Those who marched steadfastly in lock step to the drum roll that says the arrest compels the conclusion of conviction. This same conclusion coupled with the outrage of an inflamed public had placed Ron White in continuing jeopardy in among the cell block creatures who crave male sexual excitement. The problem that faces the lawyer at this point is simply that his client begins to recognize the fact that the cards have indeed been stacked against him. His presumption of innocence, so highly touted by our courts, has become in fact a presumption of guilt. Why? It is simply human nature at this point to believe the newspapers, television, radio and the law enforcement authorities. After all didn't the judge refuse to set bail for this "innocent" accused? And so we now have the beginning of that chain of events that so often lead inexorably, step by mincing step, to the final clang of the steel door as it slams behind the innocent for an eternity.

Russ knew that Ron was in deep psychological trouble. That his plea to see the Judge again to try and get him out of the security system was more than a plea. It was in fact the wailing of a frightened lost soul. One that had been given up to the system to be devoured by those who had found a way of life within this same system to suit their sadistic and erotic pleasures.

Russ picked up the phone and dialed the courthouse. He was put through to the clerk of Rachael's court and was told, in a courtroom whisper, that the Judge was still on the bench. He asked for an appointment and after a short pause, during which he could hear Rachael overrule an objection, the clerk told him to be there at four thirty and not to be late. It was already three thirty so he had to hurry. He threw on a quick five o'clock shadow shave, clean shirt, almost clean tie and a well used London Fog all weather coat against the late afternoon chill. A splash of Old Spice and he was on his way to make the appointed hour.

It took him forty five minutes to fight the cross town traffic. The problem was that once you got to the plaza square of Santa Fe it seemed that all motion stopped. Since the plaza itself had been preserved in its original state of antiquity to give the flavor of the old west, in order to attract tourism, all roads led to and through it. Although the ancient courthouse was only one block on the opposite side of the plaza, it took an eternity to get through the Indian merchants who hawked their wares all over the side walks and streets. Tourists found this to be a colorful part of the old west. Bright colored rugs and clothing, multicolored feathered headdresses, bins of beaded moccasins and the ever present handcrafted silver and topaz jewelry. The local resident found this to be no more than a kaleidoscopic nightmare of studied confusion.

As he rushed through the massive solid oak doors at the rear of the courtroom he was suddenly aware that the court was still in session. He walked down the long center aisle to the front rail dividing the spectators from the area reserved for the attorneys and litigants. As he eased his still athletic frame into a wooden arm chair his glance caught a brief smile and almost inpreceptable wink from Rachael. It caught Russ off guard so abruptly that he felt the rush of blood to his head as he nodded and smiled back.

After one final outburst by the defendants attorney which was quickly joined in battle by the prosecution, Rachael said she had heard enough bickering by both sides for one day and adjourned court until nine o'clock the next morning. As she arose from the bench she beckoned to Russ to come forward. Rachael had that desirous fragrance that belongs only to the sensuous woman as she leaned forward to quietly speak to Russ. "Just give me a minute to get out of this infernally hot robe and pour a bottle of Chanel over this poor body." Their eyes locked together for just the slightest moment before they both looked away in hushed embarrassment. Russ couldn't help but feel the rush of love to his groin in that brief moment as Rachael felt the hot flush rush through her nakedness beneath the robe. She quickly departed through her private door that led from her bench to her chambers. Russ picked up his worn Indian tooled brief case and walked around the clerks desk through the back door of the court into the clerks office.

"Hi Russ. You know you still are a real hunk, honey." Hannah had on her usual unflattering dress of multi-colors that made her fatness even fatter. Russ gave her shoulder a squeeze and leaned against the door jamb to the judges chambers.

"You know, Hannah, you must really be getting hard up to try and make points with a dead broke lawyer who has one client and a desk drawer full of bills."

"Yeah, but honey you're the only lawyer I know who has twenty four hour access to a motel suite, no questions asked." With that she was on her feet locking her desk and with a look at the clock just as it struck five o'clock, she was on her way out the door.

"Tell the Judge not to forget to lock up and turn off the coffee pot. Oh, and Russ if I can help you in anyway just give me a call. I would love to see you beat the balls off of that ass, Buzz Rawlings." The outer door closed with a bang and a moment of silence invaded the court-house after a day of business as usual.

CHAPTER IIII

Dusk was beginning to slowly settle across the white capped mountains in the distance. Rachael's thoughts were suddenly turned to another time when she happily skied the steep slopes of the Sangre Christo Mountains. Those by gone days when the only problem you really had was making a selection of which young ski instructor to share a drink with after the slopes were closed. She sighed deeply, picked up her pack of Salems and carefully extracted her third cigarette of the day. Her gold engraved lighter was slowly dying from disuse but she had made a firm decision to cut back to no more than five cigarettes a day and when Rachael made a firm decision the whole courthouse knew she would stand by it. Another firm decision she had just made was to keep her distance from Russ, at least it was a decision at this point, maybe not too firm, as of now. She smoothed her white see through silk blouse over her ample breasts and straightened her straight lined navy blue linen skirt. One final pull on her panty hose and she was ready.

When the door opened Russ was leaning half against the door and half against the jamb. He momentarily lost his balance and fell against Rachael who reached out for him to steady herself. His strong arm reached out and caught her briefly as they both struggled to regain their balance and composure.

Rachael almost began to laugh when she saw the shocked look on his face, "Russ Thurston if I didn't know you to be a fine gentlemen I would swear you were taking advantage of the security guard being off duty at five."

"My God, Judge, that's one hell of a way for me to start things off, particularly when I am up here to ask for a judicial favor." Russ held her arm lightly as he spoke with those blue eyes twinkling.

"Come on in and sit down, Russ. I hope this isn't a matter that should have another lawyer present." She took a deep drag on her Salem and slowly tapped the ash into her ash tray as she eased onto the low leather couch. "I know you are well aware that there is very little ex parte business that takes place in the criminal court, much unlike the civil courts, with which you are more familiar." Her voice and demeanor had suddenly taken on a sudden aloofness as she carefully arranged her skirt just above her knees.

Russ knew this was not the time to talk about the "good ole days", nor to make light of their meeting at the door, "Judge if I am out of order being here without the prosecutor being present then just say so, right now, and I will leave until Buzz is present. However, I really think that my request to see you alone is not inappropriate under the circumstances." His eyes flashed.

"Alright, Russ, don't get all up tight about what I just said to you. You know I wasn't impugning your ethics. Maybe you are still a little gun shy after your experience with the bar committee on ethics." She swished her nylons gently as she crossed graceful legs. "Come on sit down and let's see what the problem is today." She gently patted a cushion on the couch next to her not realizing for the moment the impact of her invitation. Russ carefully chose a hard wooden chair in front of her desk and turned it sideways to face her as he eased down. As he looked up he caught a flash of familiar thigh and the sexual beauty of Rachael raced through his mind. Here he was involved in a horrible murder case, in conference with the Judge and at the moment he could only think of her beautiful body.

He suddenly realized he was staring at her legs as his thoughts raced crazily around his head and he abruptly reached for his brief case to break the silence. "Judge, after my clients appearance in court this morning I had a chance to sit down and spend some time with him in security. Now I am not here to plead his innocence to you but only to point out that I really don't think he can take jail time while we get this case to trial. His appearance and demeanor is such that I really worry about his stability." Russ was on his feet and walked over to the window overlooking the city as it began to live it's evening hours.

"I tell you he is scared to death of not just the guards but more so of the jail house Romeo's that are trying to get to him with his pants down. So all I am asking is for you to re-consider setting bail for him so he can get out of that nightmare." Russ sat back down heavily, really weary now from his first long day back in the practice of law.

Rachael stubbed out her cigarette and pulled her legs up under her on the couch. He could tell she was tired from her day on the bench and felt a heavy desire to go to her and hold her close as he had so many years before.

"Now, Russ, I want you to understand that I don't consider you out of line coming to see me alone with this request." She ran long graceful fingers through her blonde hair now in some disarray. "I know where you are coming from when you talk about that bunch of sadists in security. Some of those turkeys would rather be inside than outside just because they have a captive bunch of poor bastards to jerk around. I don't think it is just the men who have got problems. The women raise hell about the hard core lesbians going after them day and night. Why I can't even put your client in a cell by himself because we are so damned overcrowded. So you want to select who shares the other three bunks as cell mates with your man? No matter how hard you try you will still have at least one in each cell that is a butt sticking, cock licking son of a bitch."

"Then damn it, Rachael, set bail and let me try to get him out while he still has his virginity and sanity." Rachael got up and came over to her desk close to Russ and reached across him for her cigarettes. He could smell her delicious body and wanted to devour it as she lightly touched his hand as he held a light for her.

She stood with her back to him now at the darkening window, "Russ, I made a firm decision this morning that I was not going to set bail in this case. I don't have to explain my decisions. Some are good, some are not so good and some are just downright bad. But at least I make decisions and this enables the wheels of justice to continue to slowly grind, separating the good from the bad, casting some on the shore in green pastures and throwing others back in the snake pit. Your client is presently in the snake pit — for how long may depend entirely on you as his lawyer. I intend to keep him in the snake pit because he is accused of a particularly brutal crime that has in fact shocked the conscience of the community." Russ moved uncomfortably in his chair as Rachael turned slowly around to face him. "From just what I have seen in the court file I would say there is a distinct possibility that Mr. White could be guilty as charged. Finally I would point out that at this time the feelings of many of those in the community is that your client's very early demise would save the taxpayers a great deal of their hard earned dollars. Security in the present cell is considerably more safe for your client than being out on the streets of Mayor Bascom's town."

She crossed over to Russ looked down at him with great compassion as she gently placed her hand on his cheek, "Nobody ever said it would be easy, Russ" She bent over and kissed him on the forehead and moved away before he could hold her.

Russ felt a great surge of desire but she had already picked up her leather jacket and had her hand on the light switch by the door, "Come on, lets get out of this palace of justice."

Their heels clattered noisily as the echo jumped from wall to wall of the dimly lit wide corridor trimmed with straight backed wooden benches on each side. A night security guard came by and saluted Rachael who was deep in thought. The old worn wooden stairs creaked as they made their way to the ground floor.

Rachael stopped as they reached the broken sidewalk that led to the parking lot, "Russ, you know if I could have helped you out I would have done so. Particularly you, Russ." Impulsively she grabbed his hand and squeezed it hard. Russ held on to her and headed for his car.

"Come on, Rachael, let's you and I go find one of the better known after five cocktail bars." She was smiling, now laughing. "Now wait a minute, big guy. I hear rumors around town that a new up and coming lawyer is still driving a big long and black 1969 Olds convertible. Now is that true or false?"

Russ threw his arm around her shoulders and began to laugh, "I cannot tell a lie to your honor. The great black Olds, more commonly know in past years as the "Mafia Staff car" awaits the pleasure of your royal bottom." With that he had swung open the door and bowed as she slid easily across the glove leather front seat. Russ immediately put the top down and threw his London Fog around his shoulders. The early evening was superb with just one bright star shining in the east. Rachael lay her head back on the seat and breathed deeply of the clear cool New Mexico evening air. The car started with a satisfactory rumble and leaped forward with all of the power that once was its youth. It was only a short drive through the suburbs to a cozy outside taco and tequila garden with a great roaring circular fireplace in the center. The aroma of mesquite being burned and Mexican food cooking over an outside fireplace permeated the whole area.

Russ guided Rachael to a corner booth removed from the mainstream of traffic and away from the bar area.

"Oh Russ, I just haven't had the nerve to come back here since I last saw you. Then all your trouble began and I really felt like I just wanted to put that chapter out of my life. And I guess I really did until this morning."

Russ looked up at the young dark haired waitress and ordered a dry vodka martini and tequila sour.

"You do still drink sour's don't you?"

She nodded and went on, "Was it really a bad time for you Russ? All those years out of touch with your profession and friends." Her eyes were moist even though she had a thin wisp of a smile.

"Rachael, it was so bad I really felt at times that my sanity was on the line. Maybe that is why I have such great empathy for Ron White over in security. The crazy thing is it really was no ones fault but my own. I know it is easy to blame the habit on bad breaks and people too willing to put you in touch with the pushers. The whole god damned truth was and still is that I just let myself walk right into the septic tank full of drugs. I know now that I am a lot stronger for all of the adversity it caused me but that won't pick up the years of agony I went through. But that is all behind me now so if I can just find a client or two who have a few bucks for a retainer maybe I can get out of this miserable mess." He smiled up at the waitress as she placed the drinks on the table.

Rachael took a sip of her tequila sour and smiled appreciatively "You know, Russ, you are coming back into the practice the hard way. If the State has any case at all against your client then the odds are that a jury will convict him. I certainly don't lose any love over Buzz, the boy wonder, but I can tell you one thing, he is tough as hell in the courtroom with a long string of convictions to prove it. So just in case you don't bring in a winner your first time out, don't fall back on old habits or self pity. Like I said before, nobody said it would be easy."

Russ touched his glass to hers and gravely said, "Here's to justice for all."

Rachael finished her drink and shook her head when Russ motioned to the waitress. "Russ if you feel so certain your friend and client is not the perpetrator in this case then let me give you just a little bit of advice. Get your pretrial discovery motions filed, and any motions to quash the States evidence. I will try and get Buzz to bring his evidence into court without formal notice so we can go over everything informally in my chambers. After all, in this day and age, there is no such thing as a surprise witness. Once you know what evidence they are prepared to put on at the preliminary hearing you may have a better idea of your client's guilt or innocence. In the meantime run down anything that might lead to some other perp."

Rachael lit her fifth and final cigarette for the day and looked deeply into his eyes, "Russ, you are in the hard-ball game now. Don't stand there and take strikes. Come out swinging."

Russ smiled and reminded her he had been in a few pro games before and knew just how tough things could get but thanked her for the bar room advice.

"How about one more and then a plate of red hot tacos?" He called the waitress back just as Rachael put her hand over his, "Russ, I just can't tonight. I am afraid one for the road will lead to a severe case of judicial indiscretion and I am not quite ready for that, particularly with a murder case pending in front of me."

"Rachael, I want you to know that I really had no idea how much I have missed you until I saw you in court the other day. That black robe sure doesn't do anything to enhance what I know is under it but on the other hand I still have an excellent memory. So the ball is in your court now and if you want to see an old beat up tight end in action again all you have to do is pucker up and whistle." He laid some bills on the table and got up offering his arm as he bowed to her honor.

Rachael smiled and leaning toward him whispered in his ear, "I always did think you were a better tight ass than a tight end love."

As they settled into the front seat of the convertible Russ reached across Rachael and opened the glove box. After rummaging for a few minutes he produced a small object that looked like a pearl surrounded by small diamonds. Rachael gasped and then lovingly took the earring from the palm of his strong hand, "Oh, Russ where did you find this. I remember I lost it the last night we were together. God it makes me blush to think of what we were doing when I lost it. I am going to put it on right now so I won't misplace it."

As Russ started the car he glanced at her with a sly smile, "Well maybe we can try losing it again sometime. Remember just pucker up and —"

With that she kissed him with hot full lips. He crushed her in his arms and held her delicious body to his. She felt his groin stir and begin to harden. Her warm juices were ready to meet him in throbbing surrender. She whimpered as his hand pulled her thigh over his to press against his incredibly hard erection. "No, Russ. Please, not here, not now. You know I want to but it just can't happen like this. Please let's make it last this time. I have to wait until this case is over, then I promise you we can try again. Oh, Russ, please kiss me once more and then promise to wait for me to pucker up."

Russ felt like a teenager about to get laid in the front seat. His big frame was all tangled up against the steering wheel with his throbbing erection pointing up like a tent pole. His tongue searched her warm mouth as he felt her hand gently close on his erection. Her squeeze was the promise of love but even as he held her to him she pushed away. His whole body was shaking as she moved to the other side of the car. "Jesus, Rachael, you don't know what you are doing to me. I feel like I did the first time we made love together. My hands are shaking so badly I can't find the ignition." She came back to him and stroked his hands. "I promise when it is all over I will lose my earring again, darling. Now let's get me back to my car so I can go home and remember this day while I take a hot bath."

Russ pulled out on the highway and headed toward the lights of the city. Rachael moved over and put her head on his shoulder and gazed through half opened eyes at the moonless clear starlit night. She gently rested her hand on his thigh and gave that deep sigh of contentment.

Russ smiled down at her and then maliciously said, "Now judge are you sure that was a firm decision you made about setting bail?"

She reached up and clamped down hard on his ear lobe and whispered, "You bastard."


CHAPTER V

Russ was busy the rest of the week with the usual problems of running the motel coupled with trying to find time to talk to Ron about anyone who could have been involved in the murder of Elsa. Ron did mention that some of his lecherous lovers had been over to Elsa's house with him but they were only there for the free booze and whatever else they could steal while Ron and Elsa were busy upstairs. The very nature of the way she was killed led to the conclusion that it was purely an act of sexual brutality or violent jealousy. Usually in any murder you first look to the spouse, who in this case was the Mayor. Russ had checked him out as best he could without taking his deposition and from all he could come up with he had been in his suite of offices in the City Hall at the time of the murder. Of course, his office was only a fifteen minute drive from his home so it would be hard to nail down the precise time he left home or arrived at the office. Besides, there was no reason for the Mayor to want to kill his wife that Russ was aware of at the moment. Her pregnancy gave him an automatic divorce, no alimony and no child support for Ron's baby. At least at this point the motive was not there and motive was the big item at this time. On the other hand here was poor Ron with no alibi and plenty of motive — from jealousy, to kinky sex gone too far, to outright rage with his lover. Russ was determined to catch up with the Mayor next Monday afternoon to have it out with him about the re-zoning deal and at the same time try and find out a few more details about the murder.

On Friday there was a note on his desk to be in Judge Rawlings court on Monday at eleven o'clock to take up pre-trial motions and to please call the clerk of Division Six to confirm. Russ got Hannah on the phone who quickly put him on hold.

Rachael came on the line sounding somewhat breathless, "Russ I just took a short recess to talk to you. Buzz says most of your pre-trial motions to quash and to produce evidence are the usual bull shit, but nevertheless in the interest of justice — isn't that a laugh — he will put his staff to the task of getting their evidence for the preliminary hearing together so you can see just where the State is coming from in this case. As an aside he said he felt sure you would waive the prelim once you saw this mass of evidence."

Russ felt his face flush as he thought of Buzz prancing around Rachael's chambers with his entourage throwing rose petals in his path as he unleashed his evidence.

"Well then Judge, I assume he is not formally objecting to the motions I have filed and if that is so just where do we go from here?"

"Russ, as far as I can tell this will all be done informally in my chambers. If we have any problems that arise I will adjourn to the courtroom to hammer them out under oath." She was just a little upset that Russ sounded so cool and removed from her.

"That's fine with me. I assume we can set up depositions on an agreed basis at the same time. Oh, and by the way, I will want to make photo copies of any reports from the experts which I assume Buzz will have available."

"No problem, I will clear that before Monday at eleven o'clock. Well, I really have to get back on the bench so I will look forward to seeing you on Monday." She paused, then said, "And, Russ, I still have that earring. Bye."

Russ smiled as he hung up and Willis smiled with him for no apparent reason.

"Willis, I want to know when the Mayor and his little love lumps get here on Monday."

There really wasn't much for Russ to do until Monday since these were all motions he had filed with the court. He had no obligation nor desire to disclose what his defense was going to be and it was a damn good thing because as of now the only defense he had was ripping up the offense. He knew that putting Ron on the witness stand was a very dangerous tactic, since it gave the prosecution a chance to cross examine him and open the door to many avenues that otherwise would not be available to them. He decided to have one more session with Ron before Monday to see if there was anything he could use while in chambers. He grabbed a pad of legal size paper, his car keys and headed for the door.

Every time he saw Ron he looked more emaciated, like he had already decided that he couldn't win or beat the system. This time was even worse than before. He had lost weight and had a dull look in his eyes. When he saw Russ he really did not react at all. The whole meeting was a bad scene. Ron kept begging Russ to get him out of security with Russ feeling guilty that he couldn't make Rachael set bond for him. He explained very carefully to him that he really had to be of more help in preparing the defense. Ron only rambled on about how unfair the system was, how he was going broke sitting in this jail cell with a bunch of perverts and where the hell was his wife. Russ had already talked to his wife and knew that answer. She could care less about, "that smart ass fornicator." As far as she was concerned he had earned his place in prison.

Russ was totally disgusted. The longer he stayed with Ron the worse his feeling about the case became. He just simply had to get out of the depression that surrounded Ron. He left Ron still begging to get him out of his personal hell. Russ knew it was hopeless until after the preliminary hearing and the closer he got to that hearing the worse the whole case looked.

As usual the week-end was an endless chain of one problem after another. Russ was more of a maintenance man than a manager for the most part. At least he was busy which helped to keep his mind off of the big problem on Monday. He knew that Rachael would try and get Buzz to make a deal with Russ, one that would be fair to both sides. The only problem was that Ron was in no mood for any deals while he kept wailing that he was innocent. Buzz had already said no deals on the Mayors case. It was now late Saturday night. The usual Saturday night shack up's were pulling on their pants and panty hose in order to get home in time to get up and go to church on Sunday to make confession. So far he only had to call the police one time when a drunk husband tried to break the door down on one of the rooms in order to take claim of his wife who was trying to squeeze out the back bathroom window. Fortunately she got out before he got in and the cops hauled away the intruder after he bloodied his best friends nose.

Willis came in ready to take over the late night shift and complained about the crazy drivers that were loose while he checked the room board to see where the action was tonight.

Russ had only nodded when Willis gave his customary greeting. He put down the half finished crossword puzzle, got up and stretched.

Willis poured a cup of heavy black coffee and took a quick sip, Russ thought he might throw up from the face he made. "My God, Russ, how can you drink this crap? Am I the only one around here that makes a fresh pot of coffee." He walked over to pick up the crossword puzzle Russ had laid down. Russ knew the smart ass kid would finish it and leave it where Russ could see it when he came back on duty.

"Willis, for your information, I don't drink coffee after dinner. It keeps me awake and God knows I need my sleep after a Saturday night of playing nursemaid to the underfucked of Santa Fe. Now if you are ready to assume your exalted duties as night manager I will depart for the bar next door for my usual very dry night cap." He pulled on his old suede jacket and headed for the clean outside air.

"Oh, Russ, I meant to ask you how your case is going with Ron? From all I hear around town it doesn't look too good for our star boarder." He gave a wink and a big grin to Russ as he eased into the Lazy Boy chair.

Russ stopped with the door open but didn't turn around, "Willis, I don't know what you are hearing so all I can tell you is that Ron is not good for a murder rap. Now you pass that word around town and see what results you get." He turned his head to fix intense blue eyes on Willis.

Willis could feel the heat of anger as he ducked behind the newspaper, "Now, Russ, you know I was only kidding. I am sure you will get ole Ron off when the case is tried. In the meantime I will keep my eyes and ears open around here for anything that might be of help. You know most of what you hear around here is bull shit but there is about ten percent of it that is good truthful gossip."

Russ was on his way next door but had to admit Willis had a point. He knew for a fact that some very strange motel rumors had turned out to be true to the amazement of all concerned.

The bar was roaring it's way toward closing time and Manny was up to his elbows pouring everything from gallons of margaritas to buckets of draft Michelob beer. Russ found a seat at the end of the bar and signaled to Manny. He nodded and Russ nodded back and the deal was made. One very dry Vodka martini, straight up. Russ swung around on the bar stool and looked out over the crowd. The usuals were there to spend their Friday pay checks on beer and broads. Some faces he recognized as earlier patrons of the motel next door. By now they were slumped down in booths with the starry look of love stamped on their faces. He smiled and turned around just as Manny put down his martini.

"Russ, when I get a minute, I want to pass on some direct word I picked up that might help you out with Ron's case." He was off down the bar pulling a couple of drafts. Russ carefully rubbed the twist of lemon around the rim of the white lightening as his eyes followed Manny down the bar. Just maybe something good might come out of this miserable motel.

It was at least a half an hour later when Manny came back to Russ with an unasked for refill. "Russ, I am sorry but you know how it is when it gets close to closing time. Everybody wants one for the road which they really don't need and which I water down to try and keep some sense of law and order around here. Anyway I heard the other day from one of the clerks in the Mayors office that there were some really bad vibes between the Mayor and the now deceased Elsa. By that I mean there not only was a divorce coming down but apparently Elsa had been to a lawyer and on his advice had closed out the bank accounts. Now I know this isn't too much but if Ron really didn't do Elsa in, then maybe, just maybe it could have been ole Big Balls Bill Bascom himself." He paused and drew a short draft for himself. "Frankly from what I hear the Mayor is a mean enough son of a bitch to do her in." He took a long pull from his beer.

Russ didn't respond and Manny felt he shouldn't have said anything. "I really didn't mean to stick my nose into your problem Russ —" He wiped a wet circle off the bar.

Russ looked up and gave Manny a smile, "Listen, old friend, if you can't butt in then nobody can. I was just trying to put what you told me into focus. So the Mayor is pissed at Elsa for grabbing the bank accounts. Now he is smart enough to know a judge sitting in domestic relations court will freeze the accounts or if the money is hidden he will take that into account in the final settlement or judgement."

Manny put Russ on hold while he went down the bar to put on the red flashing light signaling closing time. He came back, this time with a cup of coffee in his hand, "Go ahead, Russ, it will be at least another thirty minutes before I have to call the cops to clear the joint."

Russ smiled, "Well as you may know, under our revised laws of this great State the Judge in domestic relations, known as divorce court, owns your ass when you walk in for the final count down. He controls all and I mean all of your assets; your home, bonds, stocks, corporations, cash, money hidden in safe deposit boxes and gifts to those friendly beddy-bye acquaintances." Russ was really warming to the subject which he had become intimately familiar with during his first years of practice, when Manny cut him off, "Russ so what the hell has this got to do with his excellency the Mayor?"

Russ realized that what he was really getting at was just what worried him about Mondays meeting. He was sure that there would be some hard facts against Ron, facts he wasn't ready to combat.

"Manny let me try this on you just to see where it fits. Now let us assume that the Mayor did kill Elsa, which as I say is highly unlikely." Russ pushed his glass over for a re-fill. "First of all he had better have one hell of a good alibi. And he does. His secretary, Faith, says he was in his office as usual only about five minutes late. Now it takes one hell of a lot more time than five minutes to do to Elsa what was done according to the coroner. Next we are going to get into some highly sophisticated forensic problems." He paused as he whirled the lemon peel in his frosted glass, "For instance unless I am totally out of the main stream the prosecution will have, number one, blood specimens from the accused and deceased. Now naturally if that is a match with Ron we have big problems. Second, unless I am way off base, there will be a fingerprint somewhere in that house and I will bet it belongs to Ron White. That fingerprint will be in blood and it sure as hell won't be the Mayors. Finally I would guess that there is at least one pubic hair on the bed that does not belong to the deceased. I would bet that even Ron will tell me there are good odds that he left a few pubics scattered around the bedroom and more importantly on the death bed." Russ didn't like to even hear what he was saying but he knew it was all true and he sure as hell would hear it again on Monday.

Manny was a good listener, like he should be with anyone at his bar. He shook his head and began to move away, "But Russ what the hell is Ron's alibi? Where was he when it all came down on him?"

Russ shook his head and pushed the empty glass away as he stood up to leave. He carefully laid a twenty dollar bill on the bar. "Manny I can match that bill with ten Ben Franklins if you can come up with a solid alibi for Ron other than, "I was hung over at the motel all alone in my room." Russ slid off the stool and headed for the door, "And Manny I do thank you for the item on the Mayor, never know when it just might fit in somewhere. Keep your ear to the bar." He waved and moved out into the bright crisp night.

This was the high country and the air was truly rarified. Off to his left were the twinkling lights of Santa Fe and out across the plains in the far distance were the guardian lights surrounding Los Alamos. No matter how dismal his life seemed to be, after a few minutes of absorbing the vast clear sky and unending vistas, it always put Russ right back on the line ready to go for it on the next play.

CHAPTER VI

Monday broke clear and cool so at least the courthouse would be aired out and ready for it's usual influx of worried litigants and anxious attorneys. Russ was not due in Division Six until eleven o'clock that morning but he got his files together early and filled his briefcase ready to go at nine o'clock. He downed a final cup of black coffee and decided to get to court early. He told the day girl on the desk he was going to court and should be back shortly after noon. As he put the top down on the "staff car" he had that old feeling of importance that he used to have when he was "in court" all day. There was a feeling about being in combat in the courtroom that was hard to describe. Only a small percentage of those law students who became lawyers actually took on the role of trial lawyer. Some of the finest legal minds and jurists would absolutely turn green and throw up at the sight of a jury sitting in the jury box impatiently waiting for opening statements. However, to those few who took to the point and counter point of trial work there was nothing more challenging. True there were those days when the somber jury foreman returned the verdict against you and the world whirled dizzily at your feet, but hopefully those times were few and far between. The sheer exhilaration of winning was really what trial work was all about.

As Russ walked in on the ground floor of the old courthouse with it's scales of justice balanced precariously over the main entrance, he realized how little had changed in the time he had been banned from his chosen profession. The smell of a closed building trapping in all the agonies of defeat during the week-end was the first assault on your sensibilities. The "No Smoking" signs along the main corridor were discolored and faded from years of tobacco smoke being exhaled from the lungs of litigants and lawyers. And, of course, there was the aged sweeper who spent his days going from one level to the next sweeping up the litter carelessly thrown by the owners of this hall of justice, the taxpayers. Russ smiled and nodded to the gray haired old gentleman known only as Willie, as he pushed his broom across the landing on the stairs. Willie had worked the broom as long as Russ remembered and before that had served fifteen years for a rape he didn't commit. When the true perpetrator of the rape admitted his guilt, Willie was released amid grand fan fare, divorced and dead broke. The great State of New Mexico had graciously made amends for it's error by giving Willie the job of courthouse sweeper for the rest of his days of freedom.

Russ was early so he went into one of the conference rooms and sat down to arrange his files and thoughts. The main purpose of this meeting today was to get answers to all of the motions he had filed with the court. If he did, in fact, get these answers then he would have a good idea of where he stood and just how good the states case was against Ron. He felt certain that Rachael would keep the pressure on Buzz to divulge all of the main evidence he had to present in his case in chief at the preliminary hearing. The big problem was, if he was to believe Ron, that there was still a murderer running loose in Santa Fe. The only possible clue to this person's identity had been what Manny had told Russ and realistically this didn't seem to make much sense. The Mayor had every reason to let nature take it's course with Elsa's baby and let justice take it's course in the divorce court. Never the less he intended to check out the Mayor's alibi beginning this afternoon at the motel. He glanced at his watch and saw it was time to get one of Hannah's vicious cups of coffee and prepare for the evidence he wanted to hear but still dreaded it's total impact.

Buzz was regaling his associates and anyone who would listen with his latest story of a hard fought victory last week.

"The case really wasn't worthy of my time and effort but since the prosecutor assigned to the case, Joe Sestric, had fallen ill after opening statements, I agreed to take over and prosecute to the fullest." He paused, sipped his coffee as he glanced over the rim of the cup at Russ. Buzz smiled pleasantly and inquired, "Well Russ how is the practice going these days? Any new murders I should know about?" He turned away and continued his story without taking a breath, "Well it turns out this is a burglary case. Seems that a dry cleaning store was broken into and most of the clothing removed by the defendant. After we had put our case on, up jumps the defendant, B.J. Bobo, and says he wants to testify. His lawyer is saying no way and for him to sit down but he insists so he climbs up on the witness stand. Now this guy is a three time looser, most of it petty crap, which will all come out for the jury to hear if he testifies. Well, he settles down on the stand and his story is a true masterpiece. It seems he had just gotten out of the county work house where he had just finished serving one year on a reduced burglary charge and on his way home he notices this cleaning establishment has had the store front broken in by an unknown criminal. He being the fine upstanding citizen he is, takes all of these clothes and furs home to keep them safe from the likes of those who might remove them with ulterior purposes in mind. I couldn't believe my ears and I started laughing so hard the judge called a recess." "Buzz had begun to laugh again and pulled out his initialed silk pocket handkerchief to wipe his eyes, "His lawyer argued God, country, the flag and don't pick on Bobo to the jury. I just stood up shook my head, began to laugh again and sat down. It was my most eloquent closing argument to a jury. The Jury was out thirty minutes and off went Mr. Bobo to the state rock farm for five years."

Russ moved over next to Buzz and inquired, "Anything you want to go over before we go into chambers in order to save some time?"

Buzz gave Russ his "my life is an open book" look as he motioned to one of his prettier assistants, "Russ these files are open for you to inspect at anytime after we see the judge and get her rulings."

With that Hannah told them they could go in now and handed Russ the courts file to take into the judge.

Rachael was determined to keep this meeting short and to the point without the usual petty bickering and blustery bull shit that Buzz was famous for in chambers. So she kept her robe on and presented a grim visage as they all trooped into her chambers. Russ and Buzz took seats in front of her great desk while the assistants scattered around the room on various easy chairs and the lone sofa.

"Now, gentlemen, I have an extremely heavy docket today so please let us get right down to business." She paused picked up a cigarette and then put it down unlit on the ash tray.

"Russ, these are your pre-trial motions and I have reviewed them very carefully. I don't think you are asking for anything out of the ordinary and as far as I am concerned Buzz should comply with your requests to produce."

"Now, Judge, it seems to me that Russ wants me to open up the whole corral so he can pick what ever pony he wants to ride." Buzz lit up a huge black cigar and puffed out large bluish billows of smoke. "If I turn over all that he wants in his motions, why there just won't be any fun left in putting this punk away for good."

"Buzz, you know god damned well I am entitled to know who you intend to call as witnesses and for what purposes. I intend to take their depositions and issue a truck load of interrogatories to be answered in writing under oath." Russ felt the old scar begin to throb just as the judge surprisingly banged her gavel down on a book on the side of her desk.

"That is enough. I want each of you to address your remarks to the court unless otherwise directed. Now Buzz I want you to sit here and calmly and methodically tell Russ who your witnesses are and their purpose of testifying. Russ I will ask Buzz the questions that should satisfy your various pre-trial motions. When I have finished you may proceed." She picked up the unlit cigarette and this time lit it. Russ noted her hands were steady as she glared at Buzz.

Buzz motioned to an assistant who brought over a file about six inches thick and laid it on the desk in front of him. "Alright lets get started. Remember this is just a preliminary hearing so all the State has to do is make enough of a case to hold White for murder one." He paused for effect and then opened the file. "First there is the Mayor, who will testify to what he found when he walked into the bedroom. Next there is the mailman on the route who heard moaning that morning when he delivered the mail. Next is the nosey neighbor who can identify the perp's car. Then we have the lab experts who will identify the type "O" blood found at the scene as being the same type as White's, and an expert on fibre who will match fibres found at the scene with those taken from the defendants pants that were dug out of a dumpster at the motel where he and his lawyer live, and identification of some pubic hair found on the death bed that did not belong to the deceased. Finally we will have the fingerprint expert who not only found the defendants prints on the hose but also in the blood at the scene." He paused and then went on as he turned over one more page of typewritten material in the file. "I might, in all fairness, add that we could possibly have one more bit of evidence that could be used at the trial, but since I am not sure of its probative value nor whether it will be admissible in evidence, I will not go into any speculation at this time." He sat back and slowly closed the file looking directly into the eyes of the Judge with just a trace of smirk on his lips. An associate leaned forward from behind Buzz exposing her well endowed cleavage and whispered in his ear.

"Oh yes, Miss Cleavage just mentioned to me that we hope to match cloth fibers found on the death bed with fibers taken from the defendants pants, just one more tid bit for you Russ." He smiled that "I love you" smile at Miss Cleavage who was flushed as she buttoned the top two buttons of her flimsy blouse.

Russ felt the whole impact of the case coming down on him. It didn't take much of a defense lawyer to figure out that the State had a damn good case against Ron White. Russ still wanted to believe that Ron was innocent but with the mass of evidence presented here for only a preliminary hearing it was hard not to go to Ron with some kind of deal from the prosecution. In the past Russ had been lied to by clients who were afraid to confess the truth to their lawyer, so he wouldn't be shocked if Ron had been the perpetrator, instead of an innocent victim of the system. The fact that Ron was his friend from the past really made no difference when it came down to testimony that meant the difference between acquittal or conviction.

Rachael looked at Russ with eyes that said more than any words. The probability of a conviction hung heavily in the courts chambers. Rachael carefully arranged a wisp of blonde hair as she looked across the desk at Buzz, "Just a couple of questions to make sure you have fully complied with the pre-trial motions filed by Russ. Do you have any evidence as to where the weapon, the hose, that caused the massive internal hemorrhaging of the victim came from. That would certainly have some bearing on the case."

Buzz leaned back to get the answer from another associate, "Yes, your Honor, it was cut off of a piece of garden hose in the victim's garage. It was a piece of hose about a foot long and one inch in diameter. Incidentally while we are discussing this point I should also mention that the ropes used to tie the victim in bondage also came from the garage where remaining pieces were found."

The Judge looked over at Russ inquiringly, "Well, Russ, there you have it. Is there anything else you would need to know to comply with your motions?" She paused. "One more question, Buzz. You say you have a witness to the perp's car leaving the garage near the time of death. Do you have a description of the car and the time is was observed?"

Again Buzz looked to his associates who indicated his file on the Judge's desk. After a moment of leafing through it he held up a sheet of paper. "Here we have it. She says that the car was a metallic silver Cadillac Eldorado, fairly late model. She saw it just as it pulled out of the driveway onto the street at approximately ten forty five in the morning."

Russ shifted in his chair to look directly at Buzz, "Are there any other witnesses you haven't told us about today, whether they are expert witnesses or witnesses to the happening of the crime?"

Buzz again looked over his shoulder and all the associates shook their heads in the negative.

"Now, Buzz, I assume that you will provide me with the names and addresses of all the witnesses as well as a resume of the testimony you expect them to give at the trial.."

Buzz nodded affirmatively as Russ continued, "And you will put all of this in writing under oath and filed with the court and a copy to me at my office in the Motel."

This brought an ill concealed snicker from the associates as Buzz inquired with excessive politeness as to just which room did Russ use as his combined residence and office?

Rachael snapped an icy stare at each associate that silenced the room. "Russ, if that's all you have and you think Buzz has answered all of your motions to produce and so forth, then I think we can conclude this part of the hearing. Buzz I would like for your associates to step out of chambers while I take up some informal matters with counsel."

Buzz began to object but then saw that familiar look in Rachael's eyes that had been a warning of impending disaster during their marriage. He waved a hand nonchalantly to them as they all scrambled for the door.

Rachael got up and stretched revealing a blouse stretched taut across her finely molded bosoms. She lit another cigarette and then turned to look directly at Russ, "Russ, I hate to say this but if all that Buzz has said in here today comes to pass in front of a jury, then your boy is in deep deep shit. Apparently he was sure as hell there at the scene and so far he is the only one who has been fingered as a possible perpetrator. Now I have to assume that you still think he is not guilty as charged. This is in the truest tradition of a good defense lawyer but it sure as hell won't cut any slack for him in front of a jury. Even if he gets on the stand and denies his guilt it probably will not overcome all of the evidence against him, not without a damn good alibi and someone else to point to as the real bad guy."

Buzz smiled his most gracious winners smile at Russ as he stated, "Judge, I doubt that Mr. White will be taking the witness stand in his own defense. You see Russ, he really isn't the Mr. lilly White that you think he is. We ran a check on him and came up with a conviction for bum checks, another for assault and an arrest for assault on his wife. So I am sure you wouldn't want all that to come out in court, which, of course, it will if he takes the witness stand in his own defense."

Rachael wanted to reach over and take Russ in her arms and hold him while she told him it happens to the best of trial lawyers when they have a loser on their hands. She knew she was falling in love with him all over again and just wanted to get this damn case out of the way so they could pick up where they had left off before.

"Buzz, you, on the other hand, sure as hell don't have a solid twenty four carat gold murder one case. So far no one has come up with any motive that I know about. Therefore it looks like this is the typical spur of the moment violent crime with no premeditation. Now we all know without premeditation in the case you cannot make a first degree murder case." She slowly eased herself back down in her chair as she stubbed out her half smoked cigarette.

No one said a word for a few moments and then it was Buzz, "Well, what the hell are you getting at, Judge? I certainly don't feel like making a reduced offer at this point in the game. Before we go to trial we can probably come up with the motive in this case. Until then Murder One is the way it stays."

Rachael began to show her irritation with both lawyers now. Buzz for being uncompromising and Russ for remaining stubbornly silent. "Alright, here is the way it looks to me. Buzz, you should be happy if Russ would plea bargain to voluntary manslaughter which would carry a fifteen year load with it. Russ, the way I see it your boy would be damned lucky if the State would recommend that deal to him." Russ began to get up and protest about Ron's proclaimed innocence, but Rachael put her hand out to wave him back down. "Just hold it a minute and think it over — both of you. I think this would be the best deal for all concerned and one that the court can live with if it is a made deal."

Russ began to stuff legal pads and files back in his brief case. He snapped it closed, took out a cigarette, and carefully tapped it against his thumb nail. He looked up into the solemn face of Rachael as she waited for his answer.

"Judge, I am not saying that you aren't on the right track with this deal and I really appreciate your efforts to settle this case. I admit from what I have heard today the State has a damn good case. I will be obliged as an attorney to take any plea bargaining possibility back to my client for his consideration. I will also lay out in detail all of the evidence that I became aware of today, along with my recommendation. The basic problem I have in this case is that I have a client who says he is not guilty of any crime, much less even manslaughter."

Buzz got up in disgust and started for the door, "I told you at the outset Thurston that I was not going to make any deals on this case and by God I meant it. The only reason I am even considering what the Judge has recommended is because I happen to intimately know she has one hell of a fine legal mind and probably has a more unbiased and logical overview of this case that either one of us. But when you come up with this crap that your boy is innocent in the face of all this expert evidence that puts him at the scene, then as far as I am concerned all bets are off and we will let the jury do its job." He saluted the Judge and wheeled around to go out the door just as Hannah opened it to tell the Judge that the parties were ready for trial in the next case.

Rachael looked tired as she told Hannah she would be right out. "Russ, please think this deal over and recommend it to your client. The only out I see for him is if you can come up with someone else who could have committed the crime and you know how tough that can be."

Russ walked around the desk and took her hands in his, "Honey, I know you feel this is the way to go at this point. and I must admit it looks like a good out for Ron but there are still a few things I need to check out before I put any pressure on him to cop a plea to manslaughter — that is if the State is still offering that deal." He bent over her very slowly and tilted her chin up so that his lips brushed her forehead and then held her lips against his for a moment of eternity

"Oh, Russ, you know how I love to kiss you — so please help me to behave myself until this is over." Her hand gently stroked his cheek as her lips sought his once more. "Now I have to get back on the bench and you have a load of work to do before next week. I will see you in court, lover." With that she was out the private door to the bench with the bailiff calling the court to order.

It was not quite twelve o'clock so Russ decided to go directly from the courthouse to see Ron and go over the evidence he now knew about. Really the only surprise that morning had been the eye-witness that had properly identified Ron's car. That was just the icing on the cake since the lab experts had already put Ron in the garage, bathroom and bedroom.

The usual grim faced deputy checked Russ through the security area and put a call into the second floor to bring White down to the conference room. Then through the usual clanging and slamming of great steel doors that led to the lawyers conference tables, Ron came hobbling in with a wan smile on his sallow face. They shook hands and Russ laid a fresh pack of cigarettes on the worn desk top.

"Well, how did it go in the Judge's Chambers? Did we make any points?" Russ had a quizzical look on his face that made Ron laugh. "Russ, don't you know this jail house has a grapevine that exceeds AT&T for speed and efficiency. I knew about your meeting today five minutes after the Judge called you to give you the date time and place."

Russ smiled as he lit a cigarette, "Well, I can't say we made any points but at least we know what the evidence is going to be. There may be one small piece that Buzz is holding out but he said he would let me have it as soon as he was sure they were going to use it and that it was admissible in evidence. Ron you know all the details of the lab evidence since you and I have already discussed the problem of your fingerprints and so forth. The only way out of this mess is to find the person who really did kill Elsa or put you on the stand to try and convince the jury that you are not the perpetrator."

Ron sat up in his chair and grabbed the coat sleeve of Russ, "I want to testify. I have got to tell it the way it was, to tell them that I am no murderer!"

Russ frowned, "But Ron we have a problem if you take the witness stand. If you don't testify in your own behalf then the state cannot bring out any of your previous convictions. If you do testify then they will parade out all of those prior convictions which will dirty you up in the eyes of the jury."

Ron was highly agitated, "What convictions? You mean those little bull shit assault cases and I guess those bum check cases also. Well what the hell has any of that got to do with a murder one case? What kind of God damned legal system is this that tries to paint a man black before he is even tried? It is just like all the brothers in here keep saying, "Guilty until proven innocent." Well, by God, I am going to testify and if you don't like it then I will just get another lawyer!"

Russ was furious, he had been patient enough with this former magazine magnet who had stupidly walked his way into a jail cell, "Now you just listen to me, you smart ass bastard, so we can determine whether we want to see each other again. You have gotten yourself into this nasty situation through your own greed and horny conduct. You were stupid enough to knock Elsa up and then spit in her face. You were horny enough that you just had to go back for one more piece of ass. Well, that was your final undoing and now your ass belongs to the State of New Mexico if you don't play your cards right. You had to have me as your lawyer. Well then, you will do exactly what I tell you to do from now on in this case. Don't you forget for one minute that I am calling the shots from here on in. If I want your opinion I will ask for it, otherwise keep your mouth shut."

Russ got up to leave and looked at Ron who looked like a small crushed boy. He couldn't help but feel sorry for him as he put his hand on his shoulder, "Well, it looks like you will have to testify in any event. I will get back to you to prepare you for the hearing. Ron, please keep in mind that this is only a preliminary hearing to determine whether the State has sufficient evidence against you to make a case for the jury on Murder One. If the Judge feels there is sufficient evidence then she will order you held for trial. No matter what the outcome is on Monday, it is not the end of the line." Ron nodded and slowly stood to leave. "In the meantime, Ron, spend some time writing out in detail what happened and what you did on the day of the murder." Russ began to move toward the guard at the door.

"Russ, would you please try to get me out of here right away. I mean it Russ, I can't sleep for fear of getting raped. One son of a bitch caught me in the shower and tried to force me to suck his cock. One of the trustees saw what was happening and came in and beat him with a mop handle." Ron was beginning to weep again.

"Now the guy that saved me says I belong to him. He keeps fondling me at night and says he won't hurt me when he sticks it in me." He sobbed. "Jesus Christ, Russ, can't you do something to get me out of this fucking house of crazies?"

Russ looked at a beaten man, certainly not the wheeler dealer magazine boss. "Ron, I will keep trying. Believe me, I have tried to get bail set but to no avail. Just hang in tough and keep fighting them off for one more week."

Ron shuffled out, his orange jail coveralls sagging over his slight drooping shoulders. Russ couldn't even imagine the horror of being trapped in a cell with sexual perverts, but he knew he had run the rope out with the Judge concerning the setting of bail. The only way out now was through the preliminary hearing and Russ had grave doubts about any help in that regard.

CHAPTER VII

When Russ returned to his office in the motel Willis had already checked in for the afternoon shift. Much as Willis got on his nerves, Russ had to admit the boy was honest, prompt and finally beginning to show some signs of maturing.

"Hi Russ. How did it go today?" He lit up a cigarette that was dangling from the corner of his mouth.

Russ had never seen Willis smoke before, only chew gum incessantly, "Just when the hell did you start smoking?"

Willis smiled broadly while he exhaled through his nose, "I just tried it out the other night while out on a date and I liked it. I haven't learned to inhale yet but I'll catch on soon."

"Outside of taking drugs that is about the worst habit you can start." Russ flopped his briefcase on the desk.

Willis was visibly shaken by his comment, "Well, since you smoke I sure didn't think you would care."

Russ poured a cup of day old black coffee, took a sip and grimaced "I wouldn't care if I didn't like you, Willis. Since I have become accustomed to your honest smiling face around here, I hate to see those white teeth stained yellow and your lungs turned black." He lit up a cigarette and held it out toward Willis. "I will tell you what I will do Willis. I will stop smoking if you will — after this last cigarette." He knew there was no chance that he would quit since he had tried many times before and the longest period of time he had stopped had been from noon until midnight. He might have gone a little longer but when the phone awakened him at midnight the first thing he did was reach for a cigarette. Anyway he might be able to get Willis to stop and he could catch a smoke when he wasn't around.

Willis put out his half smoked cigarette in the ashtray, took out his pack of cigarettes and threw them in the trash basket. Russ with great mock bravado did the same thing.

"Now that is settled suppose you tell me what is going on around here."

Willis checked the guest board for filled rooms, "Well no real problems other than the usual plumbing mess and no clean towels in some of the rooms. Oh, and the Mayor checked in about a half an hour ago. From past experience he will be good for about an hour." He snickered like the school kid he was and pulled out some gum.

"What room is he in today?" Russ moved to the phone.

"He is in his usual room that we put him in each time. Room 118. Do you want me to go get him?", he asked eagerly.

Russ already had the phone in his hands dialing 118, "No Willis, I can handle it. No free girlie shows for you today."

The phone rang repeatedly with no answer. Russ hung up and looked at Willis, "Check the board. Are you sure he is in Room 118?"

Willis smiled, "I don't have to check the board because I gave him the key to 118. Maybe she won't let him up to answer the phone. I can go knock on the door."

Russ was dialing again and this time after about a dozen rings a woman answered the phone. Russ asked to speak with Mayor Bascom.

He could hear a mans voice in the background and then, "I am very sorry but you must have the wrong room." With that the line went dead.

Russ was instantly a bundle of fire. That miserable son of a bitch had her hang up on him. "Okay, Willis, get ready to bang on the door to room 118. Take your pager with you and when you are at the door beep me in the office. Then you start banging on the door and I will phone the room. That will sure as hell get his attention."

Willis whooped with glee as he grabbed the pager and ran out the door for 118. When he got there he beeped the office and then began to try to knock the door down. He could hear the phone ringing on the other side of the door. Suddenly the door swung open and the Mayor stood there with only his pants on, "What the fuck is going on around here?"

Behind the Mayor, Willis caught a glimpse of her beauty as she nakedly leaned over to answer the phone by the bed. One leg carelessly flung to one side of the bed to expose moist, pink lips of pure heaven between her thighs. Her eyes glowed with cat like fever as she stared straight at Willis and slowly put the phone to her ear.

Willis felt an enormous pulsating erection as he locked his eyes on her magnificient full black mound. He barely heard the Mayor as he slammed the door in his face and went to the phone.

Faith reached out and stroked his unzipped crotch as he picked up the phone, "Thurston, just what the hell is it that is so urgent? This is a very private business meeting we are having with a valued foreign trade representative. This kind of interruption is inexcusable."

"Cut the bull shit Bill. Our whole front office knows you have a regular matinee scheduled each week. I don't give a damn about your personal love life, but I do need to see you about a re-zoning matter before you leave today. I will be right here in my office waiting for you." Russ could feel the phone cool in his hand as the Mayor hesitated to respond.

"Well, that is certainly no problem for me since this representative has a good deal of paper work to go over that can be accomplished while you and I chat. Suppose I meet you in about fifteen minutes in your office?"

Russ smiled at the change from outraged lover to the pure politician. No wonder the town kept electing the bastard for term after term of office.

Willis came slowly in the door just as Russ told the Mayor that fifteen minutes would be just fine.

"Is he going to bring his girl friend with him?" Willis asked hopefully.

"Not hardly, Willis, and I would guess she is more of a nympho lover than a girl friend."

All Willis could do was nod and smile blissfully at the memory of Room 118.

True to his word the Honorable Bill Bascom was at the front office fifteen minutes later. As usual he was dressed in a black suit with black tie and shoes. This mourners attire had been his hallmark since his first post mortem interview and he had sworn to continue to honor his dear departed Elsa until the murderer was convicted. His face was still flushed and a large greenish black cigar was held tightly between his teeth.

"Give me a light Russ. Can't this cheap ass motel afford a little public relations by putting some matches in the rooms?" He held the cigar steady between diamond studded fingers.

Russ was determined to keep the upper hand in this meeting so he simply threw some matches on the low table in front of the old worn out couch. "You can keep those as a memento of the last time you saw me in the official capacity as manager of this honeymoon heaven."

He glanced up at Russ as he puffed out blue smoke in a haze around the overheated room. "Don't tell me one murder case is enough to send you into permanent retirement? I guess you know I have total contempt for you because you are defending that miserable bastard." He sat down heavily on the creaking couch.

"Before we get into just who is the most contemptible person here today will you please zip up your pants or is this your day to be a fucking exhibitionist? Now before you get all puffed up lets cool things down a little." The Mayor stood up and hastily began to tug on his zipper as Russ pulled an old ladderback chair around the table near to the couch.

"First of all I do not want to talk about your wife's murder. I can tell you that from the few times that I met Elsa socially, I found her to be most charming and gracious. She was certainly an asset to you as the so called leader of the community. I also want to make it crystal clear to you that I truly do not believe that my client murdered your wife." Russ held his hand up to quiet him before he exploded.

"Secondly, what I do want to talk about is getting this miserable piece of pornographic property re-zoned so a decent motel and shopping complex can be constructed. Now I know this does not come as a great surprise to you since this is the hot issue on the agenda for next Tuesday nights board meeting. Before you start to give me some of the famous Bill Bascom bull shit, let me just lay this whole program flat on this table so you can see where all the players are coming from." Russ paused and nodded to Willis to leave the room. He slowly lit a cigarette while he kept his ice blue eyes locked on the bridge of the Mayor's nose.

"CLK Corporation through its usual devious means knows that the vote on Tuesday will, in all likelihood, be a tie. This means it is up to you to break that tie vote and it is with baited breath that CLK will await the good news and I repeat, the good news."

"Now just a God damn minute. Just who the hell do you think you are to be pre-supposing my vote? This is a tremendous project that is being suggested and very confidentially I do not see any of the goodies slipping into the old Mayors trick bag. Now you boys have been around long enough to know how the wheels of government are oiled. I can assure you that a pile of Ben Franklins can start this old Mayors wheels turning a lot faster than some WD-40." He leaned forward to drop an ash the size of Faith's nipple off the end of his cigar and gave Russ the traditional conspiratorial wink. Russ showed no emotion or interest in the game.

"There aren't any Ben Franklins or gold bullion in this deal for you. Not this time. You know, of course, that there is no confidentiality in this business. That from the very first time you wheeled in here with little miss crazy crotch all of the owners of CLK saw true deliverance from this run down delight to the proposal that is now before the board. Let me assure you, Mr. Mayor, it was not my loyalty to the corporation that was your undoing. Nevertheless, I can assure you that you will be undone by the boys at CLK if the swing vote comes down on the wrong side of the playground." Russ carefully stubbed out his cigarette and gazed flatly at the flushed and now uneasy Mayor.

"I am only a messenger for the company. I am not it's lawyer nor am I acting in my capacity as a lawyer. Let us just say in a one on one situation I have conveyed to you my evaluation of some very deep shit you have stepped in and that CLK is well aware of your continuing matinees." He reached into his inside pocket and pulled out a CLK envelope and with a slap laid it on the table in front of the Mayor, "For you from them."

Russ got up and moved across the room to the coffee stand and selected a styrofoam cup. He could hear the envelope being opened and he wondered about the contents. The Mayor gave a short grunt, then leaned back and lazily blew a solid oval smoke ring. The buzzer went off signaling business at the outside drive up window. Russ crossed the room and opened the window to extend the guest registry card which usually came back Mr. and Mrs. Bill Smith and today was no exception. He took down a key, gave directions and put the twenty dollar bill in the cash register. As he turned around he saw the Mayor flip a piece of letter size paper on the coffee table and held up what looked like a key to one of the rooms in the motel. He beckoned to Russ and held out the paper to him. Russ looked down at that familiar scrawl of Cahills' and read, "Bill Boy, Thanks for your vote of confidence. Keep the key. It is your private room now and also in the new CLK Towers Motel." It was signed The Boys.

Russ dropped the note on the table and looked at the Mayor who had a slight crooked grin on his face while he continued to throw the key to Room 118 in the air.

"Well, Russ, just tell your people that as of this Monday night I will be the proud owner of Room 118." With that he stuck the key in his pocket and dropped his cigar in Russ' cold black coffee. He still was smiling but his eyes were staring past Russ into the dark past. Suddenly he looked at Russ, "Now that your game is over I have a few questions for you, off the record, of course. Why the hell don't you plead that client of yours guilty to a lesser charge and save us all from going through the routine of testifying against him to put him where he belongs? Buzz tells me they have him cold. Blood samples are type "O", same as those found at the scene, fingerprints all over the place and he even pulls out of my driveway at the time of death established by the coroner. Why in the hell waste everybody's time?"

Russ started to tell him to just forget it and send him back to Room 118, then decided to at least answer him with a question. "Well let's put it this way. How many people do you think have type "O" blood in this town? It is the most common blood type. For instance I am type "O". What type is your blood?"

"Well, so it is type "O," also, but how about all the rest of the lab evidence?"

"What about all the rest of the technical evidence? Here you are type "O", you have fingerprints all over the room and you arrived at your office a little late that day, which according to your argument could mean that in fact you killed your wife." Russ almost began to believe what he was saying.

"Now just a minute. I certainly had nothing to gain by doing in my wife. Your client had a real motive because he had knocked her up. So what the hell would my motive be under these circumstances?

Russ smiled and slowly picked up the other key to Room 118 where the Mayor had carelessly thrown it on the desk when he came into the front office, "Your motive is waiting for you in Room 118."

CHAPTER VIII

Russ was up early Tuesday in anticipation of the meeting with the CLK group. For a day that should be the highlight of his miserable career with CLK everything began on the left foot. His electric razor quit just as he began to shave. Next a violent electrical storm cut loose right over the motel and knocked out the television in the front office just as the news came on. In disgust he began to look for a safety razor in the drawer beneath the sink and found it by promptly cutting his finger. It was just a bad day and he should have started all over again. He lathered his face with some Ivory soap and grimaced as he began to scrap away a heavy one day growth of beard. He noted with some casual interest that his beard was flecked with some gray. Well, he was certainly entitled to a little middle age maturity. He had earned all of the gray he could carry. Naturally he had to nick himself with the old safety razor and he dabbed the bright red splotch with a Kleenex. He absently thought of his short conversation with Bill Bascom yesterday concerning Elsa's murder. His impression of the Mayor had always been that he was a deceitful womanizer. Russ was certainly not naive about womanizers or their counter parts since he had handled many divorces. Sex was one of the great causes of the rending apart of domestic tranquility. From his experience, the next major cause of divorce was money, either the lack of money or the greed for more of it. Certainly the Mayor couldn't have had much sex life with Elsa. After all Ron was spreading her thighs on a regular basis and the Mayor was a regular visitor to Room 118. As far as money was concerned Russ was sure there was plenty of that to support the Mayor and all of his philandering needs. But there was still the possibility that he could not stand to see the marriage come apart and Elsa begin to split the spoils of a lifetime of marriage. Ron and the Mayor both came down the line as being hatched from the same egg. They both had type "O" blood, each had fingerprints all over the bedroom, possibly each had left pubic hairs at the murder scene, and each had a so called alibi. Naturally the police would normally look to the husband in a murder case like this but not when he was his eminence the Mayor with an iron clad alibi as to when he arrived at the office. He had no reason to murder his wife who was pregnant by Ron. In divorce court he would walk away without paying any alimony or child support and he would be awarded the lions share of all of the assets accumulated during the marriage.

Russ threw the old razor blade in the waste container and slowly rinsed the soap from his shaggy shave.

Then there was Ron White, the great adulterer, the defiler of women, corruptor of young children, user of child labor for his own personal gain. Russ could just see the jury living every minute of the sex riddled background about his client. Then finally the motive comes bursting forth. Here was the true fornicator who had enjoyed the pleasures of his married lover until she had trapped him with pregnancy and then the bubble burst.

After all, the jury would hear, he only wanted the pleasure of this forbidden tryst not the fruit of his sexual exploits. But poor loving Elsa wanted it all. She had her man now, would have the baby and get rid of her equally adulterous husband. Then there is the usual violent lovers quarrel over aborting the baby with much begging, pleading and weeping. The scene rapidly changes to sudden violence and spiteful hatred, spewing out of the same mouths that once were interlocked with love. The abortion comes quickly and crudely on the blood soaked bed where suddenly not just one small life is taken, but two shall perish.

Russ found himself staring in the mirror now lost in his own thoughts of what really had happened on that most fateful day. He had to believe his client but he had to admit the prosecutions physical evidence and the motive for murder would sure as hell play well with the jury.

He slapped some Old Spice on his face and winced when it hit the nick on his chin. If is wasn't Ron who murdered her then who the hell was the real perp? It had to be Bill Bascom. That was the only other suspect the investigation had come up with and he had a solid alibi and no apparent motive. Or was there a motive, a blind spot in his logic that had blocked out the possible motive of Mayor Bill Bascom.

The incessant ringing of the phone brought him out of his realistic day dream. He had forgotten that Willis did not come on duty until noon today.

"This is Russ speaking." He walked to the front office with the portable phone.

"Cahill here Russ. I know we were supposed to meet today but I wanted to find out where we are on this re-zoning matter ahead of time."

"I talked to Bascom yesterday afternoon and it looks like he will be the swing vote in favor of the re-zoning, if it comes down to that. I made it clear to him that I was only a messenger boy and not a lawyer in this deal. I would suggest that from now on you make direct contact with him rather than through me."

"Hey Russ, let's not make a big deal out of this. I think the Mayor has probably been on our side all along."

Russ was not in a mood for finessing each other, "I agree he probably was in favor of the re-zoning. Anything would beat this flop house. Let me get to the point, Jack. Now that I am reinstated as a lawyer I just do not want to be a manager of a motel or a messenger boy. I know I have a long hard road ahead of me but I might just get lucky and get a job with some law firm. So let us just call it quits and shake hands as friends from the past. I will stick around until you get someone to take my place and then I am history in the CLK book."

There was a long silence. "Russ are you sure you don't want to hang in there so you can take over the management of the new complex? You know being a trial lawyer can be a long tough road and not much income at first. Why don't you get this God damned murder case over with, then see how you feel about all of this?"

"Jack, I won't say that this job hasn't been interesting. It sure as hell has been. All of the dregs of humanity ultimately come into this run down sin city. But it is time for me to move on up the ladder if I ever expect to do anything with that law degree that hangs on the wall in my one room suite. So just get yourself a new manager and give me a couple of days notice to clear out."

He hung up the phone as a great sense of well being came over him. He really had not intended to get out so fast since he sure as hell had no where to go and no income, but he had high hopes that he would get hired by someone or some law firm that remembered just how good he had been as a trial lawyer. After all, just a touch of gray around the temples never hurt that jury appeal.

CHAPTER IX

The week had been busy but had produced some interesting developments in the life of Russ Thurston.

The meeting with CLK did not develop since Russ had assured Cahill that the re-zoning was in the bag with the mayors swing vote guaranteed. Not only that but Cahill and the rest of the CLK group were, what is commonly know as, pissed off at Russ for his ungrateful attitude toward them. The search was now on for a new manager.

Rachael had called Russ on Thursday about producing a hair sample, well not just a hair sample but a pubic hair sample, from Ron for examination by the experts. She said that Buzz had already filed formal motions for not only this but also for a blood sample. Unless Russ agreed to the motions without formal hearing the preliminary motion now set for hearing on Monday would have to be continued. She personally felt the motions were well taken and would probably be sustained after a formal hearing. Russ took the matter up with Ron who said under no circumstances did he want to prolong the hearing. He was ready to pull pubic hairs and spill blood right in the conference room. All he could think about was getting the hell out of that cell. The preliminary hearing at least gave him a chance to get out on bond if nothing else. So Russ stipulated to the motions.

When he had called Rachael back, agreeing to the motions by Buzz, she had just gotten off the bench for the day and was in a more relaxed mood. She had a new client for Russ, an old friend who had been through two husbands and was now ready to dump number three. Her name was Susan and would be in touch with Russ for an appointment. She warned Russ to keep it in his pants since Susan was a long limbed, full busted, border line sex maniac. Russ laughed and told Rachael to just make sure Susan had a five hundred dollar retainer and the hell with the sex. Rachael didn't see much humor in the situation and told him all he needed was one nympho in his life and she wore a black robe with nothing on under it. She blew him a kiss over the phone and said she would see him Monday.

True to her word, Susan Thomas called Russ for an appointment. The only problem Russ had was where to meet her. He had a mental picture of this bundle of sex meeting him at the motel for a one on one conference. He arranged to meet her at the lawyers lounge in the court house on Friday at four o'clock in the afternoon. By four o'clock on a Friday the court house was almost deserted so the lounge would give them privacy.

Friday morning Russ met with Ron one final time before the Monday hearing. He was appalled at Ron's appearance. He had lost at least ten pounds, his eyes were red rimmed and sunken. His hair was uncombed and he had an odor about him that spelled out days without bathing. He almost looked as if he had shrunk since he had been in security. Russ took the limp hand shake Ron offered and slowly eased into the hard backed oak chair.

"Well, Russ, I guess this is our final run down on the evidence. I still want to testify no matter what you say. At least I want the Judge to hear my side of the story." He rubbed the piece of adhesive on his arm where they had taken blood earlier in the day.

"Ron, I still think you are wrong to take the stand. All you can do is give the prosecution more ammunition and lord knows they have enough already." Ron began to protest but Russ stopped him with a quick gesture. "Never the less, I will put you on the stand and you can tell it your way." Ron visibly relaxed and reached for a cigarette.

"Ron, you have to know I believe you are innocent but there is one hell of a lot of evidence that points to you as the one who did the job on Elsa. There is no other suspect at this time and I will not be surprised if the judge finds that this is a Murder One case. I think she will find this way whether or not you testify, so you are going up on that witness stand to give it your best shot."

Russ backed off from the little table between them to get some fresh air. "Now I have asked you to spend some time re-living the days that led up to your arrest to see if you could come up with any evidence that might help us or implicate someone else as the perpetrator.

Ron slowly shook his head and stared past Russ through the barred window. "Did the Mayor know you were screwing his wife and, even more importantly, how did he know you made her pregnant?"

"I guess she must of told him sometime before she was murdered. I know when I saw her for the last time he didn't know about me or even her being pregnant as far as I know."

"Did Elsa ever complain about the Mayors temper, or that he had beat her on any occasion?"

Ron hesitated, slowly blew smoke across the table, "Are you thinking the same thing I am Russ? Do you think he did it or had it done?"

"Well, I just do not see who else it could have been since robbery was not the motive, and it wasn't a rape-murder scenario. But what was the motive? Where was the gain for him to murder her? He had all the aces. She was pregnant, by you, they both wanted a divorce and she would have come out of it with no alimony or child support. She would get a share of the marital assets and probably even have to pay her own attorney fees. All he had to do was sit back and let it happen. He would have ended up the poor misunderstood husband pitied by all of his supporters."

"Russ, I don't disagree with what you are saying," Ron again stared out the window, then suddenly got to his feet and slammed his fist on the table, "but, God damn it, some son of a bitch is letting me take the fall for a murder he committed and the only person it could be has a type "O" blood, left some hair samples around and some fingerprints. Now, damn it Russ, there is just one other person who will fit that description and that is the son of a bitch Bill Bascom!"

"His alibi is what really makes the difference, along with no motive." Russ began to put his file together, "But maybe we can get some admissions out of him on the witness stand Monday. Ron, for God's sake, take a shower and wear some clean clothes on Monday or the Judge will rule against us just to get you out of the courtroom."

Ron's eyes suddenly were full of tears, "Russ, I can't even bend over to brush my teeth without some gorilla giving me a crotch job. They have a pool going on who will get my cherry and the date and time I will go down. I am scared shitless to go into the showers because that is just where it will happen. But if that is what it takes I will wait until the last minute on Monday and make a dash for the showers."

Russ snapped his briefcase shut and grabbed Ron roughly by the shoulder, "You just hang tough and we will make it through this."

CHAPTER X

As Russ stepped into the lawyers lounge, promptly at four o'clock, his stomach growled and rolled over. He knew better than to eat a Mexican chili dog with onions and jalapeno peppers. He was on his second roll of Tums and no relief in sight. As a matter of fact, there was no new client in sight either. He began to wonder if he was being stood up. The lounge was empty except for a lawyer frantically talking to his office on the pay phone in the corner. The green leather couch was worn and showed dark spots where perspiring heads had lain back in sheer exhaustion. The wooden coffee table showed heel marks and cigarette burns that gave it a special antique look. The carpet was heavily worn between the couch and the men's restroom where many a sweat stained, nervous, lawyer squeezed out one last drop before going back in the court room. The two conference rooms, each about the size of a confessional, were equipped with a beat up desk with its share of scars from cigarette burns and two vinyl covered straight backed chairs that looked like they had been confiscated from a doctors office. The whole room was illuminated by a super bright overhead one bar fluorescent light. Naturally each room was windowless with a partial glass door to give semi-privacy. As Russ turned from examining the room with the least smoke haze in it he could smell her. At the same time the lawyer on the pay phone stopped talking as he openly stared at her partially bared full breasts with a delicious crease burying itself beneath a sheer light blue blouse of Taiwan see thru fabric. As she moved toward Russ there was the gentle sound of the swishing of sheer silk panty hose. The enchanting aroma of Gorgio perfume rolled up from the movement of her hips.

"Mr. Thurston, I presume." Her white gloved hand was extending as Russ looked into green eyes and dazzling white teeth. He gently took her hand as he watched her tongue wisp across perfect full lips.

"Susan it is nice to meet you. Sorry about the office furniture but I have been in court all day and I figured this was the best place to meet." He lied with a slight blush. She smiled magnificently as she shook her shoulder length auburn hair. "No need to apologize, I have met men in a lot worse places than this and had one hell of a great time."

They both laughed as Russ escorted her to one of the vinyl chairs. He sat across from her as she crossed a superb pair of long graceful legs under a short ivory cream skirt.

"Well, I guess Rachael filled you in on my problem. So where do we start?"

Russ loosened his tie and squirmed uncomfortably on the cracked upholstered chair. She absolutely reeked sensual aggressiveness yet all she was doing was looking at Russ with wide longing eyes, into the very depths of his groin. Her every movement sent a sexual stimulation raging through his over wrought nervous system. He wanted to hold her and stroke her as he led her to his bed to make vicious rampaging love to her, flooding her body with his love.

She slowly removed her gloves and again ran the tip of her beautiful pink tongue over her full upper lip.

"As a matter of fact, Susan, the Judge told me nothing of your problems with your husband, only that you had been married twice before and apparently this marriage is ready for some expert severance."

She smiled, almost demurely, as she placed her gloves on her purse, "I never should have married the old son of a bitch in the first place, but I needed security and a place in society. I got both of those but had to put up with his whining all the time because he couldn't keep it hard long enough to fuck me."

Russ couldn't believe anyone would be unable to keep it hard with this sexual, beautiful animal wrapped around him.

"I can see you are like all the rest, you cannot believe it is true. First of all, Bradley is an only child who was totally confused by his parents. His mother used to take him into her bed when he was a young child and make him kiss her until she had an orgasm all over his little hard cock. Well papa walked in on this little arrangement and that was the end of mama. From then on Bradley was told to go in the closet and fuck his fist but never to put it in a woman, unless he wanted to make a baby. How confused can you get with parents like this?"

She took out a non filtered cigarette and held the lighter to Russ for a light. He really didn't want to touch her but he knew he had to when he lit her cigarette. She leaned forward and the scent of an aroused woman escaped between her firm breasts. Her hands didn't just touch Russ, they held his hand firmly as she looked into the very depths of his thoughts.

"Anyway, Bradley got married to a cold bitch who only compounded his frustration. She wanted a baby because by now Bradley had inherited a fortune from his father, but something was haywire with one or both of them so she couldn't get pregnant. That was when she decided to charge Bradley for her favors. A hand job for one hundred dollars, blow job, but you couldn't come in her mouth, for one hundred and fifty, and a quick fuck for two hundred. Naturally he divorced her when he was in his prime at forty years of age. As far as I know he spent the next twenty five years going to X-rated movies, reading Hustler magazines and giving himself refined hand jobs."

Her cigarette had fallen off of the ash tray and burned just one more hole in the desk top as she quickly put it out.

"So, would you believe I am working for this fag interior decorator, who has made up some new drapes and furniture covers for Mr. Bradley Thomas. He sends me out to put up the drapes and fix the furniture. By this time, I am thirty five years old and have been through two, so called, husbands, both of whom are very big on spreading my legs, but always short on the money. So I am out on my ass in the big cold world with my best recommendation for a job being that I am simply superb in the sack."

Russ, as usual, is fascinated with this real life story that rings of fiction, but for the fact that he has the real live main character in this dingy little conference room, it would be unbelievable.

"Well, I am busy doing my work on a ladder hanging drapes and sure enough I feel a gentle stroke on the right cheek of my ass. There is old T. Bradley Thomas just grinning up my legs like he owns me. The rest is history. As I said all I wanted was security and all he wanted was sex. I fulfilled my end of the bargain but he couldn't get the job done."

"What do you mean you held up your end of the deal? I guess you know he will deny that you gave him sex when he wanted it. Then it is his word against yours, Susan."

"First of all, Russ, I would assume you can tell I have had plenty of cock in my day. I am also known around some of the better bistros in this State as one unbelievable head job. I am constantly ready for sex, like right now. I spend an inordinate amount of my waking hours just thinking about sex and when will be the next time I will be holding some great hunk between my legs."

Russ could see the thin line of perspiration on her upper lip. She was continually moving, as if in constant agitation.

"But whether you believe me or not, and I am willing to prove it to you, I have proof in living, moving, moaning color." She produced a flat key from her purse, "This is a key to a safe deposit box. This box contains three video tapes of some action packed drama in a super king sized bed between T. Bradley and his loving wife Susan."

Russ leaned back in his chair and shook his head in disbelief as he got up to get a pad of paper. He felt her hand on his inner thigh as he looked into her pleading eyes.

"My God, Russ, I am so hot. Can't we get out of here and finish this meeting in a more comfortable atmosphere?"

Russ felt his hand tremble as he reached for her. He held her by the shoulders as she laid her head against his hands.

"Susan, the second thing I want the most in the world right now is to unzip my pants and let you lay me right on this desk."

She smiled and put his hand inside her blouse over her full hard nipple, she murmured, "So, what's the first thing you want the most, honey?"

"I want to keep my ticket to practice law now that I have gotten it back. One sure way for me to lose it is to commit adultery with my client."

He gently pulled his hand out of her dress and lifted her chin up to look into those magnificent eyes, "I will promise you this that the day you are divorced is the day I will show you all of my other talents."

With that she jumped up and kissed him with passion full on the lips, "Now that is a promise I can't refuse. Let's get this divorce on the way."

Russ smiled and sat down again. "Alright so you have him by the short hair with videos and I assume you could find others to vouch for your sexual prowess? No need to answer that question, but let me ask you this. Just what did blow up your marriage? You had your security and I assume sex on the outside to keep you calmed down."

"I will tell you just what did it. That son of a bitching Mayor Bill Bascom got to drinking vodka with T. Bradley one evening and told him he ought to get me to sign a post nuptial agreement so if there was a divorce I couldn't clean him out. Well, next thing I know he comes marching in with this fifty page blue bound document and tells me that he is being more than fair and I should sign it in front of two witnesses, which he will provide."

Russ made a quick note, then looked up at those blazing eyes, "Well, was it fair or not?"

"I knew it wouldn't be fair if Bill Bascom had anything to do with it and sure as hell I was right. You know, Elsa and I were pretty close friends. Oh, not to the point where we gave out our lovers names and physical attributes, but at least to the point where we could talk about our rotten marriages to ass hole husbands. She told me just before someone murdered her, that she had transferred all C.D.'s, money markets and cash investments into her name so when Bascom came at her with this post-nuptial thing she was ready for him. Anyway, T. Bradley's idea of fair was that I got about one fourth of his bank account, which of course did not include the house, trusts, stocks, C.D.'s and about a million dollars worth of other assets. I tore up those fifty pages of legal larceny and told him to cover his balls because the judge in divorce court was going to lay the gavel on them."

Russ couldn't help but laugh as he envisioned old T. Bradley Thomas in a state of shock as Susan flounced out of the room with fifty pages, now shredded, flying through the air.

"Now, Susan, let me tell you about our divorce laws in New Mexico. We are a community property state like California. Which simply means that you automatically get half of all property acquired during the marriage. It is possible, however, that you may get more or less depending on your good or bad behavior during the marriage." He paused to see if she was understanding what he was saying, then went on, "The court may or may not award attorney fees and court costs against either party depending on their financial circumstances. Naturally, in this case, I would assume the court would award my fees against your husband due to his well known wealth. However, I must still ask you for a retainer fee which will be refunded to you from any award of fees against your husband."

"Alright, I understand all of that but I want some idea of where you think I will fall on the property settlement." She had carefully laid ten one hundred dollar bills on the desk in front of Russ.

"Susan, I have to just assume we will end up with around one half of the assets and cash and probably a lump sum amount of alimony payable over ten years and one month to give T. Bradley the break to write it off as an income tax deduction."

Russ tore off a piece of yellow legal size paper with a receipt written on it and shoved it across the table to Susan. She gently stroked his hand as she picked it up and folded it into her purse.

"Russ, let's the two of us get that bastard. Now what do you need to know?"

Russ went through the usual necessities to draw up the petition for divorce and told her he would call her in a couple of days to come in and sign it. At that time they would have another in depth conference.

"Just a couple of other things before you leave. Since we will allege that you were separated as of today, you had better move into another bed room and wear a chastity belt. Put your super sex drive in double low gear until this is concluded. Now do you need any money while we are going through the divorce? You know this could take a full year before it is heard as a contested case. If you need some walking around money we can file a motion for temporary allowances."

Susan gave Russ that flash of angel white teeth and leaned forward seductively, "Russ, honey, my deceased friend, Elsa Bascom, taught me how to squirrel away fun money and if that runs out I have a few available friends who will gleefully help me out — on an exchange basis for future favors."

Russ stirred uncomfortably as she locked onto his crotch with those emerald eyes. He got up to end the conference and moved toward the door, "One other thing that occurred to me. You and Elsa were very close friends. Did she ever indicate to you that she had been physically abused by the Mayor?"

"No, she never mentioned any physical abuse by him. She was mentally abused by him for years since he always had a daytime hustler that kept him satisfied. She knew about it but really did not care since they had separate bedrooms. I do know that just before her murder she had put everything in her name alone. He would be really furious about being outsmarted by Elsa. I have seen him with fire in his eyes when Elsa would pull his chain a little too hard. I would guess he could lose control pretty easily when you stepped on his balls just a wee bit too hard." She stood up to leave and pressed gently against Russ as she moved toward the door, "Most men hate to get balled without benefit of a good screwing." She brushed a kiss across his cheek. "Hold that thought big man until we meet again."

She was gone but her instant replay lingered on as Russ tried to shakily light a Lucky.

CHAPTER XI

It was a spectacular New Mexico day. The clean air of the high country had rolled into Santa Fe during the night and had cleared away the hundreds of hangovers before the first mass at St. Michaels. Father Sebastian had long ago learned to sit as far away as possible from the repentant sinners as they made their usual weekly confessions. After twenty years of holding mass at St. Michaels and as many confessions, he knew most of those who assailed the confessional on Sunday by voice or, with a wry smile, by their breath taking confessions. As he walked slowly up the worn stone steps of the church, hands clasped behind his back, he smiled at the thought of telling Patrick Gonzales O'Toole that his pennance today would not be one hundred hail Marys but instead he must run naked around the town square carrying two full bottles of tequila, loudly professing that he is the biggest drunk in Santa Fe. The old cracked church bells began to ring slightly out of harmony and the good Father quickly crossed himself and asked forgiveness for thinking such ill thoughts of poor Patrick Gonzales O'Toole. But it just might cure his drinking problem.

Russ opened the massive, oak inlaid, front door of the church for the good Father who stood only five feet two inches tall in his high heeled black Tony Lama boots. Russ towered over the slightly built prelate as they entered the church together.

"Thank you, my son, and may the good Lord bless you on this heaven sent day."

"Indeed it is that Father. I can certainly use as much heaven sent help as possible in the week ahead."

"I don't recall you in attendance at Mass before and you are certainly much to big, physically, to have been over looked."

Russ smiled and leaned over to whisper in his ear, "Please don't tell anyone, Father, but I am not of the Catholic faith. I just dropped in for a little of the good Lord's help for my client who is being held for first degree murder."

Father squinted up at Russ through worn wrinkles of wisdom as he took Russ' hand in his, "The house of the Lord belongs to all mankind. Both the righteous and the sinner shall sit side by side and share equally in God's giving glory and forgiveness. This threshold is never closed to those in need. I shall keep your client —"

"His name is Ron White, Father."

"Ron White in my prayers and ask that the good Lord in all his wisdom shall forgive him his sins and lead him on the path to Heaven." He turned and started down the wide aisle of the church toward the magnificent jewel encrusted gold cross behind the alter.

"If you don't mind, Father, I do not want to get him started on the road to heaven during the trial." Russ smiled and sat in the last pew on the aisle and quietly made his peace with the almighty as the bells carried out their off key hallelujah.

It was always the same the day before trail. The tension that had been there all of the time had finally reached a gut wrenching crescendo. Soft boiled eggs and coffee, with lots of cream, took care of breakfast. The morning paper had the usual repetitive story about the murder and that the preliminary hearing was set for trial on Monday. Buzz Rawlings had made it clear that it would not take long for the Judge to hold the Defendant White, for Murder One, without bond. He was just as sure that White would not take the witness stand at this time. Well, Buzz, you are in for one hell of a surprise because Ron White was sure as hell going up on the witness stand. Russ angrily threw the paper in the waste container. Nobody bothered to ask him what he thought about the case. There was just a small mention of his name as attorney for the Defendant. That was when he chewed a couple of more Malox and slammed out of the Motel. On this beautiful Sunday he put the top down on the sixty nine Olds and cruised down the still quiet streets of Santa Fe. The church had beckoned to him from a distance with its gleaming cross atop a spire of hard baked clay tile. He needed to get himself under control and knock out the tell tale gentle throb in the scar above his eye. As he sat in the coolness of the sanctuary, he began to run down the witnesses and the impact of each one on the case.

The experts would probably be first. He knew they would find Ron's hair, pubic and otherwise at the scene. After all Ron had been happily making love to a loving Elsa in the very death bed just the day before the murder. She would have no reason to change the sheets since she and the Mayor had separate beds. He knew there, also, was hair from Elsa and a cat in that bedroom.

Ron's fingerprints were all over the place and worst of all he knew Ron had touched the bloody hose in her vagina. Whoever the perpetrator might be he was too smart to leave fingerprints since the only other fingerprints were those of Elsa and the Mayor.

The blood found at the scene, interestingly enough, was all type "O", with the exception of Elsa's. This was the most common of blood types and matched Ron's, and the Mayor's.

As far as proof that the child Elsa was carrying was a product of the coupling and copulation between Ron and Elsa, there would be no problem because Ron would freely admit it was his child.

Next would be the next door neighbor who would swear to the Mayor's innocence and his alibi. She would put the finger on Ron as having been at the murder scene that morning.

Finally there would be the big man, himself, in all of his glory, the bereaved, and still shocked, Mayor who would fill in all of the details.

The big question mark was the niece, Faith Rameriez, the Mayor's secretary and lover. Certainly Buzz knew they had been sleeping together for years and her testimony would be subject to impeachment if she took the witness stand. In fact, the prosecution had enough evidence for the preliminary hearing without bringing in the sweet little Indian maiden.

The bells began to ring again and the parishioners were leaving as Russ came out of his deep thoughts. As he stood to go, the good Father came toward him and with a sly wink asked, "Now my son would a bit of confession be the icing on the cake for a fine Sunday with the Lord?"

"No, Father, I think it best that I save up a few more sins so I can make this a once in a lifetime event."

The day passed quickly into a clear, warm, early evening. Fortunately by the time Russ had finished the Sunday paper, from front to back page, it was cocktail hour. He carefully slipped exactly four ice cubes from the one man economy refrigerator into his favorite martini glass and gently swished them around until the glass was a blur of frost. He poured out any water in the glass and filled it exactly half full of vodka over the remaining ice cubes. He found a twist of lemon from last weeks cocktail hour and gently squeaked the rim of the glass and tossed the twist into the drink. He inhaled the aroma as he relished his first short sip. One would be his limit tonight since he would need a clear head to give the final touches to the preparation for tomorrow's hearing. Willis had agreed to work a double shift and sleep in the office guest room. Russ knew from past experience that it would be a rough night ahead, full of, fitful, unrewarding sleep. He walked out to the lobby to make a final check before he hung up the do not disturb sign.

"Hi, Russ. All set to give it hell tomorrow?" Willis glanced up from some home work he was engrossed in finishing.

"Willis, I have found over the years that every time I am ready to give hell to somebody that is just the time that I get the hell kicked out of me." He took a long sip from the glass, "I guess you know I am on my way out, as Manager, of this desert delight."

Willis nodded gravely and laid his pen down on the counter where he had been working. "You know, Russ, I really will miss working with you. Frankly, I will miss the job, also. I know it isn't much of a strain intellectually but is sure helps you to understand people and to realize that the world is made up of a great mass of imperfections that keep it in continuous turmoil. Without all that turmoil there sure as hell would not be any justification for lawyers. So, for that reason alone, I have decided to follow in your footsteps, oh great mentor of this motel, and become a lawyer. Not just any old lawyer mind you, but a full fledge ball busting trail lawyer. A lawyer of and for the common man." He paused with a great grin on his face.

Russ finished off his martini and threw the lemon peel into the sink behind the counter.

"Willis, you have great insight into what makes this old world whirl in never ending circles, but your idea of success leaves a lot to be desired. I am a prime example of success gone astray. Nevertheless maybe someday in the future you will say to your fellow colleagues that you were a working partner with that old fart with the cigar spittle running down his chin, Russ Thurston, and at that time and place I will be proud to be in the same courtroom with you." Russ clamped a strong hand on his shoulder and gave it a squeeze "Now give me some peace and quiet tonight so I can fight my way through the usual before trial nightmares."

Russ closed the door to his absurdly small room with a bath, called a suite. He carefully put the vodka in the freezer of the economy class refrigerator, took out a quart of milk, an apple and a piece of cold pizza and called it dinner. He flipped on the desk lamp and pulled up a folding chair. Out came the old worn briefcase and the fat file slapped down in front of him. The final preparation was underway. Not that the case hadn't been on his mind all day long but now it was the ultimate count down.

Russ, once again, reviewed what to expect from each witness. Again it struck him that all of the expert evidence pointed not only to Ron White but also just as affirmatively to Elsa's husband. The big difference was that Ron couldn't prove his alibi and the Mayor could. Also, Ron had a so called motive and the Mayor did not, but was that really a fact? It wouldn't take much imagination to see the Mayor, in a burst of uncontrollable anger over the divorce, beating his wife, not meaning to kill her but only to abort the child she bore of another. So what it really got down to was the alibi and that is just where the road came to a dead end. Russ believed Ron and, on the other hand, detested the free handed, freeloader, Mayor who continued to use Room 118 while supposedly mourning the death of his wife.

Russ stopped and stared at the paper in front of him, random disconnected thoughts criss-crossing through his mind. He knew tomorrow was just the preliminary hearing but it was important to put the seed of doubt as to Ron's guilt in the Judge's mind. This could then lead to her setting bail for Ron which Russ felt was all important at this time. It might also take the news media off of Ron's case and help remove the stigma so often called up by adverse publicity, that stigma being the presumption of guilt before any hearing or trial.

He began to write his opening statement as if he was going to try the case to a jury. He knew the judge would not want opening statements by either counsel but it was an old habit and a good one that would prove to him that he knew every facet of the case and was in fact ready for trial.

It was well past midnight when Russ finally laid down his pen on his legal pad. He was not totally exhausted but he knew he was ready for tomorrow. The last sentence of his opening statement stood out as he stared at it, "The presumption of guilt is totally repugnant to our system of justice yet that is the onus that has befallen Ron White, an innocent man."

Russ leaned back, kicked off his loafers, got up and padded to the refrigerator. One more ice cold vodka martini straight up, a final cigarette and hopefully sleep would come to him.

He had dozed into deep dream filled sleep only to awake time and again. Now it was three thirty in the morning and the last dream lingered like a bad hangover. He had been hurrying on his way to court but he could not find the right courtroom. He got on a full elevator to go to the third floor but the elevator just kept on going at a terrifying speed until it crashed through the roof. Everyone glared at him and blamed him for not stopping it at the third floor. He began to run down the steps to the third floor but when he got there the courtroom was locked. He turned around just in time to see his client leaving the corridor but he had no head. He rushed after him but could never catch him. He awoke with his face buried in a wet pillow. He lay there motionless, then rolled over and stared at the black ceiling above him. The whole case rolled across the room like a computer print out. He closed his eyes but his mind continued to churn. He turned his head to look at the glowing clock beside his bed again. Four o'clock and he was wide awake. He tried to make his mind a blank but could not control his wildly gyrating thoughts.

He finally decided instead of counting sheep, to count all of the women he had slept with during his life and see if he could remember their names. The very first one had been a whore in downtown Santa Fe. He had been in high school and scared to death of what would happen. He had kept his undershorts on and one foot on the floor ready to bolt out of the room in case of any trouble. Her name was Jerry and she had coaxed him gently up on top of her and carefully put his throbbing erection in her. It was all over so fast it was hard to believe it had really happened. She patted him on the rump, smiled up at him and said now he was ready to got out and satisfy all those little girls in high school. He immediately tried to show his new found prowess to his girl friend Betty but she would have none of his clumsy back seat gymnastics unless he had the necessary protection to keep her from getting pregnant. All of this led to the usual embarrassing moment in the drug store when some nice older lady, about his mother's age, asked if she could help him. When he finally whispered what he wanted she horrified him by asking what brand he preferred.

Russ smiled to himself in the darkness and finally began to drift off to sleep thinking of all the camp followers and groupies he had sexually devoured during his pro football days.

The trial was well under way and every time Russ would object the Judge would bang down the gavel and roar "Overruled!" before he could finish his objection. Everyone in the courtroom snickered and kept pointing at his client who had slumped so far down in his chair that his face was hidden, just his shoulders heaved as he sobbed uncontrollably. There was no one on the witness stand but the Judge kept saying, "Step down. Call your next witness." Russ began to feel a sudden rush of panic as the nearness of impending doom loomed closer to his client. He turned to tell him to sit up in the chair and get ready to take the witness stand but the Judge had already told the bailiff to bring the criminal forward to face the Judge for sentencing. Russ frantically tried to stop the hearing but the Judge only intoned "Overruled. Bring me the criminal." As Russ took his place beside his client he saw Rachael in her black robe with a black hood seated in the jury box smiling at Russ and nodding that everything was alright. But is wasn't alright, it was all wrong. He looked back at the Judge who slammed down his gavel as he shouted, "This case is closed. Take the criminal away Mr. Bailiff. This court is in permanent recess." But how could the case be over, what was the verdict, where were they taking his sobbing client?

He turned to appeal to Rachael for help but the jury box was empty, the courtroom was empty. As he rushed to leave the courtroom to find his client he found the doors were locked. It was all over but he did not know the final verdict.

Dawn was just beginning to filter through the windows above his head as he lay there exhausted from a trial with no ending. It was always the same way. There never was a final decision, only that apprehension that he had lost the case. It had been years since he had tossed and turned through those pre-trial nightmares. He wondered at their similarity. Always the utter panic of not being fully prepared and the wildly vacillating Judge who never pronounced the verdict one way or the other. He had never been able to figure out if there was some sort of fatal omen in these dreams telling him the final outcome of the case since by the time the case was finished the dream was forgotten. He shuddered involuntarily and then swung his long legs over the side of the bed and reached for a cigarette. He knew this would be a pack and a half day with a gallon of coffee.

CHAPTER XII

In spite of an almost sleepless night Russ was ready to do battle. There was that same rush of adrenalin that he always had just before the game would start many years ago. He felt ready to give Ron White his best defense. He looked every bit as good as he felt. As he walked down the corridor to Division Six, his tall frame with broad shoulders accentuated the tailored cut of his dark blue suit. A blue button down Oxford cloth shirt with a red and blue striped tie caught the sparkle of his light blue penetrating eyes. These were eyes that smiled so easily but could change in an instant to cut a witness to the quick.

Rachael came rushing around the corner and gave him a radiant smile. "Hi, Russ. Come on back to the clerks office and contribute to the coffee kitty. It will be a while before they bring your client over from the lock up." She moved in close to him and let her hand briefly brush against his hand. "My but you look good enough to eat for breakfast, Mr. Thurston." Her lips glistened and her eyes met his for the briefest moments.

"That is exactly what I had in mind for you this morning Judge but I guess I will have to settle for coffee." They both laughed as she stopped at her chambers door, key in hand.

"Just for today, Russ. Tomorrow the rules change." She pouted a quick kiss at him as she opened her door, "Oh, by the way, any idea how long this hearing will take? There isn't any rush but I just thought you might have some idea."

"I really can only guess since most of the evidence will come from the prosecution. I would say not more than a couple of days depending on your schedule."

"Don't worry about me. This case is big time and the sooner we get this preliminary hearing over with and get on to the main trial the better I will like it."

Russ held her gently by the arm and swung her to face him, "Aren't you pre-supposing there is going to be a finding of guilt at this hearing?"

She turned away and as she closed her door said, "Don't you worry, Russ, if anyone is going to get a fair trial in this courtroom it is going to be you. I will lean over backwards for you and I mean that in more than one way."

She was gone and Russ knew if there were any breaks to be given by the court they would come his way. He turned into the clerks office where the usual Monday morning lawyer small talk was already in progress.

Hannah waved a greeting at Russ and pointed to the coffee pot as she continued talking on the phone. Russ obediently threw a quarter in the tin kitty cup and drew down a hot black cup of real coffee. De Caf was served in the Cantina located in the hundred year old basement that was frequented by flying cockroaches from time to time. Short time prisoners, guilty of misdemeanors, were used to spray and swat the flying invaders every Monday morning before the court house opened. Needless to say their efforts were less than strenuous and on occasion a few high flyers would invade Hannah's third floor domain causing unmitigated hell to break loose as she screamed and stomped her feet while the lawyers all had a hilarious time swatting the fat monsters with yellow legal pads and any loose court files on Hannah's desk.

"Russ, are you going to try that preliminary on White today?" Charlie London, a criminal lawyer, well known through out the southwest, poured himself a cup of coffee as he fattened the kitty with a dollar bill.

"Well, I am ready to go, so if the prosecution will show up I guess we are all ready. I know the Judge is counting on disposing of the prelim today."

"I heard she was going to pass all of the other cases down so she could get this one out of the way. From all I have heard it sounds like you may be in some really deep shit on this one, Russ." He glanced up at Russ as he stirred in some powdered creme.

"Charlie, you and I have known each other one hell of a long time and you know I respect your opinion, so please don't make my ulcer any worse than it is right now."

Charlie grinned and then grimaced over the sip of coffee, "Russ it has been a while since you have been in the court room so I would be glad to help you out by riding back seat at this prelim if you think it would help."

"You are right about that, Charlie. I haven't been a prominent figure in the courtroom for quite a spell but I think I can keep the Judge from nodding off during the hearing. Any inside trader information you might have will be gratefully accepted."

They both walked out into the corridor away from the Judge's door and out of the ear shot of Hannah. Charlie lowered his voice, "The first problem you have to face with Judge Rawlings is whether it is her time of the month. If it is, she can be hell on wheels in the courtroom and as the old saying goes, "she thinks only with her ovaries" not with that beautiful head of hers. Keep your questioning short and to the point, don't wander around just to kill time, she hates that approach. Keep your cross examination to a minimum but make your point. Remember the old adage, "a good trial lawyer never asks a question that he doesn't already know the answer to." Finally, and this one is only my gut feeling, if I were you I wouldn't put White on the witness stand, but that is only a close side line call." He took out a cigarette and offered one to Russ. They both lit up and inhaled deeply.

"Thanks, Charlie. The only problem I have is that my client insists on taking the stand to tell his story. I know all that will do is give the prosecution additional ammunition if or when there is a trial later, but he still says he wants the world to know he is innocent."

"Then you had better make it damn clear to him that you do not agree with him and that you are advising him not to take the stand. When you get to that point in the case you had better make a record with the court so there isn't any doubt about where you stand on this issue. Clients have a funny way of forgetting some of our advice when the case is lost. That is just when your ass is up before the God damned disciplinary committee for lack of competency."

Russ smiled and slowly shook his head, "Hey, Charlie, you don't have to tell me about bar committees, remember, I already bought the farm once. If I can keep him off of the stand I sure as hell will, but I have my doubts that I will be successful. Anyway, thanks for your thoughts. Who knows, I may even walk him right out of the court house after the hearing."

"You wouldn't be worth a damn as a trial lawyer if you didn't ultimately believe you had a winner. My personal opinion is that you haven't got a prayer of walking him at the preliminary. Maybe second degree murder, no less, then out on bond. This is a bad case, Russ, with a lot of public out cry to hang the bastard. Judge sweet lips in there will be under a lot of pressure to keep your boy in the slammer until the final verdict by those twelve grand citizens called his peers." Charlie carelessly stepped on his cigarette butt on the tile floor.

"She is a tough broad when it comes to taking the public heat. I have seen that before so at least I have the best Judge to give me a break if there is a chance. All I can do is give it hell and grab my balls when the gavel comes down."

"You got the picture, Russ. Well, looks like my case will get passed for sure. Good luck and Russ give me a call when all of this bull shit calms down. I have an open office, maybe we can work something out." Charlie retrieved his briefcase from the clerks office, blew Hannah a kiss and headed for the stairs.

"Judge wants to know if you are ready Russ? Take that final nervous piss? Comb your hair? One more cup of coffee? Need some gum to chew?" Hannah was already gathering up files and heading for the Judges chambers.

"Cut it out Hannah, just tell her excellency I am ready when she is as long as the friendly jailors have brought my boy over from his temporary lodging. Where the hell is Buzz and his entourage?"

"Oh, the Prince of Prosecutors had his little darling call in for him to advise he was eagerly awaiting the opening of the hearing." She opened the Judge's door and told her that all parties were ready to proceed.

Russ was not prepared for the explosive panorama in the courtroom as he left the clerks office and entered the court through the rear door. The clock on the back wall showed five minutes to nine and already the courtroom was almost full. With studied casualness he walked over to the long counsel table and carefully opened his briefcase and removed his files. Since there would be no jurors at this hearing it made no difference which side of the table he sat at since both counsel would be facing forward, toward the raised witness stand and the judges raised bench above the witness. The row of chairs in front of the spectators rail was filled with curious lawyers and members of the prosecutors staff. The constant hum of voices from the spectators made it hard to concentrate. The noise level had risen noticeably when Russ entered the court room. He looked for the bailiff who should have been at his desk against the wall opposite the jury box. Finally his attention was focused on the open doors of the court room where the bailiff and four sheriff deputies appeared to be searching each person allowed to enter. Two of the deputies were women who carefully searched each woman's hand bag and gave them a professional patting down. Russ was amazed at all of this since he had attended many criminal trials and never had seen such precautions taken. Suddenly the crescendo of voices again increased and all heads turned like robots to the door that led to the jury room. Russ also turned and saw not one but four deputies escorting his client into the courtroom and over to the counsel table. Russ couldn't help but feel sorry for this forlorn sight as Ron White, the accused, stood waiting for his hand cuffs to be removed. Russ could hear the stage whispers from the assembled audience, "Murderer," "Sadist", even "Son of a bitch." At least he was out of his usual orange jump suit even though he had lost so much weight that his once tailored dark gray suit hung grotesquely on his scare crow shoulders. His tie was neatly done in a Windsor knot. His shrunken neck left a great gap between it and his collar. The crease had long ago left his pants that bagged not only at the knees but around his waist and for some unknown reason his socks had been stolen so he showed bare feet in his tightly laced black shoes.

Russ threw his arm around his shoulders and shook his hand to the delight of the hecklers who had become more boisterous. "What the hell is going on back there?" Russ motioned toward the deputies.

Ron looked back at the crowd and said, "I thought you would have heard it on the morning news. The guards couldn't wait to tell me all about it. Apparently the Santa Fe herald received a phone call saying the caller was going to cut this hearing short by putting a bullet in my head and that he hoped you would get in the way so he could get rid of that shister, son of a bitch, also." Ron was smiling but his eyes were dull and dead serious. "All of the deputies are wearing bullet proof vests and the big joke in the guard room is just how is that big breasted Judge going to fit into a bullet proof vest."

"Well, I can guarantee you there will not be any problem today with the security I saw at the courtroom doors. So just keep cool Ron and we will get this dog and pony show underway." Ron smiled broadly and gave Russ a pat on the back as he sat down behind him.

"Now, Ron, I will be busy concentrating on the witnesses as they testify, so if you have something you think I should know or should ask the witness, just write it down on this yellow pad because I cannot listen to you and the witness at the same time. I will look over all of your notes before I release the witness. Okay?"

"Fine, Russ. How about my testifying, when will that happen?"

"We will talk about that later after we see how the prosecution's case comes in. We have plenty of time to decide."

Ron started to say something when the bailiff's gavel slammed down on his solid block of mahogany and snapped the courtroom to attention. Harry glared out at the noisy audience which began to quiet down as the Judge entered from behind her bench. Russ could tell she was not wearing a bullet proof vest, not the way the robe shook. Harry gaveled three solid times and then entoned the solemn greeting of the court to all those present. Once more the gavel came down after the moment of silent prayer and all were seated for one hushed moment before the trial began.

The great oak doors to the court room were flung open and in came Buzz followed by his usual four assistant lawyers, all with fat ominous looking expensive briefcases. Suddenly the two by two column came to a disheveled halt as the deputies let Buzz pass through but stopped the rest of his team for the shakedown given every one else. Russ couldn't help but laugh as he watched the shocked look on the young attorneys' faces. One green eyed blonde, blushed furiously as the matrons hands moved down her body and she suddenly bolted from the room not to be seen again until morning recess.

"This is totally ridiculous. I suppose we should all be wearing bullet proof vests and side arms." Buzz was obviously thrown off balance by the unexpected interruption. He dabbed at a moist droplet over his upper lip, then carefully folded his handkerchief and placed it in the breast pocket of his gray flannel suit. "Russ have you got any good news for me this morning that might save us a couple of days of wasted jousting? Such as waiving this prelim so we can move ahead to trial time?"

"Buzz, I haven't seen your highly touted court room soft shoe dance in a long time. I hear that the edge is getting a little worn and every now and then you slip a cog or two. Anyway I can't think of a better way to get a free look at the States case than to drag you through a preliminary hearing in front of your ex-wife. Should be interesting." Russ smiled up at Buzz.

The last of the prosecutors team and some witnesses had finally settled down in seats provided by the bailiff just as Buzz whispered across the table, "You won't see it all today, Russ, just enough to give the Judge reason to believe he should be held for trial on Murder One. Jail house word has it I will get a free look at your boy on the stand and get a chance to rip his ass on cross. Should be a fun day."

"Good morning, Ladies and Gentlemen." Rachael smiled down on the crowd benevolently as they murmured a good morning judge.

"This is a court of law and you will respect the rules as I set them out for you. If you do not, then, I can assure you that my bailiff, Mr. Bates, over here on my right, or one of the numerous deputies in the court room, today, will promptly escort you to the outside corridor to permit you to regain your composure."

Rachael surveyed the packed courtroom with a flat gaze that conveyed no nonsense as she recited a few basic rules of the court, "There will be no talking, smoking or reading while the court is in session. You may take notes and you may use a tape recorder if you so desire. However, no portable radios will be allowed. If you leave the courtroom for personal necessity during the trail there is no assurance you will be re-admitted since I am informed that there is a crowd outside waiting for vacancies to occur. There will be at least one fifteen minute recess during the morning session at which time you may move about, talk, read and smoke out in the corridor. No smoking is allowed in the courtroom at any time." She paused, thoughtfully, then continued, "There has been a serious threat made against the life of the defendant and his attorney. Do not make light of this matter nor make inappropriate comments that could lead to your involuntary removal from the court room and possible lengthy interrogations while being incarcerated."

"The son of a bitch ought to be shot, that's what I think." A square jawed, short, two hundred pound, red haired woman, in the second row, glared, red faced, at Ron as she furiously chewed her gum.

Before Rachael said one word, Harry was on his feet, holster unsnapped ready to move.

"Mr. Bailiff, remove that woman in the second row and obtain her name for contempt of court proceedings later today."

Harry's long legs took him quickly to the swinging gate separating the lawyers from the spectators. He moved to the woman with the grace of a panther and as he glared down at her he motioned for her to get up and come out to the center aisle. She was frightened to the point where she trembled violently and released a great loud burst of gas as she struggled to get past the person seated next to the aisle. Harry put one hand under her fleshy upper arm and lifted her up so that she was rushed out the doors on her tip toes.

Ron leaned forward and whispered to Russ, "Jesus, how can a Judge give me a fair trial with people in here calling me a murderer and wanting to shoot me?"

"You just let me worry about that. We have the one Judge that is fair minded in this court house."

Rachael nodded to both attorneys, "Gentlemen, will you step up to the side bar at the bench, please?"

Russ and Buzz walked around behind the court reporter and took one step up toward the bench to rest their elbows on the side bar next to the Judge's bench. "Well, that is one hell of a great way to start the day. Of course, your tardy appearance did not help things, Buzz." She flushed with anger.

"Now wait a minute, when I came through those doors it was nine o'clock straight up."

"Just goes to show you, Russ, those cheap Rolexes he wears never did keep accurate time. Well, gentlemen, have we any stipulations to make that might help to shorten this hearing?" She looked first at Russ.

"Your Honor, I may be able to stipulate as we go along but right now I am not sure just how much evidence Buzz intends to put on. We can probably cut short some of the expert testimony by admitting their qualifications and even make some admissions as to their findings but right now I would be premature in so stipulating."

Rachael smiled beautifully at Russ, "In other words — No."

Russ smiled back at her and nodded.

"Okay. Lets get this show on the road. We will take a fifteen minute break around ten thirty so I can meet with the court en banc briefly. I have to be at the women's bar association luncheon as a guest speaker so we will break for lunch from twelve fifteen to one thirty. I intend to get all of the state's case on today so we may have to work past the cocktail hour. Buzz call your first witness and please remember what I used to tell you years ago — K.I.S.S. Keep It Short Smartass."

Russ tried to stifle a smile as he walked back to the counsel table and Ron wanted to know if anything was wrong. Buzz had already produced his first witness who had come forward to take the oath. He was the fingerprint expert whose name oddly enough was William Fingerhut. Russ knew damn well that Ron's fingerprints were all over the murder scene so after waving qualifying testimony he let Buzz take his witness quickly through the process of identifying Ron's fingerprints as States exhibits one through five.

"Now, Mr. Fingerhut, did you find these same fingerprints all over the bed room and bathroom?"

Russ stood, "Object, your Honor, as to the form of the question. Too broad."

"Yes. Sustained. Let's limit the scope of the question counsel."

"Very well, Mr. Fingerhut, did you find these same fingerprints at any other locations other than on the door into the kitchen from the garage?"

"Yes, sir, I did. I found —"

"And can you tell us at how many different locations you found them?"

"Yes, sir, there were five separate locations, including the kitchen door knob."

Buzz relaxed as he got set to ease through the experts testimony, which had already been well rehearsed, "So just tell us where the next set of the defendant's prints were found."

"On the stair rail leading to the upstairs bedroom. We found a distinct thumb print and an index finger of the right hand."

"How are you sure it was of the defendants right hand."

"Well the stair rail was on the right hand side of the stairs as you go up. The thumb print was pointing generally up the hand rail and other smudged prints from the hand were on the inside of the rail near the wall behind the thumb."

"Where else did you find his fingerprints?"

"On one of the faucet handles in the upstairs bathroom. There again we found a clear thumb print, an index and middle finger." Without waiting for the next question he glanced at some notes on his lap and stated, "Then we found a palm print and fingerprints on one of the bed posts where the victim had been tied."

Buzz paused and seemed to be finished with the witness, then looked up at the Judge and asked, "Mr. Fingerhut that is just four locations. Where was the fifth location of the defendants fingerprints?"

"They were on the hose that was removed from the victims vagina."

The courtroom began to rumble with first a gasp, then the spectators began making obscene out cries at Ron's back. Harry's gavel brought order and silence once more.

"Again, could you determine which hand these fingerprints came from?"

"Oh, yes, it was the defendants right hand. You could clearly see all four fingers and a portion of the thumb above them."

With that Buzz nodded to the witness and turned to the Judge, "That is all I have of this witness your Honor."

"Very well. Mr. Thurston you may cross examine the witness."

Russ was on his feet immediately. "Now, Mr. Fingerhut, did you find any other fingerprints in the victims bedroom?"

"Well, yes, but they were the usual you would expect to find in a bedroom of a married couple. Mayor Bascom's prints, the victims fingerprints and one set of unidentified smudges."

"Now where did you find the Mayor's fingerprints?"

"All over the room. The dresser, door knob, bathroom, lamp —"

"Well, did you find them on the victims bed posts?"

"Yes, I think we did."

"Tell me would you "expect to find" all of the Mayor's fingerprints in this bedroom if I told you the Mayor had not shared the victim's bed for the past eight years?"

"Object your Honor," Buzz was on his feet, "Calls for a conclusion by this witness based on facts not in evidence."

"Judge, I will make an offer of proof and state to the court that we will have evidence that the Mayor and his wife were estranged within their home and had not shared a bedroom or bed for at least eight years."

Rachael leaned back and concentrated on a fly walking on the high ceiling, "Since this is not a jury trial and I shall render the final decision and further based on your offer of forth coming evidence, I will overrule the objection." Turning to the witness, "You may answer the question, Mr. Fingerhut."

The witness looked confused, then looking up at the Judge said, "Maybe he went in the bedroom when she wasn't there. I really cannot answer that question except to say he must have spent some time in that bedroom."

Russ moved to another subject, "Now, the so called murder weapon, the hose that caused the fatal hemorrhaging by the victim, you, of course, were able to determine which end of the hose had been inserted into the victim's vagina."

"Yes, we were particularly careful about how we handled the hose."

"And these fingerprints you found on the hose clearly indicated someone had wrapped their entire hand around it. Is that correct?" Russ seemed to be wandering.

"Yes, the entire hand."

"Now we have the hose right here in protective covering so you can show us just where the prints were and how the hose was held." Russ handed the witness the stipulated States exhibit which was in fact the murder weapon.

"Now, Mr. Fingerhut, you are sure you have this hose held as the defendants fingerprints indicated?"

"Yes, I am absolutely certain."

"You will notice that the portion of the hose that was inserted in the victim is furthest away from the thumb and forefinger prints on the hose which would indicate the insertion was made in a back handed manner."

"I don't know. I guess so."

"Now where were these unidentifiable smudges you found in the bedroom? Are there any on this hose, per chance?"

The witness began to see where the questioning was leading and glanced over at Buzz who seemed to be engrossed in other matters at the moment.

"Yes, the smudges were on the hose. They were just above the defendants fingerprints and appeared to be with the thumb closest to the bloody end of the hose."

"Object, your Honor. What some smudges appeared to be is a pure conclusion by the witness." Buzz was obviously more interested in the testimony than it appeared.

"Yes, Mr. Thurston, I will sustain his objection and strike the last answer. Let's move ahead."

Russ, was satisfied he had made his point to the Judge and would not quarrel over her ruling. If Ron was the perpetrator he had to do the job in an awkward back hand manner while whoever owned the smudges gave the hose a good strong fore hand insertion.

"That is all I have of this witness, your Honor."

"Very well. You may step down, Mr. Fingerhut. Call your next witness."

One of the assistant prosecutors beckoned to a distinguished white haired gentleman seated in front of the spectator's rail. His name was Edward Woodworth and he would identify the blood samples taken from the scene. After being sworn in, he smiled graciously at the Judge who acknowledged him with a nod, "Nice to see you again, Edward, but not under these circumstances."

He nodded back as he carefully arranged his sport coat and adjusted his tie as he took the witness stand.

Buzz took him through the usual preliminaries qualifying him as an expert and then got to the essence of his testimony.

"You took a blood sample from the defendant, Ronald White, did you not?"

"Yes I did. As a matter of fact, it was just last week."

"And will you tell the court what type blood the defendant has?"
He glanced briefly at his notes, "Yes. It was type "O" blood."

Buzz got up and moved to the exhibits on the table in front of the courts bench. He picked up what were obviously three separate blood samples and had them marked States exhibits six thru eight.

"Now, Mr. Woodworth, I will show you States exhibit six for identification and ask you what that is?"

"This is the type "O" blood sample taken from the defendant."

"Now look at States exhibit seven and tell us what that is."

"This is another type "O" blood sample which was obtained from the pillow beneath the victims head."

Rachael gave Buzz a quizzical look implying that the chain of evidence was a little shaky at this point.

"Now, Mr. Woodworth, did you take a blood sample from the victim, also?"

"Yes, I did. That would be States exhibit eight right here." He held it up and handed it to Buzz.

"And did you determine just what the blood type of the victim was?"

"She was "RHO Negative" blood type."

Buzz approached the bench with the three states exhibits in his hands, "Your Honor, I will offer States exhibits six, seven, and eight into evidence."

"Any objection, Mr. Thurston?"

"No, your Honor, none."

"Very well, States exhibits six, seven and eight are admitted into evidence. Mr. Thurston, you may cross examine the witness."

Russ stood and approached the witness with the States exhibits in his hands. Mr. Woodworth smiled pleasantly but his eyes betrayed the fact that he dreaded cross examinations.

"I am going to call you Ed because you and I have known each other for many years." Russ gave a broad smile as the witness nodded.

"Ed, when you went to the murder scene were you instructed on just what to look for at that time?"

"Yes, I was told by our supervisor at the lab to get a blood sample of the victim and any other blood samples that I felt were inconsistent with the victims blood."

"Now why did you choose to take a blood sample from the pillow?"

"Because the blood on the pillow was inconsistent with the mass of blood on the bed all below the waist of the victim. Incidentally I did take other blood samples in the bedroom all of which turned out to be the victims type blood, RHO Negative."

"RHO Negative is not a very common type of blood is it?"

"No. It is not found in the majority of people."

"But type O blood is probably your most common type blood, isn't that true?"

"No question about it. The majority of people in this country are blood type O."

"So what you are really telling us today is that you found some person's blood at the scene of the murder that was type O?"

"Well I guess — ", he paused as he looked at Buzz for help.

Buzz was on his feet, "Your Honor he has testified that the defendant has the same type blood as that found on the pillow. It is obvious that it is in fact —."

"There is no such obvious conclusion. I object to counsels interruption of my cross examination and I ask the court to disregard his conclusion as to what is obvious. The defendant has yet to be placed at the murder scene."

Rachael held up her hands for silence, "Easy, Russ, there is no objection before the court to rule on. Mr. Woodworth, you may answer the question."

The witness turned appealing eyes to the Judge, "I am sorry, Judge, but I forgot what the question was."

"No problem, sir. I will have the court reporter read it back to you." She nodded to the court reporter who quickly scanned her steno type tape and read back Russ's prior question.

"My answer is yes, that is correct."

"So all of this talk about type O blood does not necessarily mean that the defendant was the person who deposited the blood on the pillow, correct?"

"Yes, that is true."

"As at matter of fact you have no way of knowing exactly how long that blood was on the pillow."

"Well, we can tell within some time frame, about how long a blood stain or deposit has been present, but again you are correct that we cannot tell exactly."

Russ was towering over the witness now asking the questions that he already had the answer to from his pre-trial preparation. "And, as a matter of fact, no one even bothered to determine how long this blood stain had been present on the pillow."

A slight murmur went through the spectators and a few nervous coughs were heard.

"I have no knowledge of that fact one way or the other." He was desperately looking through his notes for help that wasn't there.

Russ persued him now, "So to make this crystal clear the type O blood could belong to anyone, correct?"

"Yes, sir, that is correct."

"There is no way you can say that the blood you found on that pillow is blood from, Ron White, the defendant."

Woodworth continued to look at his notes as he answered, "There is no way to determine who is the carrier of that particular blood type O."

Russ turned around and started to walk away from the witness, who had a look of relief on his face.

"One more question, Ed." Russ had turned suddenly, an

official looking paper in his hand, "Were you aware that the victims' husband, Mayor Bascom, has type O blood?"

Before he could answer Buzz was objecting to the question which the Judge quickly sustained since there was no prior evidence to support this statement. Russ just smiled and walked away from the witness. He had made his point and he knew the Judge was now fully aware that both the defendant and the Mayor had the same blood type. Very interesting indeed.

Rachael stood, looked at the bailiff and nodded. She picked up her voluminous notes as the bailiff announced a fifteen minute recess.

Russ turned around to Ron and took the yellow pad from him. No notes or questions just the usual doodles.

"So far so good." Russ slapped him on the back.

"What do you mean so far so good. My God, my fingerprints all over the place, somebodies type O blood on the pillow, and a Judge that looks at me like I crawled out from under a rock. Just great!"

"Well, I admit it looks like a one sided ball game but you have to keep in mind that this is just a preliminary hearing. All we are trying to do at this point is put enough doubt in the Judge's mind that will enable you to get out on bond. It is very seldom that a major felony is dismissed at the preliminary hearing stage. We could have a chance of getting the charge reduced to manslaughter but don't count on it."

Russ got up and walked to the rear doors of the courtroom and was aware of the whispered curses and glares of hatred as he passed through the spectators. Outside at the drinking fountain he saw Charlie London again.

"I take it your boy was at the scene of the crime.", he said with a wry smile.

"It would seem so. The big question is was he there when the murder was committed? He says he was a late comer after the murder. So who the hell did the job?"

Charlie shrugged and lit a cigarette, "That is the tough part, but just from what little I heard today and what you have told me I sure as hell would not count out, that pompous son of a bitch, the Mayor."

"I agree totally, but the big problem is that the Mayor has a locked in alibi with a neighbor who has the hots for the grieving widower and will get him out of the house before the murder. Also, a niece he has been screwing that is his secretary, who swears he arrived at the office at the usual time."

"Just hang tough, in there, Russ. Maybe I can help out with some investigators before the final trial."

The bailiff called for Russ to get back in the courtroom. The Judge was ready to resume the trial."

The rest of the morning was quickly taken up with testimony from additional experts who identified clothing fibers from the murder scene that matched the fabric retrieved at the motel. There were other clothing fibers that were found on the bed, also, but were not further identified.

The final expert identified pubic hairs found on the bed as being an identical match to those pubic hairs removed from the defendant this past week.

None of this was a surprise to Russ since he was well aware that Ron had been in that bedroom the day before the murder and had sexual relations with the victim in that very same death bed. There really wasn't much sense in fighting the obvious, particularly when the only trier of fact was the Judge. But he continually made it clear that there was a distinct possibility that the murderer was someone other than his client. That was the question that had to be answered.

Promptly at twelve fifteen the Judge adjourned court for the noon recess. She asked both lawyers to stop back in her chambers for a brief conference. Ron was handcuffed again and the crowd cheered as he was shackled around his ankles.

"Don't let it get to you, Ron. We still have a long way to go. Just stay cool and don't panic." Russ knew his words of advice had fallen on deaf ears. He could tell from Ron's eyes that panic was the order of the day. He grabbed up his files and his briefcase and rushed back to the Judge's chambers. Rachael was obviously in a hurry to make her luncheon meeting. The room already had a blue haze of cigarette smoke.

Rachael, unthinking, started to unzip her robe then stopped just below that delicious cleft between those magnificent breasts. Russ smiled as he lit a cigarette and saw her blush as she quickly pulled up the zipper.

"As you both know, I have a bar association meeting to attend so I have to get out of here. Buzz, I just want you to know that all of this technical evidence is only helpful to the court and to your cause if you can place the defendant at the murder scene. That you have not done thus far. At this point the court has some serious misgivings about holding this defendant for any crime much less murder one."

Buzz stood looking out the window at the snow capped mountains in the distance, "For Christs sake, Judge, you must know that I have been a prosecutor long enough to know where I am and where I am going. Just don't you worry, I will put that little bastard at the murder scene." Buzz sounded tired and he flopped down on the long sofa in front of the picture window.

"Alright, then, let's get on with this hearing promptly at one thirty. Russ tell your client to quit making faces and shaking his head when he doesn't like the testimony. It does not help his cause one bit."

"With all due respect, your Honor, I think if I was charged with murder one and staring at a death sentence, I would show some emotion in the courtroom."

"Just tell him, Russ. Now get out of here so I can change clothes!" With that she rushed into the bathroom as she unzipped her robe.

Russ turned to Buzz as they walked out the door, "How many more witnesses do you have, Buzz?"

"Three. One will be brief, the others may be lengthy depending on your cross."

Russ nodded and headed for the downstairs cafeteria.

Charlie London caught up with him just as he got to the top of the stairs. "Hey, Russ, can I buy you a lunch at the Branding Iron?"

"Well, I guess that beats a half cooked hot dog and orange juice in a cardboard carton." They followed the noon time crowd down to the street level and started across the street to the local lawyers' restaurant and watering hole.

"Let's not eat in the cafeteria. We can get a table downstairs and relax for a few minutes." Charlie waved to some judges and fellow lawyers as they walked through the lunch room to the stairs leading to the downstairs bar and restaurant.

"I eat here almost every day, at lunch, and frequently for evening meals when I am working late on a case. I got the owner out of a tough case about two years ago when he busted a chair over a drunks' head that was playing grab ass with his mistress. Not his wife, mind you, but his mistress. Killed the drunk. Good ole Buzz hits our hero with a manslaughter charge." He signaled to a waitress who nodded as he moved through the crowded room to a very private table in the corner. "The jury walked my boy clean as a whistle. Don't ask me how or why because as far as I could see he was good for some slammer time." He smiled as he pulled out his chair, "I really think the all male jury fell in love with that sweet ass on his mistress as she wept copious tears on the witness stand. Anyway ever since then I have had the prized possession of a reserved table in the corner of the lower level Branding Iron."

He looked up as the waitress put a vodka on the rocks with two anchovy olives down at his elbow. "Hi, Shirley, want you to meet a good friend of mine, Russ Thurston. We just might put a team together one of these days. Turn around Shirley. I want Russ to see that famous jury killing ass of yours."

Shirley laughed and her dark brown eyes flashed as she held up her tray in one hand and did a graceful pirouette which truly did show off a fine set of cheeks in brief white bikini panties beneath a rather sheer white uniform.

Russ smiled and shook his head, "Maybe I can work you in as a witness when or if we go to a jury trial on this case."

She leaned over and in a throaty voice almost whispered, "My price as a witness is pretty stiff and as you know I have a really jealous boy friend." They all laughed and Charlie asked Russ if he wanted a drink which he refused since he was in trial. They both ordered rare roast beef sandwiches on rye with a side order of fried onions rings, which were the specialty of the house. Shirley swished away to pick up a second vodka on the rocks for Charlie under the admiring eyes of Russ.

"Russ, so far you have put a lot of questions in front of Rachael. As I sat there watching and listening, it was apparent that you had made some good points as to reasonable doubt. I am sure the Judge got the point that the Mayor has the same blood type as the defendant." He paused to twirl the ice in the new drink Shirley had put before him. "Also, she has to be aware that both the Mayor and the defendants fingerprints were all over the place. Since the Judge knows little about this case, except what is coming at her from the witness stand, it would seem that you really have no choice but to put your man on the stand to explain away all that technical evidence and just why he was at the murder scene."

Russ sipped his coffee and knew he had to agree with Charlie, much as he had hoped to keep Ron off of the witness stand during the preliminary hearing.

"Just how bad is your client's past history? Has he served any time for a felony? Is he wanted anywhere else?"

"No, it's not so much his past history but is just the fact that I am not a bit sure he can hold up under cross examination by Buzz. He is in deep depression right now and is about to hit the panic switch for real. You know how that is Charlie, your whole case falls apart and all of a sudden you feel like a junior associate in a store front law firm." Russ was deep in thought and hardly noticed his lunch being served.

"Well, I can tell you one thing, you are going to have your hands full when you go after the Mayor on cross. He is a wily old bastard and if he really is good for this murder then you can bet he is ready for you. In the meantime, if you want me to talk to your client I will, just to see if I can give you a snap judgement and maybe at the same time give him a shot in the arm."

Charlie was dead serious and Russ appreciated his willingness to help, "I will tell you what Charlie, let's get back to the courtroom about fifteen minutes early and I will get Ron in a private room, give you a big build up and excuse myself while you talk to him. Then you can give me your opinion before we start trial at one thirty."

Charlie was signing the check as he looked up at Russ and nodded, "Sounds right to me." He gave Shirley a generous tip and a gentle pat on that famous ass.

Russ could see Ron warm to Charlie right away. After all Charlie was a top flight criminal lawyer that Ron had heard of before his introduction. Also, Charlie was a sharp dresser and in excellent physical shape. This was Ron's type of man and he willingly opened up to him.

Just a few minutes before the opening of court, Charlie came out of the jury room with Ron following him in the custody of the deputies.

Charlie and Russ sat down in the far corner of the jury box.

"Well, you were right Russ. Your boy is as tight as a g-string on Mamma Pearl. He is smart in the head and also street smart. He trusts you completely which is good. He wants to take the witness stand and thinks he can stand up to that "son of a bitch, prosecutor." I am not too sure he can hold up but maybe you can get Buzz off balance with some bull shit objections that will give Ron time to think before he answers. Of course, you can use the old trick of answering the questions for Ron in your objection. Rachael will get pissed but that's just the way the game is played."

Russ stood as the bailiff called the court to order just as a flushed and irritated Judge took the bench. Russ whispered "Thanks Charlie for all of your help. He will be going up on the stand so hold onto your balls."

"Do you have business with this court, Mr. London?" This was not the smiling Judge from the morning session, but a frowning black robed taskmaster.

"No, your Honor. I just had a message for Mr. Thurston," he turned to leave and as he passed by, Russ murmured, "Bitch."

Russ showed no emotion but knew it was going to be a long afternoon. He had been around Rachael long enough to know that when she got in a down mood she could be hell on wheels. As he took his seat at counsel table, looking at those full sexual lips, he knew the fastest way to get her out of her blue funk was to give her a full sixty minutes of strenuous sexual activity in the sack.

Buzz had already called his first witness to the stand. He was in the uniform of a U.S. mailman. Russ could tell he was proud of his uniform and also overwhelmed by his responsibility as a witness for the great state of New Mexico. He was short, about five feet five inches tall, with an Adolph Hitler mustache and a nervous tic at the corner of his left eye. On direct examination, he gave his name as Adolphus P. Schwartz and he had delivered mail to the Bascom home for the past six years. He had, in the immediate past, seen the defendant as he drove his car into the Bascom garage. He positively identified the driver of the car as the defendant, Ron White. On the day of the murder he had been on his route at the usual time, which was shortly after nine o'clock in the morning. It was a clear cool day so the windows and doors were closed on the homes along his route. When he got to the Bascom home he noticed the garage door closed. He stopped on the front stoop to select the Bascom mail. As he was putting it through the mail slot in the front door, he heard a male voice that was angry and then heard what he though was a woman's call for help and then a sob or a moan. He heard nothing else so he rang the bell to announce the mail delivery and moved on to the next house.

Buzz was about ready to turn the witness over to Russ and then asked another question almost as an after thought, "Now Mr. Schwartz was it customary for the garage door to be closed when you made your delivery?"

"No, as a matter of fact, it was usually open with Mrs. Bascom's car in the garage. I never saw the Mayor's car in there since he had to be at work by nine o'clock."

Russ held up a hand, "Object to when the Mayor had to be at the City Hall. Speculation by the witness."

The Judge nodded, "Yes, sustained, and that portion of the answer is stricken from the record."

Buzz smiled knowing the nine o'clock start up for the Mayor was now before the Judge even though it had been stricken, "One more thing Mr. Schwartz, did you ever see the defendants car in the Bascom garage?"

"Yes, and I have seen the defendant drive into the garage, get out and push the automatic closer to close the garage door."

Before Russ took over the witness he quickly reviewed the testimony before the court. None of the evidence placed his client at the scene of the murder on the day in question.

"Mr. Schwartz, you have never heard my clients voice have you?"

"No sir, I have not."

"So, of course, you are not saying the man's voice you heard in the Bascom home was the voice of Mr. White."

"No, I cannot identify the voice as that of Mr. White or anyone else for that matter."

Russ paused and smiled at the witness, "You are not telling the court that you saw Mr. White or his car at the Bascom home on the day of the murder, are you?"

"No, I am not. I had seen him there before, as I stated, but not on that day."

"One final question, Mr. Schwartz. You heard a woman in distress, presumably Elsa Bascom, and yet you did nothing to assist her or come to her aide. Was this because you felt some moral indignation about her affair with the defendant?"

His left eye twitched and he visibly reddened as he sought to compose himself, "To tell you the truth, I was sure she was committing adultery with this man. When I heard her in distress my thoughts were that if her husband had caught her at her little game then she was deserving of a little heavy handed straightening up. It wasn't until later that I realized I was at the front door after the Mayor was at work."

"But your first impression was that it was the Mayor administering justice to his wife?"

"Yes sir, that is true. I was wrong."

"I wouldn't be too sure of that Mr. Schwartz, not too sure. You can step down sir." Russ turned to Buzz to see if he had any rebuttal questions. He shook his head.

Buzz turned around to point his finger at a sharp nosed woman in her early fifties. She was dressed in a gray flannel skirt, green turtle neck sweater and a mannish green and gray plaid jacket. Her hair was in a tight bun and her large black framed glasses gave her a distinct owlish look. She and the Mayor exchanged smiles as she approached the witness stand. Russ knew this was the only eye witness to his client being at the Bascom house on the day of the murder. Mrs. Amelia Gray was the next door neighbor of the Bascom's. She had been a widow for the past ten years. She was financially independent and spent most of her time reading by the front bay window of her home where she had an excellent view of all the happenings in front of her home and to either side. She had refused to discuss the case with Russ but from his short conversation with her it was apparent she held the Mayor in the highest esteem, had no use for his high society slut of a wife and would tell her story in court. Goodbye, Mr. Thurston. With that the door slammed as Russ retrieved his briefcase. But Manny, the bartender, knew another side of Mrs., Holier than thou, Gray. It seemed about once a month she would frequent the lounge and always sat alone at the dark end of the bar. Her limit was two doubles of dry Tangeray martinis on the rocks. Manny always gave her more than full measure since she had complained once that his double looked like a single. Her bar room conversation always played the same tune. First it was how lonely life was without her husband. Next it was how difficult it was for a genteel lady to find a proper man to be seen with in public and finally, inevitably what a fine, outstanding and gentle man her neighbor was. That he deserved better than that woman he was married to and finally how she could show him what a real woman was all about. It was after Elsa's murder that she had made it known, after her second helping of gin, that she was sure she and the Mayor would soon be a matched pair in public and in the boudoir. Manny had pressed her on this and she had told him that after all these years the Mayor had finally seen what true sexuality was and was prepared, after a decent waiting period, to combine their two neighboring households. Manny had passed this bit of gossip on to Russ thinking it might help him out at the trial.

Russ smiled up at her on the witness stand as she carefully tugged at her already too long skirt. She simply looked away with a shrug.

She was a good witness. Well coached, direct and precise in her answers. As usual on the day of the murder she had been reading at her front window. She had seen the Mayor leave the house at his usual time and they had exchanged casual waves to each other. The time had been shortly before eight thirty when he left — his usual time. She had put down her book after he left, gone to the kitchen and poured herself a cup of coffee and toasted a piece of whole wheat bread. She had eaten her sparse breakfast in the kitchen while she read a recipe for Italian sausage soup. She had then gone to her bedroom and prepared herself for the day which took about thirty minutes. She then poured herself another cup of coffee just as the door bell rang for the morning mail. She retrieved the mail and separated the bills from the junk mail. She went to the kitchen and threw away the junk mail, then opened and read a letter from her cousin on the East coast. When she returned to the front room and her chair by the window it was almost ten o'clock. As she sat down she saw the defendant pull his car into the Bascom garage. It was simply disgusting the way that woman carried on with the defendant while her poor husband slaved away to make this a better place for all of us to live. It was shortly after the defendants arrival that she heard his car start and looked out to see it come hurrying out of the driveway onto the street. With a screech of tires he was gone. That was the last she saw of him until he was on TV as the murderer of Elsa Bascom.

Buzz smiled graciously at his star witness, "Mrs. Gray, you are here under subpoena are you not?"

She straightened in her chair and looked at the Mayor, "Yes, I was subpoenaed, but I can assure you I would appear as a witness for Mayor Bascom at any time voluntarily."

"That will be all Mrs. Gray. Thank you." As he turned to offer the witness to Russ she got up from the stand and began to leave.

"Just a moment Mrs. Gray." The Judge held out a restraining hand, "Unless I am mistaken the defendants lawyer will have some questions for you."

The witness looked confused as she slowly took her seat again and looked at Buzz for help.

"Mrs. Gray, there just isn't any reason for this court to think that you are an impartial witness, is there?" Russ was on his feet, voice booming, his whole demeanor menacing.

"I don't know what you mean." She shrank back in the chair.

"What I mean is that you obviously are having an affair with Mayor Bascom." The hushed courtroom rumbled with shocked voices.

"Object, Object your Honor, no foundation for this statement." Buzz was visibly upset.

Before the Judge could rule Russ went on, "Do you remember a conversation with Manny Blake, the bartender at the Red Wing Lounge, shortly after this murder took place?"

"Well I can't say that I —"

"Mrs. Gray I want to remind you that you are under solemn oath here today. Further that I am prepared to produce Manny Blake to testify about his conversation with you."

The witness was visibly distraught at this point and tugged at a small Kleenex in her hand.

"Now more specifically, Mrs. Gray, do you recall telling Manny Blake on a Friday evening two weeks ago that, and I quote, "the Mayor and I will soon be a matched pair" and that through you he had found what true sexuality was all about?" Russ held a typewritten statement before him as he glared at the witness.

"Well, I might have said words to that effect. But that doesn't mean I would lie for the Mayor."

Russ ignored her last statement, "And didn't you also tell Manny Blake that same night that you and Mayor Bascom would soon combine your two households?" He swung around to look directly at the Mayor who registered shocked disbelief at this turn of events.

The pause was deafening as all eyes focused on the now humbled witness.

"Object, your Honor. I am sure the witness cannot remember some off hand remark like that."

"Yes — that is right I don't recall saying —"

The scar over Russ's eye throbbed as he bore down on the witness, "Then I will bring in Manny Blake about his conversation and about your drinking habits."

She was visibly trembling now as she reconsidered her testimony. "Well I guess I could have said those words, in jest, of course."

"Now is it not true that the Mayor went to work on this day later than usual?" Russ had moved toward the witness almost in a threatening manner.

"Well, it could have been a little later."

"When you say a little later, as a matter of fact, wasn't it just a few minutes before the defendant arrived at ten o'clock?"

"Oh, I really don't know Mr. Thurston."

"Well, was it nine fifteen, nine thirty, nine forty five, do you, in fact, know what time it was?"

"It would just be a guess. I thought he left at the same time as usual but as I think about it he did leave a little later." She smiled weakly at Mayor Bascom who now glared back at her.

Russ eased back to the counsel table and let the witness regain some of her composure, "When you saw the defendant arrive, it was close to ten o'clock, right?"

"Yes sir, that is correct."

"Now just how long was it after his arrival that he left and as you say screeched down the road?"

"Oh, I don't know perhaps an half an hour or so."

"Mrs. Gray, an half an hour or so is no answer. Think back to what you were doing as you sat at the front window."

"I was reading a romance novel." She blushed slightly.

"Well, where were you in the book when the defendant arrived?"

"I was almost to the end of it."

"And when he hurriedly left had you finished the book?"

"No, not quite. So I guess he was not there too long." It was almost a question but it was enough of an answer for Russ.

"That is right, Mrs. Gray, he wasn't there too long. Thank you. That is all I have of this witness your Honor."

"Mr. Rawlings, any further questions?" Rachael smiled for the first time at Russ as she looked past him to where Buzz was in rapid fire conversation with Mayor Bascom. "No, that is all your Honor."

Buzz thanked Mrs. Gray and then turned to the courtroom and loudly announced, "I will call his Honor, Mayor William Bascom, to the stand."

Russ turned around to see how Ron was making it and saw to his relief a smile on his face as he gave Russ a thumbs up. He leaned forward and whispered, "Did you just make that up about Manny, cause it sure as hell made a Christian out of Amelia Gray?"

"You are right about her getting religion on the witness stand but Manny really was ready to testify if she lied." Russ scowled a little then and in a stage whisper said, "You know what Ron? I think this son of a bitch on the witness stand killed his wife."

Buzz looked over at Russ and in his best stage whisper said, "Bull shit, prove it." He turned to the witness who had just been sworn.

"We all know that you are the Mayor of this town and the husband of the late Elsa Bascom who was murdered on the 26th day of February at approximately ten o'clock in the morning."

Russ stood up slowly and held out a hand to stop Buzz. "Judge I will have to object to counsel testifying in this case. This is not closing argument and — "

"Yes, yes, I know. Sustained. Let's get the evidence from the witness, Mr. Rawlings, I am sure you know how the game is played. Let us proceed." She was obviously irritated as she glanced up at the clock at the rear of the courtroom.

Buzz nodded and gave Rachael his most ingratiating smile as he referred to his notes. "Mayor Bascom what time did you leave your home for the office on Friday, February 26th?"

"The usual time, about eight forty five since I like to arrive at the office promptly at nine o'clock."

"And did you go directly to your office and arrive there at nine o'clock?"

"Well, the traffic was rather heavy that day so I was a few minutes late, perhaps ten minutes after nine."

Buzz took States Exhibit 9 from the table and showed the grizzly photograph to the Mayor. "When was the first time you saw your wife in this condition?"

He visibly shuddered as he looked at the exhibit, "As I have said before, I went back home about eleven o'clock to get our savings passbook to withdraw funds to purchase an anniversary present. The day she was murdered was our anniversary, your Honor."

"When you arrived home was the garage door open or closed?"

"Why it was closed and I had opened it when I left for the office."

Buzz produced a length of garden hose which had been carefully preserved in a cellophane bag. "Have you ever seen this hose before?"

"Only when I saw my murdered wife. I went upstairs on that morning and she was lying in a sea of blood with this hose inserted — "

"Your Honor, I believe the photograph will speak for itself." Horror and grief hung heavily in the courtroom.

Russ nodded and Buzz placed the photograph back with the other exhibits.

"Mr. Mayor, do you have a garden hose similar to the one shown in States Exhibit #5?"

"Yes, I do and this piece has been hacked off of one end of that hose."

"What did you do after you saw your wife on the bed?"

"I threw up in the sink. Then I went downstairs and called the police."

"When you left your home for the office that morning had your wife been fully clothed?"

"Yes she was. When I returned she was totally naked and her clothes had apparently been violently ripped from her body. They were strewn all around the bedroom."

"Were there any valuables or money missing?"

"No. There was nothing missing except the hatchet that was used to cut off the hose. This was the work of a maniac."

Russ stood to object and then sat back down knowing full well the Judge would cull out the conclusion of the witness.

Buzz paused then got up and stood behind Ron White, "Mayor Bascom do you know the defendant, Ron White?"

"No. I only knew my wife had mentioned his name as some sort of salesman. After her murder the police uncovered some letters she had written to him at this sleazy motel. They had been returned as not at that address and no forwarding address. The next door neighbor had seen him use our garage before, unbeknownst to me."

"I know this has been difficult for you, Mayor, but just one more question. Were you aware that your wife was pregnant?"

"No. Absolutely not. It is embarrassing, but years ago we found out that I was incapable of producing a child. So it came as a great shock to me to find out not only that my wife had committed adultery with this man but that apparently she was bearing his child. Our marriage seemed so secure, it was and is just unbelievable."

Buzz sat down and turned to Russ, "Your witness, counselor."

Russ smiled up at the Mayor on the witness stand, "Now, Mayor Bascom, I am going to call you Bill, if that is alright with you, since you and I have known each other for some time out at the motel I manage."

The Mayor's smile froze on his face as he saw what was coming next.

"As a matter of fact, Bill, you frequent that motel at least once a week, don't you?"

Rachael had leaned back in her massive chair so that only the twinkle in her eyes could be seen as she glanced at the Mayor.

"Well, I have used a suite of rooms for certain business meetings that were not ripe for disclosure to the news media." He glared at Russ as he slowly rolled his massive diamond encrusted gold ring around his little finger.

"So, I can assume that one of those persons who were in regular attendance at those, so called business meetings, is a Faith Rameriez, your niece?"

"Object your Honor, the Mayor is not on trial today. This is a preliminary hearing to determine whether or not to hold the defendant for trial."

Through all of this the Mayor could be heard angrily saying that naturally his secretary would be present at a business meeting.

The Judge beckoned to both lawyers to approach the side bar at the bench. She covered her microphone with her hand as she smiled down at both attorneys, "This dog and pony show is beginning to get interesting. I gather the old boy cannot make babies but can still cut a wide swath in the sack?"

Russ said, "Maybe I should take the stand to vouch for that your Honor."

"No, I have heard enough about the Mayors outside activities to know his marriage was probably on the rocks for a long time. Now let us get off of this subject and onto some relevant cross examination. The hour is getting late and much as I hate to say it I am afraid we will have to recess until tomorrow morning to finish this testimony if you have much more cross examination." She looked at Russ with the question in her eyes.

It was always a good game plan to have the opportunity to carry a witness over to the following day on cross examination. It gave you time to re-think your position and check out some of the answers given earlier. "Well, Judge, I really don't think I will finish with ole Bill before six o'clock."

With that the Judge turned away and both lawyers returned to the counsel table. Russ picked up where he had stopped when he was interrupted.

"Now, Bill, let's talk about the day of the murder. When you left your home did anyone see you leave other than Mrs. Gray?"

"Not that I am aware of other than my wife."

"As you say traffic was bad so you were a little late arriving at your office. Who knows exactly what time you arrived at the office?"

"Why my secretary was already there when I arrived. She mentioned I was a little late."

Russ smiled at the witness, "Now this secretary is the same Faith Rameriez who accompanies you to the motel for these, quote "business meetings," unquote."

"I only have one secretary, Mr. Thurston."

"So you are saying that between the time you left home at eight forty five that morning and eleven o'clock when you returned some maniac rushed in and brutally attacked your wife with a chopped off piece of hose after beating her and tying her to the bed."

"That is exactly what happened."

"What is your blood type, sir?"

"Type O."

"That is the same blood type that was found at the murder scene, is it not?"

"I believe it is and as you know it is the most common blood type," he smiled benevolently at Russ.

"You and your wife had separate bedrooms, did you not?"

"Yes. For some time Elsa had objected to my snoring so we used different bedrooms — for that reason only."

"Then perhaps you can explain your fingerprints on the four poster bed, the dresser and in her bathroom?"

"Well, after all, just because a man snores doesn't mean it is the end of his sex life with his wife."

The courtroom rippled with laughter and some snide comments were made about the horny old son of a bitch. The bailiff gaveled for silence.

Rachael admonished the witness to simply answer the question.

"Yes, I can explain those fingerprints. We had sex the night before so I was in her room, her bed and her bathroom after we had sex."

Ron leaned forward and whispered, "That lying bastard. He hadn't had sex with Elsa for years and she refused to let him in her room for any reason."

Russ shrugged and moved ahead, "Did you find the passbook you went home to retrieve on the day of the murder?"

"Yes, I did, but it was sometime later after things had calmed down."

"Isn't it true that when you found the pass book, it had been changed from a joint account in both of your names to an account in you wife's name only?"

"The account was in her name alone."

"And isn't it also true that certain certificates of deposit and a checking account were taken out of joint names and put in your wife's name alone?"

"That is true, it was done with my knowledge. It was done for estate planning purposes on advice of our attorney." He had begun to roll his ring again.

"The only advice given by an attorney was to your wife to change these accounts in preparation for a divorce, wasn't it?" Russ was on his feet holding a sheaf of legal looking papers.

Before he could answer, Russ went on, "And this secure marriage you were telling us about had just come to an abrupt halt and divorce was the next step."

"No, that is not true."

"Well, if your marriage was so secure why did you tell your lover, Mrs. Gray, that you had found true sexuality through your relationship with her?"

He was furious and could no longer keep his calm exterior, "Mr. Thurston, I have never made any such comment to that woman. I have never had any sexual contact with her and never intend to do so. In short, I do not know where she came up with such a preposterous thought."

"No sir. As a matter of fact, in short, you are calling her a liar aren't you?"

The Mayor was stunned. He needed her testimony to backup his departure from the house and as an eye witness but now he had just called her a liar.

"Well, I guess she was just mistaken in her use of words."

Russ slammed his huge hand palm down on the table, "Was her statement the truth or not the truth?"

The courtroom was silent as all of the actors were frozen in position waiting for the answer.

Almost, in a whisper, "I guess it has to be untrue."

"So you are saying that she lied under oath, aren't you?"

"Well, at least she was not correct about those statements she said I made to her."

"Did you ever make any such statements to Mrs. Gray?"

"No, I never did."

"You are telling us the solemn truth now. You are not mistaken, incorrect or lying under oath?"

"Yes. I know I have never made any such statements to her."

"Then it follows that Mrs. Amelia Gray, knowingly, told an untruth to this court, is that correct?"

He had become somewhat confused and had lost his self confidence as this neighbor's testimony plagued him. "Yes, that is correct."

"And isn't it also true that she either lied or was incorrect about your activities on the day of the murder?"

"No. She was correct in all of the rest of her testimony."

"Come now, Bill. You are asking this court to believe bits and pieces of evidence and disbelieve what you don't like. Maybe you and Amelia should get together and re-arrange her testimony."

Buzz was objecting, but it was too late, the Judge had already put a large red question mark next to her notes on Amelia Gray's testimony.

Russ began to put away his trial notes even before the Judge adjourned court until the next morning at nine o'clock. She moved quickly off of the bench into her chambers without a glance at either attorney.

Buzz leaned across the table and quietly said, "You are in tough shape on this one, counselor, but if you want to talk about a plea, now is the time to do it."

Russ looked back at Ron and he could tell he had overheard the statement. He leaned toward Buzz and said loudly enough for Ron to hear it clearly, "Buzz, let's not play games. It has been a long day. Whatever you have on your mind just lay it out on the table so we can both hear what it is and then I will leave the decision up to Ron."

"Well, this is not the usual way to plea bargain but if that is the way you want to play the game it's alright with me. I still think he is good for a murder one rap but just to get rid of this without further embarrassment to the community I am willing to reduce the charge to manslaughter with the maximum time of ten years." He looked directly at Ron and said, "You had better think long and hard on this offer sonny boy, because it is the last one you are going to get. All bets are off once we start trial tomorrow at nine o'clock.

He snapped his suede Hartman briefcase shut and strolled out of the courtroom as he lit a cigar followed by his admiring staff.

Russ looked at Ron without saying anything, just waiting for his answer. Ron kept his head down looking at what he had doodled on the yellow note pad. Finally he looked up with tears in his eyes and shook his head, "I can't do it, Russ. I didn't do it so just don't ask me to take a plea."

Russ stood up and beckoned to the deputies to come get Ron as he placed a firm hand on his shoulder. "It is your ball game Ron to win or lose. Tomorrow you take the stand. Get some rest and we will give it hell tomorrow." Ron smiled up at him through blurred eyes, "Just remember, Ron, it ain't over until the fat lady sings and the only fat lady I saw in the courtroom was thrown out early this morning."

Ron shuffled away under guard as Russ picked up the doodled yellow note pad. The only notes were in bold print that said, "That Bastard Murdered Elsa!"

CHAPTER XIII

"All rise, this honorable court is again in session." The bailiff scowled out at the full courtroom as the Judge closed her private door behind her and quickly took the bench. She smiled pleasantly out at the spectators and said she was sorry for the delay in continuing the proceedings from yesterday but she was obliged to take some guilty pleas earlier before moving ahead with this preliminary hearing. "Mr. Thurston, am I correct in assuming that you are ready to proceed with the defendant's case?"

Russ stood and announced he was if the prosecution had no more evidence to present. Buzz nodded that he had completed the prosecutions case and turned to the Mayor to continue a whispered conversation.

"Very well, then you may proceed. Call your first witness."

"If it please the court, at this time, I would like to make an oral motion to dismiss the States case against my client. First of all there has been no showing of any motive by my client to commit this murder. Secondly, by the States own evidence, it would be impossible for Ron White to have entered the Bascom premises and found a murder weapon, struggled with the deceased, brutally attacked and murdered her in the short period of time he is alleged to have been in the home of the deceased."

Buzz was on his feet about to interrupt Russ when the Judge waved him back down in his chair, "Now, Russ, I am sure you are sincere in your motion to dismiss but there simply is no basis for dismissal at this point. It may well be after I have heard all of the evidence for the defense, that I will entertain such a motion again. Your motion to dismiss is overruled. Let's proceed."

Russ turned to Ron and beckoned to him, as he said, "I will call the defendant, Ronald White, to the witness stand." There was a stirring and some loud obscenities heard as Ron approached the clerk to be sworn. Rachael swiftly brought down her gavel on the cherry wood pedestal, "Any further demonstrations like this and I will clear the entire courtroom. This is a hearing to determine whether or not there is enough reasonable, convincing evidence to bind this defendant over for trial in the alleged murder of the deceased. He has not been found guilty nor will he be found guilty of any crime today. Therefore, I shall expect all of those in attendance today to keep their personal thoughts and utterances to themselves." Only the hum of the overhead fan could be heard over the hush in the courtroom. Rachael let the silence hang heavily for a dramatic moment and then slowly turned to the clerk and nodded.

"Raise your right hand, please, and place your left hand on the bible" Ron straightened his shoulders and looked the clerk in the eye as he took the oath. She read from a typed card well worn by the years of use in the courtroom, "Do you solemnly swear to tell the truth and nothing but the truth in these proceedings, so help you God?"

Ron nodded and at the same time answered in a loud clear voice "I do." He was motioned to the witness stand by the clerk and gave his full name and address to the court reporter before taking a seat on the stand. He looked up at the Judge who seemed to be busy with other matters on her bench other than the case at hand. She finally looked up at Russ and nodded.

"Ron, you have already given your name and address to the court. Did you know the deceased in this case Elsa Bascom and, if so, over what period of time?"

"Yes. I had known her for some months prior to this."

"What was the occasion for meeting her." Russ stood and walked over to lean against the jury rail so that Ron would have to look at the Judge as he answered Russ's questions.

"I own a magazine distributing company and some of my salespersons had made contact with her and suggested that I also meet her in an effort to sell additional subscriptions. I did meet her and that led to further meetings and eventually an affair developed between us."

"I assume that such an affair was what would be commonly known as an affair of the heart?"

"Yes. It developed into a rather deep situation as far as Elsa was concerned. I did not consider it to be anything more than a casual relationship similar to others I had experienced in the past."

"Again, I assume that you and the deceased had sexual relations?"

"Of course. As a matter of fact, Elsa encouraged our sexual engagements by telling me of her husbands infidelity and her craving for sex that he withheld from her."

Mayor Bascom was on his feet, behind Buzz, eyes bulging and his face pale with fury, "That's a God damned lie." he roared. Buzz quickly pushed him back in his chair and apologized to the court for his clients outburst and at the same time told the Mayor to keep his God damned mouth shut or get out of the courtroom.

Russ moved ahead ignoring the outburst, "And did this sexual relationship continue up until the death of Mrs. Bascom?"

"Yes, it did. As a matter of fact we had sexual relations just the day before her death." Ron seemed well poised and under control as he testified.

"Was there any particular time of day or night that you would have sex with Mrs. Bascom?"

"It was usually at the same time and at her home. Since her husband always left for the City Hall promptly at 8:30 a.m., I would arrive at 10:00 a.m., shortly after he left. I would pull right into her garage and then go into the house. She liked to think that no one knew about our affair since I would pull in and out of the garage in a few seconds time. I knew better because I had seen the lady next door peeking out the window when I would arrive. On this final day I arrived in the afternoon. This was the day she told me that she was pregnant and wanted to have the child. I was against this and said she should get an abortion. She told me that she was going to get a divorce from the Mayor and that she had already changed the bank accounts and emptied the safe deposit boxes. I simply told her that I couldn't see a divorce in my future and I sure didn't need a new baby to carry around while I was on the road selling."

"Now, can you describe her reaction to your feelings?"

"She simply said it didn't matter to her whether or not I got a divorce because she loved me anyway and she was still going to go ahead with her plans to get a divorce. She said she would just say the baby was the Mayors and get child support and alimony. We both thought that would serve him right for all of the screwing around he had done. So we had a glass of wine and toasted our unborn child and her divorce then spent an hour having great sex."

The courtroom began to hum with excitement and the bailiff gaveled it back to order. All eyes were on the Mayor as he almost burst with fury. Buzz was on his feet, "Your Honor, I have to object to all of this testimony as not being relevant to any of the issues in this hearing and as not being responsive to the question posed by the defendant's counsel."

"I will have to sustain the objection unless you can show that all of this has some relevancy as to whether or not the defendant should be bound over for trial as charged?"

"Your Honor, I believe this is relevant to show that my client had absolutely no motive to murder Elsa Bascom but that perhaps the motive was within her own home." It was apparent to all within earshot that Russ was beginning to point the finger of guilt at the Mayor. Ron and the Mayor glared at each other while the legal maneuvering continued.

Rachael listened to both sides of the argument while she leaned back in her swivel chair and watched the fan blades slowly rotate. "Alright, I have heard enough gentlemen. I will overrule the States objection for the moment based upon your argument that this goes to show no motive on the part of the defendant but I want to caution counsel that we are here today concerning State versus White, we are not at the moment interested in any other person or perpetrators."

Russ turned back to Ron who refused to take his eyes off of the Mayor, "So that when you left Elsa Bascom on that final day what was the nature of your parting?"

"I told her that I had to leave the next morning for Texas with my sales force, and didn't know when I would be back in Santa Fe. I wished her luck and told her I still thought it best for her to get an abortion but she just shook her head and told me that she loved me and the next time that I would see her she would be a free woman with a beautiful baby. I got in my car in the closed garage, opened the door and left."

"Now, was that the last time you saw Elsa Bascom alive?"

"Yes, it was. The next time I saw her she was apparently dead on her bed in her bedroom."

Russ seemed almost confused, "But I thought you testified that you told her you were leaving for Texas the next day?"

"That's right, I did, but something happened to change my mind. That afternoon after I had said a final goodbye to her I went back to my motel and told the manager to get my bill ready because I was checking out early the next day. Well, that night I went to my favorite bar next door to the motel and began to drown myself in about a vat of martinis. The more I drank the more I began to feel sorry for Elsa and want to see her ... I finally staggered into bed about midnight. The next day I woke up with an immense hangover and just as a big desire to split the sheets just one more time with Elsa."

"What time was it when you woke up on that Friday?"

"It was 9:00 a.m. I got up, cleaned up, had a quick cup of coffee and got in my car and headed for Elsa's house."

"Was this the usual time that you would go to her home?"

"Yes. Oddly enough, it just seemed natural for me to wake up at the usual time and make the usual trip over to her house for a good morning matinee. So, I arrived there at 10:00 o'clock. Everything seemed the same, the garage door was open as always, the back door was unlocked and I could hear the TV somewhere in the house. The only thing different was that I could smell the strong odor of cigar smoke in the house."

The Judge who had seemed bored before this seemed to suddenly take an interest in the testimony. Russ caught the change in her attitude so he quickly persued the last answer, "Just why would the smell of cigar smoke in the house be unusual?"

Ron looked away from Russ and stared into the bloodshot eyes of the Mayor. "Elsa hated the smell of cigar smoke in the house and always made it a point to air out the house or spray lots of deodorant around before I would arrive. Since the smell was so strong I knew that the Mayor must have just left. This was unusual since he always left his home in time to be at the office no later than 9:00 a.m." Ron continued to stare at the Mayor who self consciously fingered two long cigars in the breast pocket of his sport coat.

"What did you find upon entering the house?"

"I found Elsa tied to the bed posts, with this piece of garden hose in her. She was dead." Ron's voice was hardly audible as he answered and his hands were visibly shaking. Russ paused and poured a glass of water from the metal pitcher on the counsel table and took it to Ron as he asked his next question. "What was the first thing you did upon seeing her on the bed?"

"At first, I really wasn't sure that she was dead since the blood looked so fresh, so I took her head between my hands and screamed at her to look at me. Then I saw this grotesque hose protruding from her and I reached down to pull it out. At the same time it dawned on me that I could be a suspect so I released the hose without pulling it out."

"Ron, I have a section of hose here." Russ removed a new one foot section of rubber hose from his briefcase and handed it to Ron. "I want you to show the Judge just exactly how you put your hand around that hose that was inserted into Elsa."

Ron carefully took the hose from Russ, "Assuming that the portion of the hose inserted in her was where the exhibit sticker is then I grabbed it like this."

"Now, Ron, your little finger would have been on the upper part of the hose and your thumb furthest from Elsa's body, correct?"

Ron nodded and then answered for the record, "Yes. That is correct."

"Why did you grasp the hose in that manner? It seems to be an awkward way to take ahold of it."

"I couldn't look at her or the mess on the bed so I simply turned away and reached down to pull it out. But I quickly let it loose when I realized I could be a suspect. You can't believe the mass of blood on the bed, splattered and — " he couldn't go on for the moment. The Judge offered a brief recess if Russ thought it was necessary but he declined for fear of losing his impact on the court.

"Now, Ron, had you ever seen that hose that was inserted in Elsa before that day?"

"I saw that type of rubber hose every time I went through the garage to meet Elsa. It was rolled up and hung on the wall."

"What did you do next?"

"Well, somewhere in time, I don't know when, I became violently ill and threw up in the bathroom sink, which, incidentally had the water running in it when I went in to throw up. After that I just purely panicked and ran down the stairs, got in my car and went back to the motel."

"Just a couple of more questions Ron. Was Elsa tied in the same bed you had used for your sexual relations the day before?"

"Yes. That was the same bed we used all the time. It was in her bedroom, her private room." Ron gave an audible sob as he answered.

"And just one final question, and this may seem superfluous to you, but just for the record, did you in any way harm Elsa Bascom or cause her murder?"

"My God, no. Why would I want to murder the mother of my unborn child? I had absolutely nothing to gain by such a horrible crime." Ron was shattered.

"That's all I have, your Honor, the Defense rests it case." Rachael was looking hard at the subdued and slumping witness on the stand as if to try and glean out the wheat from the chaff, the truth from the half truths or out right lies. She slowly turned to Russ and then looked over to Buzz, and nodded as she said, "Very well, you may cross examine, Mr. Rawlings."

Buzz was on his feet in an instant and Russ feared the worst was yet to come for his client. "You say, and I quote, "Why would I want to murder the mother of my unborn child?" — and yet you were perfectly willing to murder your unborn child by abortion, weren't you?" Buzz smirked at the defendant as the noise level in the courtroom raised to the point where the bailiffs gavel was poised to strike the pedestal.

Ron seemed helpless as he looked at Russ for some kind of guidance. Russ stood and thundered an objection, "Object your Honor. We are not here to indulge in the classic argument of just when a fetus becomes a living creature."

"Yes. I am inclined to agree with you counsel. In any event we have all heard the defendant's testimony that he did in fact encourage the deceased to have an abortion. Let us proceed." Rachael glanced at the clock in the rear of the courtroom and Russ only hoped she wouldn't take the noon recess until the cross examination was completed. He didn't want the prosecution to have more time to prepare to harass his client.

"Now, Mr. White, do you really expect this court to believe your far fetched story of the happenings on the day Elsa Bascom was murdered?"

"I told you exactly what happened on that day and the day before." Ron seemed confused by the line of questioning and couldn't figure out just where Buzz was going.

Buzz picked up his yellow legal pad and referred to his notes, "Let us just look at all of the coincidences that have occurred, according to your testimony. First, just coincidentally the blood found at the scene, other than the deceased's, is type "O", the same as yours, correct?"

Ron nodded and the Judge admonished him to answer the question so the court reporter could take down his response.

"Yes, that is right, but so do a lot of other people have type "O" blood."

Buzz ignored the voluntary statements of the witness and continued, "And just coincidentally again your fingerprints are not only all over the house but are on the very hose that caused the deceased to hemorrhage to death. Now that's two fortuitous coincidences Mr. White."

Since he had not been asked a question, Ron simply sat there and looked at Russ who was busy taking notes at the time.

"The third coincidence is that a pubic hair that matches yours was found in the very death bed. Now aren't these three coincidences alone enough to cause reasonable persons to believe that you just might have been at the scene of the murder and, in fact, murdered Elsa Bascom?"

"No. I don't think so, not when you look at the reasons behind the so called coincidences. After all, I had been seeing the deceased for months so my fingerprints would be in every room. As far as the pubic hair is concerned I am sure even you are aware that after having sex with a woman it is not unusual to leave not only a sample of your semen but also pubic hairs from both parties."

Buzz seemed annoyed at the answer that was not really responsive to his question, "Just answer my question Mr. White without adding your exculpating statements and we will move along much faster. Now it is true, or is it not, that on the day before the murder took place you said goodbye to the deceased for the last time? You had no intention of ever seeing her again, isn't that true?"

Ron hesitated then shrugged and said, "Yes, I suppose that is true, but I wasn't entirely sure I could stay away from her if I was back in town on business."

"Nevertheless, this final goodbye led to a great deal of emotion on the part of the deceased, particularly since she had just told you that you were the father of her unborn child?"

"Well, she was upset because I suggested the abortion and, also, because it was apparent to her that I wasn't going to run home, get a divorce and then come back and marry her. I guess you could say that she was emotional, but then again I was emotional, also."

"But you want this court to believe that after hearing such damning and unnerving news from the deceased you blithely gulped down a glass of wine, had an hour of furious fornication, gave her a pat on the butt and disappeared over the horizon?"

Before Ron could answer, Buzz came out of his chair and came menacingly toward the witness stand, "You know damn well that isn't the way it happened, don't you. What really happened is that she was furious with you for not wanting to marry her and she threatened to go to your wife about your affair and to hang you with child support for your baby, and that's the reason you were back there the next day, to straighten out this whole mess with the deceased, but it just didn't work out did it?"

"That's not true. No it didn't work out because when I got to her house she had been murdered. Why the hell would I want to murder Elsa? Coincidentally, Mr. Rawlings, the Mayor has Type "O" blood and his fingerprints are all over the bedroom and if anyone had a motive it was the about to be divorced husband of the deceased."

"Your Honor, I really must object to the voluntary statement of the defendant and ask that it be stricken from the record." Buzz had his famous "I am pained" look on his face.

The Judge asked the court reporter to read back the question and answer, then looked at Russ and said, "I will sustain the objection and strike all of the defendant's answer after the word "murdered." She turned to the witness and gently said, "Mr. White, will you please simply answer the question. Any further explanation of your answer can be brought out by your competent attorney on re-direct examination. Thank you." Russ thought he detected a softening in the Judge's attitude toward Ron as she spoke to him.

"In short then, Mr. White, you admit that you were in the deceaseds' home shortly after the murder?"

"Yes. I was there but she was already dead."

"You also admit that the day before this murder took place, you and the deceased had a parting of the ways which was not to her liking."

"I guess you could say that, but there was no violence."

"And even though you knew a murder had just been committed you did not call the police or an ambulance, but instead bolted from the house and hid out until the police came and arrested you and dragged you off to jail! ... I think that's all I have of this witness, your Honor." Buzz slapped his yellow legal pad down on the counsel table and gave a knowing smile to the courtroom audience.

Rachael turned to Russ and asked, "Mr. Thurston do you have any further questions of this defendant?"

"Nothing further your Honor." Russ motioned to Ron to step down from the witness stand. The Judge looked at Ron and nodded. With an audible sigh Ron stepped down and returned to his chair, behind Russ, at the counsel table. With that, Russ stood and announced that the defense rested it's case. Ron leaned forward and whispered in his ear, "How did I do? Did I talk too much? What do you think the Judge will do?" Russ quieted him with a wave of his hand as the Judge gaveled for attention.

"Mr. White, the evidence in this preliminary hearing is now concluded and the matter will be taken under submission by the court. I assume that your attorney has explained to you that should this court bind you over for trial in this matter it in no way implies or suggests your guilt in this case. You would still be entitled to a full and complete trial before a jury to determine your guilt or innocence." Rachael paused looking openly at Ron who could feel a grid lock in his stomach. Her gaze moved to the attorneys who were both standing, "Gentlemen, I will hear your concluding remarks, if any, informally in my chambers. In the meantime, until such time as I have made a decision, the defendant will be held in custody." Rachael looked at the clock and said, "Since it is almost one o'clock this court will be in noon recess until two o'clock." Harry's gavel crashed down on it's pedestal as Rachael gathered up her file and her notes while beckoning to the two attorneys to come back to her chambers.

Ron frantically grabbed Russ' sleeve and implored him to do his best to get the case dismissed and not to forget about getting a bond set if they should lose. Russ turned to Ron and tried to reassure him that everything had gone as well as it could for them, under the circumstances, "You know I will do my best for you, Ron. You did a good job on the witness stand and I think the Judge was impressed with your honesty. It may be awhile before the Judge makes up her mind so you just go on back with the deputies and try and get some rest."

"Russ, I have to tell you I am scared shitless of those rape happy bastards in that jail. If I get hit on by them I don't think I could face the outside world again. So, for Christs sake, get me out of that God damned asshole of creation, now. Please, Russ, please believe me and get me out." He was already shuffling away in his leg irons between two guards. Russ turned to Buzz and said, "Isn't there something you can do to help him out over there?"

"Oh, hell Russ, you know how they all exaggerate about the jail full of butt stickers. I know it happens once in awhile but most of the time it is just a bunch of tough pros that want to scare the shit out of the first timers with no intention of following through with their threats." he paused and lit a cigarette. "But I will call over there and tell the jailers to keep a close eye on your client since there have been threats of bodily abuse made to him."

They both packed up their briefcases and started for the Judge's chambers. "Where did your star witness, the Mayor, rush off to in such a hurry?"

"Who knows probably some important luncheon meeting about the damned deficit budget this town lives on."

The Judge's door was open since the clerk had already gone to lunch. Rachael had removed her robe and looked absolutely ravishing in her favorite white silk shear blouse open at the throat and showing just enough cleavage to make Russ feel a stirring in his groin. She flopped down in her leather chair behind her desk and put two beautifully stockinged feet up on the credenza. "You know the general public thinks that all a Judge has to do is sit on his or her ass up on that bench all day and make great, Soloman like, decisions, collect the old pay check and go home promptly at five o'clock." She gestured at the stacks of files on her desk and on her floor next to her desk. "These are all cases that I have to decide, most of them with some knotty legal problem that has to be researched. There isn't any law clerk to do that research in this courthouse, you are your own law clerk and opinion writer."

Russ smiled at her as he sat down on the low couch the better to appreciate those long slim legs, "Well Judge, you at least have had lots of practice in the research department before you took the bench."

She playfully threw a pencil at him and winked, "There's nothing I hate more than a pure bred legal smart ass." She leaned back and put her hands behind her head giving a casual stretch that forced her full nipples against her blouse. She caught Russ staring and self consciously leaned forward and put her feet under her desk "Alright Buzz, you can go first if you feel the need to enlighten me on your position, which I doubt you do."

"As a matter of fact, Judge, I don't think there is one hell of a lot to talk about. As we all know, it is truly within your sole discretion to decide whether or not there is sufficient evidence to bind the defendant over for trial on the charge of either first or second degree murder. Now that amount of evidence required to compel a finding against the defendant is really only the merest amount, that is an amount that would cause a reasonable person to have some cause to believe that the defendant murdered, one, Elsa Bascom. Without reviewing all of the evidence, suffice it to say that it is admitted the defendant was at the murder scene in close proximity to the time of the murder and all the other circumstantial evidence would be more than enough to cause the court to bind him over for trial. I have seen cases, with far less evidence against a defendant, that have been bound over, and later the case tried by my office and a conviction obtained."

Rachael looked at the ceiling, "Please, Buzz, spare us your usual recitation of the great trials and exploits you have seen in your lifetime." She was carefully looking at her trial notes, "I think I have heard enough from the prosecution. I will tell you quite frankly, Russ, that I am inclined to agree with the position of the prosecution but there are some things in this case that really bother me, so perhaps you will touch on those problems during your argument."

Russ nodded and after briefly referring to his notes, got up and took a chair near the desk in order to look the Judge squarely in the eye. "You are right there are some things that are bothersome about his case. What really bothers me is that this man did not murder Elsa Bascom. What also bothers me is the fact that there is enough evidence in this case to indict the husband of the deceased just as easily as you can my client."

Buzz started to interrupt, but the Judge quickly quieted him down with a short admonition, to give Russ the courtesy of not interrupting while he was addressing his remarks to the court.

"Yes, it is true that the defendant was at the deceaseds' home close to the time of the murder but I would point out that her husband deviated from his normal time of departure for the office on that day and left his home late which places him in the home just as close to the time of the murder as the defendant. The defendant has type O blood, so does the Mayor. The defendants fingerprints are found at the scene of the crime, so are the Mayors'. The fact that one of the defendants pubic hairs was found in the death bed does nothing but give strong credence to the fact that the deceased and the defendant were, in fact, lovers. I have no doubt that some of the Mayor's pubic hairs could be found in the home if need be. Motive. Let's talk about motive. Who really has the motive to commit this murder. Certainly not the defendant since he had just become a brand new father who had nothing to do but just walk away from the scene and let his lover continue on her avowed course of divorcing her husband, the Mayor. And does the Mayor have a motive to murder his wife? Picture this scene. His excellency gets up in the morning, has a cup of coffee and then his wife smilingly drops a bombshell on the table. "Guess what darling, I have seen my lawyer and I am filing for divorce. I have cleaned out the safe deposit boxes, closed the savings accounts and taken your name off of the checking account. Oh, and by the way I am pregnant by my lover." Now there is real motive for a murder of such violence as we have here. Far be it from me to tell the prosecuting attorney how to run his office or just whom to arrest for murder, but I would strongly suggest that if justice is to be done in this case there should be an investigation into the Mayors activities before, during and after the murder." Russ found his voice booming in the closely confined chambers, and reached across the desk for one of the Judge's cigarettes.

"Thank you, Russ. I have quite a few reservations about this case, also, and I strongly recommend that the prosecutor's staff get off their sanctimonious behinds and dig into this case to make sure we are protecting the rights of the innocent and not persecuting them. There is a presumption of innocence in these courts even though it would appear to the defendant that there is only a presumption of guilt, in his case. I am still inclined to bind him over for trial since there is sufficient evidence to warrant such action." She paused and gazed, for a moment, out the dirty windows at the majestic Sangre de Christo mountains in the back drop, "but I want some time to make up my mind and perhaps a good cup of coffee and some lunch will help me make that, Soloman like, decision. I will make a decision before the afternoon is out and should it be against the defendant I will most certainly set bail for him. I feel that there are a lot of loose ends in this case that need to be tied down and the defendant must be free to assist his attorney in any preparation for trial. So, both of you give thought to the amount of the bond in the event I do not set Mr. White free. I would suggest that both of you be back here at three o'clock for my decision."

Russ had the feeling that the third ball in a juggling act was still in the air. It was impossible to get a handle on which way the decision would go, so the ball was still in the air.

CHAPTER XIV

It was later than usual when Willis checked the Mayor and Faith into their usual room, number 118. Willis wondered why the Mayor wasn't in court but then decided that it probably wasn't necessary for him to be there since he had already testified. He saw both of them laughing as they slipped in the front door of the room.

Mayor Bascom was in a jovial and expansive mood and he gave Faith a healthy slap on her skin tight white slacks as they entered the room. "I'll tell you one thing, baby, the old Mayor knows how to hold his own against that smart ass lawyer, Russ Thurston." He had already taken his shirt off and unzipped his pants, "I knew every question he was going to ask before he even asked it. Hurry up and get out of those clothes, we don't have much time today and I am ready to get down to some serious fucking."

Faith slowly and tantalizingly slipped out of her shear panties and carefully massaged her magnificent bush between her thighs, then unhooked her bra and revealed those firm full pink nipples that quivered with her every movement. The Mayor told her to get busy on his already full erection and she obediently slipped her hand around it and gently pulled the full throbbing head of it into her warmth. In seconds the Mayor moaned he was about to blow his load and she quickly released him. He reached down and frantically tried to pull her down on him again but she resisted. He grabbed her by her jet black hair and forced her over on her back and propped two pillows beneath her thighs. By now she was laughing hysterically as he hoisted his bulk on top of her and tried to jab his erection in her. "God damn, you, I'll teach you to be a laughing prick teaser." With that he grabbed her by the throat and began to squeeze until it frightened her so she took his erection fully and deeply in her. In a few strokes he had exploded and she held him as he continued to plunge with rage into her heaving mound of love. He fell heavily on her shuddering and whimpering, "Oh God, oh God you are so good."

Willis had watched all of this through the well worn peep hole that gave him a clear view of Faith's widely spread legs revealing her now deliciously wet bush with it's gleaming pink lips and above that the Mayors quivering ass. She gently pushed him off of her and down her now moist and writhing body until she could take his failing erection and ease it from within her. Willis had a great erection just watching the performers at work.

Now Faith was talking to him, "Come on baby, you can do it again just keep pumping and I will keep getting hotter and hold you in me." Now she had her legs up over his shoulders and her hands were grasping great hunks of his ass as she jerked him into her faster and faster until she threw her legs down and lifted him off of the bed as she reached a screaming orgasm, "Fuck me, you son of a bitch, fuck me. Now, now, oh, my God, I love it, fuck me." She lay under him slick with sweat as he slowly withdrew from her and rolled over on his back, eyes bulging and mouth slack. It was moments before either of them moved and then it was Faith who again began to gently stroke his now totally exhausted organ.

"Now that Elsa is resting in heaven, there is nothing to keep us from being seen out in public, together, is there?" She continued to massage his un-responding penis as she looked at him with those large black eyes.

"Now, I would think you would know the answer to that question. How would it look for me to be dating my niece who is young enough to be my daughter? Why the news media would have a virtual field day with that one. No, honey, we will just keep this the same way we have been doing it in the past." He felt a slight stirring in his crotch and vaguely wondered if he could possibly take her once more before they had to leave.

Faith rolled over on her side with her back to him, "I don't want it to be the same way that is was in the past. I want to be with you all the time, not just in this God damned, shack up motel." She paused a minute then smilingly turned back to him and pressed his face into her breasts. "The least you could do is to take me to your house so we could make love in your bedroom. Maybe I could even move in, since I am your niece no one would think anything of it. Just say you needed someone to take care of the house and to cook your meals." Her eyes sparkled with delight and anticipation as she waited for his answer.

With that he sat up and swung his legs over the side of the bed and icily glared at her, "If you think I got rid of Elsa just so I could move you into her bedroom then you are the craziest Indian that ever came off the reservation." He was heading for the shower as he turned around and said, "I've got enough trouble keeping the heat on this idiot magazine salesman for the murder rap without complicating my life with a nymphomaniac in the house."

Willis almost gasped loud enough to be heard. He couldn't believe what he had just heard. He put his ear to the peep hole to hear better. Faith said, "I always had a feeling you murdered her, particularly when you needed an alibi about the time you got to work." Faith was wiping herself with a hand towel.

The Mayor called from the shower, "Well, honey, as it turned out, I really didn't need an alibi since I was lucky enough to have that White character get a big hangover hard on and show up at the house right after I left. That was one hell of a good break for me."

Faith was slowly pulling on her shear panties as she stared in the hazy mirror on the wall. "You really don't think of me as anything more than your personal whore do you?"

"Now, come on, honey, you know it isn't that way at all. It's just that things have to calm down in this wind blown town for a little while before we can parade down main street." he lied.

Faith smiled in the mirror as she hoisted her full breasts into her lace bra. "Then you really will take me to nice places for dinner and show me off to your friends?"

"Now, honey, have I ever treated you badly? Haven't I always told everyone that you were the prettiest little Injun in the southwest territory? And after all we are kin folks." He came out of the shower and threw his towel on the bed as he came to her and put her hand on his still limp penis and gave her a heavy wet kiss. She responded with a tongue that slid down to his nipple and then dropped to her knees. He stroked her hair and then almost as a father said that Daddy had enough for the day and had to go to work. He gently lifted her by the arms and pulled her to him as her nipples showed hard through her bra, "Now you are Daddy's little girl, aren't you honey?"

She put her head on his shoulder and sighed deeply, "Yes, Daddy, you know I am and always will be."

"Now, let's get dressed and get out of here because I have an important meeting to attend at three o'clock and we are already late. We will take the short cut back to the city hall on the back roads. It's faster and more private."

Willis rushed out of the adjoining room to get to the front office and the phone to call Russ about what he had just heard. As he opened the front door, the Mayor's, new pale blue Cadillac Beritz flashed out the front entrance. As he looked after it he saw the Mayors' arm go around Faith's head and pull her down on his lap.

"Now you keep your head down, while we get out of the busy part of town, and don't fool around or I might run off the God damned road." He stopped at the intersection of Broadview and Shadow Tree Lane and swung quickly onto the narrow blacktop lane.

Faith giggled as she began to slide her hand up and down his thigh. "I think I'll just keep my head down here on your lap, Daddy, so you won't have to worry about anyone seeing me." She already had her hand on his zipper and she could feel him begin to squirm in the seat and raise up the steering wheel.

"Now, Faith honey, I told you to behave yourself down there or I might loose control of this magnificent machine and then we will both be in some deep shit." But even as he was talking he had taken one hand off the steering wheel and had reached under her blouse and bra to squeeze and massage her hard nipple. There was no one else on the road as he looked down to see her take it in her pouting lips trying to tug it to an erection. He looked back at the road just in time to see the other car hurtling around the tight curve almost too close to miss. My God, he was on the wrong side of the road, he swung the wheel violently with his left hand while he tried to get his right hand out of her bra. The cars missed each other by inches and he could see the horrified look on the young driver's face in the other car. The curve swallowed them up as the screeching tires left the roadway. Crazily he could still feel her warm mouth on his penis as the car suddenly flipped over and began to roll down the embankment with its doors flapping wildly disgorging it's passengers as it crushed them into the rocky soil. The last thing he remembered hearing was the death wail of the Souix as she found a place by the side of her forefathers.

CHAPTER XV

Russ was in the clerks office promptly at three o'clock but the Judge was still on the bench hearing a brief motion for a change of Judge which in all liklihood she would grant since Russ knew she didn't care for the attorney making the motion. So she could easily be rid of him by simply granting the motion. The prosecution really didn't care one way or the other since it sent up one of it's very junior assistant prosecutors to argue the motion.

"Russ, I think you really did a good job for your client today, but I am afraid there is still enough evidence to bind him over for trial." Hannah lit up another cigarette and went back to entering a minute on the fly leaf of a file.

"Maybe you know something that I don't know. If you do you might as well tell me and I can get the hell out of here." Russ was a little irritated that the Judge might have told the clerk her decision before she told the attorneys.

"No. She would never do that, you of all people ought to know that. It's just that I heard all of the evidence and even though I really have some doubts as to whether or not he actually did murder Mrs. Bascom, still there is plenty of evidence to warrant a jury hearing the case to determine guilt or innocence."

"I know, Hannah, and you know how it is when you are in the middle of one of these things, you always feel like a winner when the case is over and before the verdict. But I'll tell you one thing, I sure couldn't get a handle on what Rachael was thinking as the evidence came in or even after the case was closed." Russ sat on the lone wooden straight backed chair by the grimy window and stretched his long firm legs out as he put his hands behind his head. He was pleasantly tired from the past two days trial and he momentarily closed his eyes.

"Tell me one thing. Just why didn't you and the Judge ever make a go of it when you were dating. I know she was really nuts about you cause there wasn't a day that went by that she didn't mention your name." Hannah had a way of putting things to you in a direct manner if she wanted an answer to something that had been nagging her.

Russ kept his eyes shut and smiled a beautiful warm smile as he reminisced. "I guess I really felt the same way about Rachael and was making some pretty good moves on her when all the shit hit the fan. I fell from the top of the mountain to the bottom of it's lowest canyon overnight. Hannah, I went into a deep, deep depression and it took me years to really look at myself in the mirror and admit that I was the only reason for my downfall, not the system, not my injury and not this country. I was my own downfall and I had to be the one to pull myself up by my own boot straps. I just couldn't face the old part of my world while I was so down and a part of that world was most certainly Rachael." He stopped a moment, and gazed out of the window, then straightened himself in the chair, "Well, it's all behind me now. I'm out of the Motel business and back in the law business with Charlie London and with a little luck and some encouragement by you I'll be back in business with Rachael."

They both heard the private door open to the Judge's chamber so they knew the court was in recess. Hannah smiled as she got up to tell the Judge that Russ was here for his three o'clock appointment and said, "You can count on me to help out all I can. It's about time she got some good old home style lovin. Might improve her disposition when she gets up in the morning."

Russ picked up his briefcase and followed Hannah to the Judge's door and entered before she had given the word to enter.

"Well, now, Mr. Thurston, it seems to me you are sure anxious to get this over with. Sit down while I go to the john. My kidneys are about to burst, one of the hazards of being a bench sitter." She smiled at him as she hurriedly began to unzip her robe and head for her private room. As he sat there in the quiet of her chambers listening to the gentle sound of her sudden relief in the water, he could see on her desk the file of his case with a memorandum on top of it. He could see the style of the case on the memo but since it was upside down he had a difficult time reading her decision. Naturally, he was tempted to casually reach over and quickly look at the last paragraph on the last page to see what decision she had made but he resisted and continued trying to read the memo from where he sat. He heard the toilet flush, water running in the sink and an appropriate time for hair combing, lip gloss, and mirrored satisfaction before Rachael slowly came back into the room. She was still pulling up her zipper and Russ could tell that she wore nothing under her black shining robe.

"Where's Buzz? Did you see him as you came in the court-house?"

"I haven't seen him since we parted company at noon time. I thought maybe you had already told him the decision since it is three thirty and he isn't here."

"I apologize for being late but these damn motions have to be heard so the wheels of justice can continue to grind out the wheat and the chaff. I'll call down at his office and see what is keeping him." She picked up her private phone and dialed the prosecutors in house number. "This is Judge Rawlings. Let me speak to Buzz." There was a pause while the connection was made, "This is Judge Rawlings, you were supposed to be here at three o'clock, so just what the hell are you doing sitting down there in your private kingdom with your harem?" She smiled and winked at Russ as he heard the loud protestation from the other end of the phone. "Listen, Mr. Prosecutor, I don't give a damn what your arrangements are with the Mayor. I want you up here right now." She put the phone back on it's hook and turned to Russ, "His excellency says that he was supposed to meet the Mayor at his office just before three o'clock and he hasn't shown up. Apparently the Mayor wanted to be here to get what he hoped would be good news, first hand. Anyway, he had better be here in five minutes or I will show him what the word contempt means, not to me as an individual, but as a Judge."

Hannah tapped on the door and stuck her head in to tell the Judge that Russ had a phone call from the Motel. Russ started to get up to go out to the clerks office and then stopped. He really didn't want to be interrupted while in conference with the Judge.

"Hannah, it probably is Willis, so just tell him I am in conference with the Judge and will call him back as soon as I can. Tell him if it can't wait, to call the owner, Mr. Cahill, at his office."

Buzz came past Hannah in the usual great huff with the usual entourage following dutifully behind him. He took a seat next to Russ at the Judge's desk while his followers sat on the old couch.

"Thank you, Mr. Rawlings, for honoring us with your presence." her voiced dripped with icy sarcasm. "Now if you would be so kind to close the door to the clerk's office we can proceed with this rather important meeting."

Buzz nodded to a beautiful number ten seated on the couch who immediately dropped her poised legal pad and swished her golden long legs toward the door.

"I really am sorry, your Honor, but the Mayor was emphatic about being in the courtroom when you handed down your decision. I am sure you can understand his concern."

Russ turned to glare at Buzz, "I can sure as hell understand his concern. As far as I am concerned, the son of a bitch ought to be the one over in security."

"Just hold it now. What you may think is not the issue in this courtroom, Russ, so I will appreciate your attention to the courts decision at this time." She turned her attention to the memorandum before her on her desk. "I must admit that there is a good deal of conflicting evidence in this case but as both of you are well aware all the court needs in order to bind the defendant over for trial, is really the merest, as they say in legal circles, scintilla of evidence. The admissions by the defendant, alone, put him at the scene of the murder in close proximity to the time of the act of violence. The presence of fingerprints, hair samples, and other forensic evidence would further implicate the defendant. The defendant's attorney has vigorously pursued the theory that the defendant is in fact innocent of the crime and, to be quite blunt about it, that her husband, Mayor Bascom, is the perpetrator. The court takes no position on the issue raised by defense counsel." She handed her typewritten decision to both attorneys who quickly turned to the final paragraph of the last page. The decision was obvious as Russ disgustedly dropped the decision on her desk and looked out the window. Buzz handed the decision to one of the followers with a broad smile on his face.

Rachael looked at Russ with deep compassion and asked for understanding of her difficult position. "Now why don't you two get together and see if you can't work this out on some kind of a deal that is fair to all concerned?"

Buzz shook his head gravely as he studied the massive diamond in his ring, "I still can't do any better than second degree murder on a plea."

"Oh shit, Buzz, you know damn well that the worst a jury would give this poor horny bastard would be second degree. Get off your self righteous ass and be reasonable. "She got up and stood behind her high backed chair.

Russ shifted uneasily, "I'll tell you the truth, Judge, I am not inclined to plea bargain on this case. I think I can walk this poor son of a bitch with a little luck and then his excellency, the Mayor, may have the well known tit in the ringer."

"Buzz, why don't you drop this down to voluntary manslaughter so I can lay five to fifteen years on him and he can be out in four counting time served?" She lit a cigarette as she glanced over at Russ to get his reaction.

"If it gets out of this meeting that the Mayor is being accused of his wife's murder by the defendant and his attorney then all bets are off. So with the understanding that there is no more talk about the

Mayor's involvement in this murder I will recommend voluntary manslaughter in order to dispose of the case without further trial."

Russ reached over to pick up his briefcase and put the Judge's decision in it, "I still don't think he is good for this murder. I will take the offer to him not because I want to or that I will recommend that he take it, but because I am obliged to, as his lawyer, under our so called Cannon of Ethics."

They all stood to leave as the Judge stubbed out her cigarette.

"Well, do the best you can, Russ. If White knows in his inner self that he did in fact kill Elsa Bascom, then he might take the offer with a little urging from you. In the meantime, I am going to hold the defendant without bail, since he is to be tried on murder one."

"Judge, I am really worried about my client being in the general jail population from what he says. He is about to have a nervous breakdown worrying about his safety, physically and sexually."

"The best I can do for the moment is call the warden and have your client isolated from the rest of the jail house gang. That should help somewhat. I want to hear from both of you on this plea bargain no later than tomorrow. Send Hannah in as you leave." With that she turned her attention to the day's mail.

As Russ passed Hannah she told him that Willis had called three or four times while they were in chambers and insisted it was urgent.

"Thanks, Hannah. Can I use the phone in the courtroom?"

"Sure, Russ, just dial nine and you will have an outside line." She got up from her desk and opened the door to the Judge's chambers as Rachael called out to Russ, "Russ give me a few minutes to get rid of this mail and then drop by before I leave for the day."

"I have to make a phone call, then I will be right there." Russ opened the door to the now empty courtroom except for the bailiff whose head rested against the wall behind his chair while he enjoyed a short nap. Russ was tempted to slam down the gavel but thought differently as he eyed the forty four magnum in his holster.

"Willis, this is Russ. What the hell is going on that is so important that it can't wait until I get back there?" Russ sat on the rail in front of the clerks courtroom desk and shined his shoe on the back of his pants leg. As he listened he smiled at first then the corners of his mouth drooped as the impact of what Willis had heard came through.

"Now, Willis, sit down and calmly think this through and write down everything you can remember in detail. Yes, even the sex part. I want it from beginning to end. It's your word against their's but it sure as hell looks like just what we need to break this case wide open." He hung up quickly and went back to the Judge's chambers. Hannah was just coming out the door and motioned for him to go in without knocking. Rachael blew him a kiss as he closed the door and began to unzip her robe. "I told Hannah she could leave a half hour early so will you please lock the door behind you? I have a few non judicial decrees to lay on you and the emphasis is on the word lay." As she came toward Russ she could tell that he was not in the same mood as she was so she stopped midway to him.

"Rachael, I just talked to my assistant manager out at the Motel, and he has passed on to me some information that I think will exonerate my client. Maybe you should get ahold of Buzz and have him come up here so we can discuss this matter?"

"I doubt if Buzz is in the office at four thirty. This is happy hour at the Branding Iron and he will be regaling all in earshot about his stunning victory today. Why don't you give me a resumé of what you have and we will see what can be done?"

Russ sat with Rachael on the couch and carefully went over his conversation with Willis. He could tell that she was visibly upset by the obviously new evidence in the case. She got up from the couch and picked up her pack of cigarettes from the desk, started to take one out and then threw them down on the desk, "Damn that son of a bitch. You know, of course, that the two of them will out swear your peeping Tom, but there is enough here to certainly cause me to re-open the case on my own motion for additional testimony. Just hold off on talking to your client about my decision and I will advise Buzz that I am at least temporarily setting it aside. I will reschedule the hearing to admit additional testimony for tomorrow afternoon."

She came back to Russ and stood before him as she slowly took his head in her hands and looked deep into his eyes, "You know of course what my decision will be if your new witness sticks with his story." She moved between his legs.

Russ reached up and put his strong arms around her slender waist and let his hands gently stroke her firm thighs, "Does this mean we can try to loose another ear ring?" he nuzzled her perfumed thighs through the robe.

"If there is a trial of your client later on you know I would have to disqualify myself. There is no way I could sit in judgement on a case you were trying and give the other attorney a fair and impartial hearing." She was already pulling down her zipper as she held him close to her warmth. Russ opened her robe to gaze at her magnificent mound as it thrust itself toward his waiting moist tongue. "Do you still get horny when you try a case, my darling?" She shuddered as he pulled her tightly to his up turned face and buried his lips in her thighs. She thrust at him wildly craving for more, moaning as his tongue found all the sensitive places. "God, Russ, I can't stand this, I'm going to come. Put me on the couch and fuck me."

Russ pulled her down on top of him as he clumsily pulled his pants down. She straddled him hovering over him like a great black winged bat sucking his erection into her rocking crotch as he hungrily devoured her swollen, sweet pink nipple. He could feel the heavy throbbing in his groin as her heat was bringing him to a raging climax. She exploded on him soaking his shorts and kept forcing herself toward another orgasm as he held himself proudly in her. She begged him to come for her, in her, hard and violent. He quickly pulled out of her just before he was ready to come in her and heard her curse him as she smothered him with her kisses. She desperately grabbed his full erection and slipped it back in her as she mounted another orgasm. He could hold back no longer and they came in blissful climax together. Sweat ran between her hanging bosoms and dripped on his lips, salty to the taste. She flung her robe off on the floor and collapsed on him. "Oh God, Russ, how did I survive all those years without your great loving mass in between my thighs. You are so good, so good, darling."

"At this point, you have, at least, reduced that loving mass to a limp loving mess," He said. She smiled as she snuggled down next to him on the couch and continued to stroke him gently.

"You know that I'm not finished with you. I have great plans for that limp love maker." Russ could feel her thighs tightening against his leg as she kissed him warmly.

"Well, I'll tell you what, baby, there is a lot more where that came from but I think I could do you more justice in a king size bed with a magnum of champagne at my elbow. So how about it, your place or mine?"

"You have to be out of your skull to think I would go to that Motel for a night of sheer delight. I just happen to have the required king size bed and some very vintage champagne given to me by a very vintage admirer."

"Do we have to get dressed for this occasion or can we just slip out the back door as we are locked together in blissful copulation?" She playfully gave his balls a squeeze bit his nipple just as her private phone rang. She glanced at the clock and saw it was just five o'clock.

She eased across Russ and beautifully naked walked across the room to her desk where she picked up the phone as the setting sun's rays shone on her still glistening blonde mound, "This is Judge Rawlings." Russ had taken off his soaked under shorts and pulled up his pants. He crossed to the private washroom where he cleaned up and wrapped his shorts in some paper towels. As he came out and put his package in his briefcase, he heard Rachael say she would try to locate Russ as soon as possible, and would give him the message.

"Russ, that was Lt. Lester of the State Patrol. It seems that Mayor Bascom and his motel mate were in a serious one car accident.

She is dead, God rest her soul, and he has suffered such grave injuries that they don't think he will live through the night. They want you and Buzz and a court stenographer to get over to Memorial West immediately."

"I don't know why the hell I should go over there to be by his side. Do you know how it happened?"

"No. I asked the Trooper the same thing, and all he said was that they were on the wrong side of the road and almost hit another car head on. They seemed to loose control of the car and it rolled throwing them out and rolling over them."

"My God, he must have been drunk."

"I don't think so. The Trooper casually mentioned that when they found the Mayor his fly was unzipped and his penis was out of his pants. My great wisdom as a Judge in the criminal division of this court tells me that he was getting a ferocious head job when he crossed over the yellow line."

"Well, as the old saying goes, he died with a smile on his face. I still don't see why I should go to Memorial West?"

"Suffice it to say, the good Father who is there to give the last rites, told the Trooper that the Mayor wanted to make a death bed confession. So get your sweet ass out of here and I'll see you later at the Rawling's private bed and breakfast."

Russ gave her a quick kiss as she wrapped her sweat stained robe around her waist, "Love you, babe. See you in a little while."

"Just in case anyone needs me from over there I will be at home — cooling champagne and warming a bed." Her smile was radiant as he went out the door.


CHAPTER XV

As Russ got off the elevator on the fourth floor it was apparent which room was the Mayors. The television crews were passing the time flirting with the nurses who were busy applying make up for their television debut. The door was guarded by two State Troopers who could pass for Saturday night wrestlers. Russ moved through the reporters, doctors and general confusion to the door where he identified himself to one of the troopers. After careful scrutiny the door was opened for his admittance.

The stark white of the room was in severe contrast to the dark blue uniforms of the State Troopers and Santa Fe police officers. The bed where the Mayor lay on his back was slightly raised, and the good Father Sebastian stood near his side speaking in hushed words as he gently caressed the gold cross and beads. Russ walked over to Buzz and nodded, "Is he still conscious?"

"Just barely, but he is still rational. He was crushed pretty badly and he has a ruptured spleen, broken ribs, collapsed lung and a broken spinal cord. He is paralyzed from the waist down and the internal bleeding can't be stopped. Both the head of orthopedics and surgery say that it is just a matter of hours before he is gone."

"Not that I care that much for the murdering bastard, but isn't there something they can do to stop the bleeding?" Russ was truly distressed to see the gasping, ashen, dying Mayor, obviously, almost in the final throes of death.

"Let me tell you something, Russ. I am a lawyer, not a doctor. I assume they know what they are doing and have done all they can do to save his miserable life. Personally, my own opinion is that he will be better off dead than he would be in prison for life." Buzz started to light a cigarette and then quickly put it away as he noticed the oxygen pumping life into the Mayor.

Father Sebastian motioned to them to come over to the bedside. Buzz beckoned to the court stenographer and to the Lt. of the State Highway Patrol, who quickly joined them. Father took the hand of the Mayor and put the beads in his hand as he spoke quietly to him, "My son you are aware that you are about to leave this earth to join the Kingdom of the Lord."

He nodded feebly as he clung to the beads and Father Sebastian's hand. Buzz whispered to him that he had to answer out loud so the stenographer could get his answers. The Mayor overheard him and said, "Yes, Father, I understand."

"Very well, my son. Now is it your desire to make a confession, to those gathered here, in contemplation of your death?"

He stared at the dimly lit ceiling for a moment and a tear slowly slid down the side of his cheek, "I wish to confess my sins Father and ask for forgiveness."

Father nodded to Buzz and Russ and they stepped forward next to the head of the bed. Buzz took out a printed piece of unlined paper and read from it, "Your name is William Bascom and you are the Mayor of Santa Fe, New Mexico, is that correct?"

"That's right." his voice was barely audible and the stenographer moved a step closer with her recorder and steno type machine.

"You are making this statement of your own free will, without coercion from anyone realizing that your statement may be self incriminating in the case of State of New Mexico versus Ronald White." Buzz paused and looked at the broken man in the bed.

"Yes I am, and I am in full control of all my mental faculties."

"You are further making this statement after having been given the last rites of the Holy Roman Catholic Church by Father Sebastian who is present here at your bedside."

He nodded slowly and then answered, "Yes, I know I am about to die and I wish to confess."

"Therefore, this is a confession in contemplation of death on your part and shall be binding upon you in a court of law should you recover from your injuries. Do you understand that?"

"I fully understand all you have said and still want to confess to the murder of my wife, Elsa." He sobbed and his hospital white pillow was suddenly damp with the flow of his tears. The room was silent except for the heart monitor and the sucking of oxygen by the Mayor. There was a hushed feeling of expectation as he struggled to compose himself and gather enough final strength to make his confession, "Forgive me Father, for I have sinned. I lost complete control of myself when she told me that she was going to divorce me and that she had already cleaned out all of our accounts and the safety deposit box. Then she told me that she was pregnant by someone else who wouldn't marry her so she was going to say it was my child and get child support as well as alimony."

Even on his death bed, you could see the fire and hatred flash in his eyes and his pale death mask turned into a cruel visage of damnation. He would confess but never would he repent. "She taunted me until I couldn't control my temper any longer. I ripped her clothes from her unclean body and began to beat her. Then I decided to tie her to the bed and force myself on her, to literally rape her, but she fought back even as she was tied. I had this piece of hose from the garage that I slammed in her while she was unconscious. I didn't think it would kill her, I just thought it would abort the child and then she might come to her senses. So I left. She was still alive when I left her so I figured to go to the office and come back in a little while and untie her. When I returned home before noon she was dead. I called the police and told them my wife had been murdered by someone. I didn't know her lover had been there in the meantime." He struggled for life as it slowly ebbed away into the monitor.

Russ knew in his own heart that the Mayor was still lying even as he fought for life, "If your wife wasn't dead at the time you left your home with her tied to the bed, then why did you need an alibi from your niece and your neighbor? Isn't it true that when you got to the office that day you told your niece to lie about the time that you arrived?" Russ knew Willis had overheard his niece in the motel mention his demand that she lie about this.

The Mayor turned away from the two attorneys and stared past Father Sebastian on the other side of the bed. Spittle drooled from the side of his mouth and sweat broke out on his forehead. A Doctor and Nurse came to him and asked if he was finished with his statement and he nodded.

The Doctor and the Nurse ushered all of them out of the room into the still jammed corridor where questions were being fired at them by reporters. The State Highway patrol trooper kept them away from Buzz while he and Russ had a quick conversation in a vacated room.

"Buzz, I guess the next thing to do is get ahold of the Judge and tell her what has happened so she can release my client from jail." Russ was standing at the window staring out, still a little dazed by the whole turn of events.

"You know, to be honest with you, I never have had this happen before. There isn't any doubt in my mind that the confession would hold up in court even if by some miracle he would survive and then recant the statement as being forced out of him while he was under sedation." He was already heading for the phone on the night stand beside the bed.

"You know what really gets to me is the fact that he had to lie, even in his death bed confession. What he did was to deliberately murder his wife. While she was tied up with her panty hose and he went downstairs in search of rope and cut off a length of hose, he had plenty of time to stop his actions, cool down and walk away from the whole mess. Instead, he followed his now premeditated plan and killed her with all the violence of a cold blooded psychopathic murderer. And why? Money pure and simple. He wasn't jealous, he didn't love her, all he loved was his ego, power and above all his money. What a God damned waste."

"All I can tell you, Russ, is that you are suited for the job as defense counsel. I don't let all of these assholes get to me either philosophically or otherwise. They get their ass in a crack, by God, I'll put them away where the sun doesn't shine. So he is a liar, even on his death bed, that isn't my problem and it sure as hell doesn't bother me. Let him lie there and worry about how he can lie himself past Saint Peter at those pearly gates." he was dialing the Judge's private number as he talked to Russ. "Rachael this is Buzz. No he isn't dead yet but he isn't long for it. He did make a death bed confession so I guess you can issue an order to the Warden to release the Defendant. Well, I suppose you are right, it should be in writing and filed in the case file before he is released." He shrugged as he looked over at Russ. "Well, we have a court stenographer right here so I can tell her to meet you at your chambers as soon as possible and you can dictate the order and file it tonight. I can pick up my copy of the order to take to the Warden. You just tell security to let Russ in when he gets to the courthouse." He smiled and then waved a hand in the air as he said, "Well, Rachael, as you well know, you can't win them all. See you tomorrow."

He moved toward the corridor outside. "As you heard, she is going to issue the release order now, so White can get out tonight. Just ring the night bell and security will let you in the courthouse. He stuck out his hand to Russ, "Good luck, Russ. I'm sure we will tangle horns again, sometime, in the future."

Russ shook hands with him, as they opened the door to the confusion in the corridor. Buzz immediately gave his best television smile as he moved into the bright lights to answer questions by the media. Russ was happy to ease out of the hospital without being questioned by anyone. He smiled to himself as he got into his convertible thinking about the days when he would be sweating and hurting with pain in the locker room after a game and always had time for the interminable, often absurd, questions by the media. In those days there was no slipping out the side door without being seen and stopped, for in depth interrogation, on how he managed to catch that pass in the end zone with three defensive players hanging onto him. He flipped the key in the ignition and the old 350 twin barreled rocket engine roared into action. He pulled out of the parking lot and headed for the courthouse about five miles away. His mind wandered over the events that had led him up to this point. It was always a good warm feeling to win a case for your client but in this instance he really had backed into a victory. True, it didn't make any difference how you won as long as the result was in your favor, but he sure as hell didn't expect the dramatic ending to this case. He wondered if Ron would go back to his wife and try to make a go of their marriage or for that matter if he would stay in the magazine hustling business. In any event, it wouldn't be the problem of Russ Thurston. He would pack his bags tonight and turn the master key to the motel over to Willis, with a handshake, a bear hug for his peeping Tom assistance, and good luck in the future as the new Manager. He was anxious to get on with his life and it looked like the opportunity would be at his door when he went into the office of Charlie London on Monday. He pulled up, in a no parking zone, in front of the courthouse and headed for the door. He rang the night bell and immediately the security guard came to open the door. He nodded to Russ and admitted him without hesitancy. "Have to use the back stairs, Mr. Thurston."

Russ took the stairs two at a time and used the back hallway to get to the Judges' chambers. He could hear the typewriter in the outer office as he approached and knew the order was already dictated. Rachael was looking over the stenographer's shoulder as she typed. "Hi Russ. It won't be a minute until she is finished. Come on in and put your feet up." She closed the door behind them as Russ took the now familiar chair at her desk. She was wearing a western shirt of pale blue and some well worn blue jeans that curved deliciously around her firm cheeks. Russ looked up as she gently stroked his hair, "Tough day for the good guys and the bad guys." Her eyes were solemn and understanding as she bent to place her lips carefully on his. She held the kiss for a long minute and then broke away with a sigh. "Probably not the time or the place but I really do think our love is here to stay. At least, I know mine is and I hope you know what the word "reciprocate" means."

Russ took her hand in his and gently kissed her perfumed fingers as there was a tap at the door. Rachael smiled and whispered "Later" as she opened the door to admit the stenographer. She handed a copy of the release order to Russ who quickly looked it over. As he stood to leave Rachael took his arm and walked out to the corridor with him, "I will try and get ahold of the night jailer to tell him that you are coming over with a release order for your client. Sometimes he is hard to get in touch with so if I am not successful by the time you get there, just give me a call at home and I will confirm the release." She looked at her watch and said, "It's just eight o'clock. Why not come by my place later for that vintage champagne?"

Russ looked down at her and smiled, "Get your sweet ass home and chill the champagne and warm up the bed." He gave her a quick pat on the ass and a kiss on the cheek as he headed for the stairs.

He told the security guard he would only be a minute over at the jail so could he please leave his car in the no parking area. He made straight for the jail which was located at the end of the block. As he approached the building, he could see the usual girl friends and wives of some of the inmates standing under the barred windows talking to them as best they could. It was always the same conversation, "I got to have money, the baby's sick and when you gettin' out?" Russ went in to the main booking desk on the ground floor which was manned by a woman deputy sheriff. She looked up pleasantly and inquired if she could be of assistance.

"Yes Maam, my name is Russ Thurston. I am a lawyer representing Ron White. I have here an order for his release signed by District Judge Rachael Rawlings." He handed the order across the desk to her. She carefully read it over and then handed it back to Russ. "I will have to get the night jailer down here and he can then take you up to your client." She turned to her intercom and placed a call to the night jailer's office. "Yes, Mike, there is a lawyer down here by the name of Thurston with a release order for one Ron White. Do you want to come down or do you just want me to put him on the elevator up to you?" She paused a moment as she carefully looked over the still firm athletic body in front of her, "Okay, I'll send him right up."

She stood and Russ appreciated the tight, dark blue shirt with it's badge. She straightened her skirt and opened a gate beside her desk to admit Russ. They walked across the room past dilapidated chairs and full ash trays from the usual daily arrests. She opened the door to the elevator and turned to Russ, "Please get in, Mr. Thurston. When the door closes the elevator will automatically take you up to the second floor where Mike will meet you when the door opens. Security you know."

Russ stepped inside the elevator and immediately noticed that there were no buttons to designate the floors, just bare steel walls. The doors slid shut and after a long pause he felt a jolt but he had no sensation of movement up or down. Suddenly there was another jolt and the doors came open to reveal a bank of bright lights glaring into his eyes. He was temporarily blinded.

He heard a voice just as the lights were turned off, "Well, it really is the great Russ Thurston. I knew it the minute I saw that hulk standing in the bright lights. Sorry about those but we bring prisoners up in that elevator and we want a good look at them when they first come in to our little house of horrors.". He stuck a heavily ringed hand out to Russ, "How you been Russ?"

"Mike, I haven't seen you since we played football together in high school. I sure didn't know you were working the jail at night."

"Yeah, I been a deputy for about ten years now. I got tired of serving summons and subpoenas so I took this cushy job watching these scuds. It ain't too bad cause I can still do a little private work during the day serving subpoenas for lawyers. Maybe you could use my services sometime?", he handed Russ his business card.

"Well, I am just getting back into the legal rat race but I will sure keep you in mind." Russ pulled out the release order and gave it to Mike.

"Yeah, the good Judge just called me a few minutes ago with the good news for your boy. I haven't had time to get him out here yet. You know, I usually don't give a shit for any of these scuds in here, but I really felt sorry for this guy. Always on the verge of crying. At first I thought he was just some kind of fruit cake but then I found out from one of my sources that these bastards were trying to bore him a new asshole and the queers were grabbing his crotch all the time." He paused to light up an enormous black cigar. "You know we do our best to keep things from happening in here but I swear to God they always seem to find some way to get ahold of the poor fucker and rape him."

"Well, that's just the reason I want him out of here right now. He told me they were after him and he was scared to death of what might happen. I can't think of anything worse than to be innocent, which he is, and to be locked up with a bunch of sexual perverts that spend day and night trying to figure out how they can get ahold of you and rape you." Russ could feel the old scar pulsating and he knew he was on the verge of really losing his temper. Rachael was right it had been a long day.

Mike walked over to his desk and picked up a ring of keys and carefully selected one to open the steel barred door behind him. He turned to Russ and said, "Do you notice how quiet it is in here tonight?" That is a sure sign that the assholes are up to some no good. Usually they are yelling at each other about who is fucking your ole lady while you're in the slammer, just to get a knee jerk out of the other guy, but when it gets quiet that's when I need to make a tour around to stop the bull shit." He pulled the massive door open that led into the main corridor with the locked cells on either side. He turned to Russ, "Come on, you can come with me to get your boy. He sure as shit will be glad to see the great Russ Thurston tonight."

Russ hesitated but then decided Ron would appreciate hearing the good news direct from him rather than from the night jailer.

Their footsteps resounded off of the steel walls and cement floor as they passed cells crowded with four men in them. There was no privacy and the lights were kept on bright until ten o'clock when they were all shut down and only dim corridor lights remained. Mike led the way past silent cells of sullen inmates toward the very end of the corridor where one smaller cell with just one bed in it was located. Russ recognized a yellow legal pad on the bed, other than that the eight by eight room was bleak with a urinal in one corner and a steel chair in the other. Mike smiled at Russ, "This ain't exactly Trump Towers but it does the job until these scuds get sent on their way to the State joint in Albuquerque." He ran his black night stick across the bars of a cell where a card game, with matches being used for money, was in progress. He called down to the end of the corridor, "Okay, Whitey, get your shit together. Your lawyer is here with some good news for you."

There was no response from the small cell and Russ could see no one in it with the glare of the lights in his eyes. From somewhere back down the corridor a voice came through the now total silence as they both stopped at the steel door to Ron's cell. "Hey, Boss Man, he ain't in his private joint. He down at the showers, been down there for bout an hour." With that the cells exploded with laughter. Mike could see that the door was slightly ajar so he slammed it shut, "Just when the hell did he get permission to go to the showers?" They were walking back toward the voice at the other end of the corridor.

"Got permission from old Warden Pete just before you came on night shift. Two trustees took him down there with his towel and soap. I saw old Charlie Hardcastle come out of the Warden's office just about that time and he went to the showers right behind your boy. Lot's of hollering and screaming down there with ole Charlie just grunting like a ruttin" stud. Finally it all stopped and Charlie came on back to his cell with a big smile on his face. Looks to me like he got himself a pure white virgin tonight." The cells gave the usual "Amen brother" and then some snickering. The voice went on. "That rotten pervert smiled right at me and said that asshole was so good he was going to make a full blown whore out of him. Said he left him in the shower trying to wash some of that big cock off his ass." There was silence and then the voice yelled out, "You lousy rotten pervert. I hope they gas your ass for this one."

Russ felt sick at the thought of poor Ron at the mercy of a depraved sex pervert. Here he was almost out of this God damned hell hole without mishap and now he had been raped.

Mike said, "Come on Russ, he is still in the shower cause I can hear the water running. Those fucking trustees are in deep shit for this one. They all knew that it was that bastard Hardcastle that was determined to get at White."

Steam was coming out of the shower room as they went through the room with a row of toilets on one side and a row of wash basins on the other. At first they couldn't see Ron as they stood at the entrance to the showers because of the dense steam rolling out of the entrance. Then Russ saw him at the far end of the shower room.

Ron White swung slowly at the end of the knotted strips of towel tied to the shower head. The bench lay on it's side below the limp undulating body. Russ could only stare in horror at the grotesque dance of death, at those still terror stricken eyes as they gazed off into nothingness, into the world of the unknown. He walked slowly and deliberately into the shower and ripped the whole shower from the wall as he parted the towel strips with one hand and held Ron to his body with his other arm. He was soaked with the hot water from the shower but he involuntarily continued to shiver as he carried the lifeless body of his client, his friend, through the jailers doors to the Warden's office where he gently lay him to rest on the night jailers bed. He covered his nakedness with a sheet and slowly closed the eyes that would weep no more. His massive frame was wracked with shudders of grief as he passed through the gathering crowd into the waiting elevator. As he walked out of the security building he licked his lips and tasted the salt from his tears being shed for the cruel injustice of the system that had brought an end to the case of State versus White.

He pulled the sodden release order from his inside pocket and slowly ripped it into pieces as he walked into the clear darkness of a New Mexico night where the stars shone brightly above the snow shrouded mountains. He hoped the soul of Ron White would burn brightly as a new star in the galaxy.

END

www.ingramcontent.com/pod-product-compliance
Lightning Source LLC
Chambersburg PA
CBHW020020030726
47499CB00007B/2196